REMEMBER TOMORROW

Arran Davies

Edlogan Publishing

Copyright © 2025 by Arran Davies

Remember Tomorrow

All rights reserved.

All rights reserved. No part of this publication may be reproduced, distributed, or transmitted in any form or by any means, including photocopying, recording, or other electronic or mechanical methods, without the prior written permission of the publisher, except as permitted by copyright law. For permission requests, write to Arran Davies.

The story, all names, characters, and incidents portrayed in this production are fictitious. No identification with actual persons (living or deceased), places, buildings, and products is intended or should be inferred.

Book cover by getcovers.com

ISBN: 978-1-9193146-0-0

First published in 2025

Edlogan Publishing

For the family.
Past, present and future.

CONTENTS

1. The Bridge 11
2. Entrapment by the Lake 16
3. Central Park 24
4. Donna Forte 32
5. Crazy Talk 43
6. Lake Garda..53
7. The Precinct 60
8. Trouble..72
9. Thorny Words..87
10. Villa of Death 100
11. Investigations 117
12. Dead Men Tell No Tales 134
13. Meeting the FBI 141
14. New York, New York..157
15. Rocco's 165
16. The Last Kill 175
17. Tea for Three 183

18. An Uninvited Guest 192

19. Voyage of the Damned 203

20. Knock Knock 220

21. The Castle 228

22. The Afterlife 234

23. Remember Yesterday 242

24. Gun for Hire? 246

25. Cryptonasia 249

26. Body Bags 268

27. Revelations 278

28. Escape 287

29. Escape Trial 291

30. Execution 300

31. Release 309

32. Army of Lost Souls 316

33. The Last Stand 322

34. An Offer 333

PART ONE

Sorrow like a ceaseless rain

Beats upon my heart.

People twist and scream in pain, —

Dawn will find them still again;

                        Sorrow by Edna St. Vincent Millay

1. The Bridge

The cool night air of the late-summer evening breezed through the streets of New York City. There were no clouds in the sky, and as day turned into night, its colour turned from a clear blue to a purple hue before the sky transitioned into the dark shade of night. The lights from the skyscrapers of Manhattan exuded a glow in the atmosphere that formed a blanket of protection over the city from the darkness above.

A black Cadillac sedan rolled calmly down East 59th Street. Drifts of steam wisped from the vents of the sidewalk and up into the ether. The motion of passing vehicles created a vacuum causing the rising steam to twist and dance. For this time of the evening, the traffic was light, allowing vehicles to flow freely without the usual commotion.

The Cadillac cruised over the intersection with Park Avenue, heading east and on towards Lexington and Bloomingdale's department store. The tinted windows created an extra layer of darkness in the car's cabin, projecting a fashionable privacy to the casual onlooker.

The driver, a young man in his late twenties, wore Gucci shades and an expensive tailored suit without a tie. He drove in silence with his eyes fixed firmly on the road ahead, an expression of tranquillity exuding from his face, hiding the pain and inner turmoil that raged inside him.

As the black Cadillac cruised past Bloomingdale's, it weaved casually through the traffic, switching lanes nonchalantly. The car continued down East 59th Street, never needing to stop and never in a hurry before reaching the intersection of East 59th Street and 2nd Avenue.

To the left stood the Tramway Plaza, the base on the east of Manhattan for the Roosevelt Island Tramway, the aerial tramway that carries passengers high in the sky over the East River from Manhattan and onto Roosevelt Island.

As the car crossed the intersection, a cable car on the tramway swooped down from the sky, carrying its passengers back down to earth. Oblivious to this sight, the man steered the Cadillac to the ramp and onto the Queensboro Bridge. Much like the tramway, the bridge crosses the East River but expands the full length of the waterway into Queens.

The Cadillac coasted along in the narrow two-lane road amongst the traffic and the large steel trusses holding up the bridge. The car drove along the middle deck and as it passed the trusses, each one made a zipping sound. Up above on the top deck, more traffic made its way to its destination, and on the lower decks on the furthest edges of the bridge, a pedestrian and cycle path allowed for non-vehicle crossing.

As the car reached the midpoint of the crossing between Manhattan and Roosevelt Island, it stopped without warning. Drivers following behind honked their horns in anger at the delay before navigating around the stationary vehicle without thinking why the car might have stopped. They cared only about reaching their destinations.

The man in the shades got out of the car and, opening a rear door, took a long chain from the back seat, looping his arm through the chain so that it hung over his shoulder like a lasso. Without looking to check for any dangers in the traffic, he casually vaulted the railings separating the roadway from the cycle lane. As he landed, he adjusted his jacket to ensure he wore it correctly.

On his left, a hundred yards away, he saw two men walking towards him. To the man's right, a cyclist ventured on towards Queens in the distance. Behind him, cars continued to honk their horns in dissatisfaction at the obstruction in the road. None of this mattered to him. All that mattered was the noise in his head, the pain that he had to stop. Despite the pain in his mind, he didn't feel anger or frustration. He was calm, almost melancholy, for he knew what had to happen. The pain hadn't always been there. It had come later, after the euphoria, but the euphoria was no more.

In front of him were another set of railings and an eight-foot fence that provided a barrier along the bridge from the river below. He secured the chain to the railings and deftly climbed to the top. From his position standing on the metal barrier, the chain fence was now a little over three feet high and easily within reach. He worked quickly, wrapping the chain around his neck and pulling hard, the cold steel links pinching his skin. He then tossed the slack of the chain over the fence.

Over his shoulder, he heard the two men walking towards him on the pedestrian walkway calling out. He glanced in their direction without moving his head. He could see they were waving their arms and running towards him. It didn't matter. He already knew they wouldn't make it. With the agility of a gymnast, he scaled the chain-link fence and balanced precariously on its summit, his arms held aloft at his sides so that his body assumed the shape of a cross.

The next second lasted an eternity, as if time had slowed down. Three hundred and fifty feet below, the water of the East River shimmered with the light from the moon. The skyscrapers of Manhattan on his left stood proud and resolute in the night sky. Behind him, the traffic had stopped on the bridge, and he heard more cries from panicked onlookers.

As he struggled to control his balance, he glimpsed the faces of a group of passengers in a tramcar that was making its way along the cable track. They were screaming at him through the glass as they passed in front of him, knowing what he was about to do. He couldn't hear them, but it didn't matter. Nothing mattered anymore.

In the final milliseconds of this eternal moment, his balance finally tipped him over the edge and he plunged towards the river below. As he fell, he looked at the passengers in the cable car, and a look of euphoria spread across his face. He gained speed rapidly. As he plummeted, the wind whipped through his hair. For an instant he felt no pain in his mind, only peace, then without warning the chain snapped tightly around his neck, cracking his cervical spine, and the bright lights of New York for him were no more.

2. Entrapment by the Lake

It was a perfect late-summer day. The sun was high in the sky and its warm rays made everyone feel happy. The romantic and quaint streets of Desenzano del Garda nestle on the southern shore of Lake Garda in the Lombardy region of Italy. They were lined with restaurants, bars, hotels, shops, and interspersed quays, and buzzed with tourists and locals alike enjoying the town's ambiance.

Sitting at a small café bar facing out onto the lake, a man watched as a father helped his small daughter onto one of the many ferries that cross the lake to the nearby town of Sirmione. The father and his daughter were laughing and joking, looking forward to the ride and an ice-cream in the sunshine at the other end of the journey.

Wearing dark shades, dressed in a light blue cotton shirt and light tan suit, the man watching the family gathering was anonymous amongst the other people sitting at the tables outside the café bar.

Darko Vidić was far from anonymous in his home country of Serbia, where, as a member Army of Republika Srpska (VRS) he had witnessed the brutal horrors of war. Numbed by conflict and abandoned by the system following his discharge from the army, he'd been driven to become an emotionless killer and had worked for notorious gangs in order to survive.

He'd fled from his home country to Switzerland as a refugee, but had become tired of the pitiful existence of an unwanted migrant. In the murky underworld of Swiss international finance, he'd found that his skills were in demand and commanded significant financial reward.

Now, he worked across Europe. From the relative calm of the west to the more politically tense former Soviet states. There was always work for a discreet, detached, and professional freelance killer.

Now, Darko sat at a small square glass table of the café opposite the ferry port just off the Viale Motta, watching the tourists on this gloriously sunny day. To his left, the tables and chairs in front of the adjacent cafés were full of tourists.

Standing at the end of the crescent of café bars was the Café Vert. Its large canopy gave shade to its customers, who enjoyed drinks and laughed amongst themselves, enjoying their holiday.

Amongst the tourists, he watched a woman, sat alone at a table on the far right, near the edge of the canopy. The photo given to him by his employers didn't do the woman justice. She had Italian looks with shoulder-length dark brown hair, dark eyes and a clear olive complexion. She was slim but not skinny and had an athletic body.

As the waiter placed her drink down on the table, she flashed a flirtatious smile. She could definitely make the most of her wares. He wondered how many times she had used that smile with men to get her way. She wouldn't get her way with him, though, he thought. He wondered whether she would try to use her smile on him when she realised he was going to kill her.

Darko hadn't decided how he would do it yet. In fact, he didn't know when he would kill her. His orders were to watch and wait. She was due to have a meeting, and until then he was to sit tight. When he killed, he preferred to do it quickly, a quick shot to the head, no fuss, no mess, out and onto the next job, easy money. That's what he liked about his job. She didn't have a chance.

Darko was a big man, six feet four and 240 lbs. The grey smudges of hair at his temples aged him beyond his thirty-nine years. His appearance was deceptive. Despite his weight, he appeared relatively slim. He took his profession seriously, keeping himself fit. When Darko wasn't working, he followed a training programme he'd adapted from his days in the army combined with various martial arts and strength conditioning exercises. When he was working, he didn't drink, smoke or get involved with women. He kept himself cold and focused only on the job he had to do.

Darko didn't suffer fools gladly and didn't let anything or anyone get in his way. He didn't know what the woman had done, and he didn't care. All he knew was that the man on the phone had sounded desperate to make sure she was dead. In Darko's experience, this was not uncommon among clients. Most people are desperate when they hire a contract killer. It is usually a last resort to rid them of a big problem.

The sound of a chair being carelessly dragged back broke his thoughts. A man's foot forced the chair to make an audible scraping sound before a pair of drinks were placed upon the table with two clunks. Darko cursed under his breath at the man's raucous manner. The man placed a tall glass of iced water in front of Darko and a Peroni beer in a tall presentation glass with a handle on the table before the empty seat. Darko had already decided he would kill this man when the job was done. He didn't enjoy working in teams, and particularly not with an idiot like Marvin.

'Any movement?' the man asked in his Southern American drawl as he sat down.

Marvin was an American. Ex-military forces, five foot nine inches tall. Medium build and about 150 pounds. In his late thirties, Marvin had life experience. He had served a tour of duty in the Middle East. He sported a semi-military haircut, with his hair cut short to his scalp. Marvin was another mercenary, fleeting from one job to the next.

He had a gung-ho attitude in his manner that was a remnant of his front-line army days, where he had been part of the American freedom force in Iraq. He was an all-American hero, signing up to the forces at eighteen and helping to free a country infiltrated by an evil dictator.

The military discharged Marvin shortly after his service in the Middle East. As a young soldier from the backwoods of Alabama, he was used to shooting and hunting animals in the woods. Easily influenced, he fell in with a shameless group in his early service years.

Together with a militant group of Kuwaiti soldiers and local rebels, Marvin had held Red Army members captive in a private prisoner of war camp, maiming and torturing them like animals. When the prisoners were driven to the brink of death and beyond recovery, the militant soldiers had shot dead the captives and buried the bodies in shallow graves in the desert.

Through his youthful naivety, Marvin had then helped the Kuwaitis extract more Red Army guards from the official POW camp to commit yet more maiming and torture, sometimes over weeks. Marvin's superior officer became suspicious of Marvin, bringing an end to the horrors.

A military court tried Marvin and discharged him dishonourably. To be discharged in such a manner forced him into employment outside the civilian norm.

Signing up as a mercenary suited him. Working in gangs suited his style. He had tried working alone, but because of his careless nature, he often found himself in trouble. Often courting the law when fulfilling contracts, he had been fortunate to escape murder convictions by becoming an informant.

'No,' Darko replied abruptly in his thick eastern accent. 'She got a drink from the waiter. No other movement, no calls and no visitors.'

'She sure is a pretty little thing,' Marvin said, taking a long draw of his drink. 'I'm lookin' forward to having a bit of fun with her before we finish her off. I bagged her first Darko buddy.'

'As you wish,' Darko sneered. He was not a molester or rapist. The woman, to him, was just another business transaction. She died, he got paid. He didn't agree with the so-called perks that other people in his line of work assumed with female victims.

'All this waitin' around watchin' her sure is getting my pants hot. She doesn't know what she has coming to her.' Marvin rumbled under his breath.

'And you don't know what is coming to you, my friend!' thought Darko. He had endured Marvin's crude comments for six days and had become bored with them.

When Darko hadn't joined in the conversation, Marvin had bragged about his exploits in Iraq and Afghanistan against the local women. It was then that Darko had decided he would kill him when the job was done. He'd debated killing Marvin at the start of the engagement when he'd learned from his employer that he would be working in a team.

He had decided against it, as his employer was insistent that the target was dangerous and that it was a two-man job. Instead, he bided his time and assessed the situation. No sense in rocking the boat.

He understood his new colleague could be professional and therefore useful, but after meeting Marvin, he felt Marvin had left him with little choice. Darko felt no remorse. He presumed Marvin's arrangement to collect his payment would be similar to his own, so he could benefit financially by removing Marvin.

Darko decided to act first, as he suspected Marvin might try to do something similar to him when the job was done.

Marvin took another slurp of his beer. They continued watching their target together in silence. Marvin considered the situation as the cool liquid travelled down his throat. He had learned that Darko wasn't a big talker. He assumed the big man couldn't understand properly. "Dumb Croatian," he thought, either that or he was just plain boring.

Either way, he didn't care. He had plans for the woman. If Darko didn't like them, tough, he didn't need him to kill her. He could enjoy himself with the woman if he wanted, it didn't matter to him. There would be trouble if Darko got in his way though. Darko was a big guy, but he was no match for his Glock 17M. He didn't like him much and wanted the woman all to himself.

Marvin turned his attention back to the woman they were watching. She didn't look dangerous to him, but he knew from the briefing he'd received that she was armed and ready to kill.

Her phone rang, and after an intense conversation, the woman got up to leave. Darko and Marvin quickly got up to follow her. They knew they couldn't afford to lose her, or it would be their necks on the line.

3. Central Park

Central Park was still. New York City was still waking up. The sky was light blue tinged with the grey of dawn. It was a cool, still morning, exactly how Sam Martin liked it. In the distance, the faint sound of traffic could be heard as the Big Apple's daily traffic of taxicabs, delivery trucks and commuters began to ramp up.

Dressed in a dark blue sports sweatshirt and shorts, Sam pushed his relentless running pace. He wasn't a particularly good runner, just above average, but overall he maintained a good level of fitness, a hangover from his military days.

As part of his routine, he liked to take a daily morning run around Central Park before getting into his office. Although invariably, his run took a back seat to an extra hour in bed because of his laziness, or most times, a mild hangover.

This morning, though, he was feeling good. He had made good time running from the Maine Monument, passing the Tavern on the Green building. A quick glance at his wristwatch showed he was thirty seconds ahead of his best time.

As he ran through the park alongside New York's Upper West Side, he was still feeling strong. He was on his third and final lap of the park. Heading up on the west side of the Onassis Reservoir, he avoided the occasional glances from the other morning runners coming from the other direction, focusing on the next curve of the pavement or the tree up ahead, keeping up momentum.

He considered himself a casual runner. The serious runners, hardened marathon runners, ultra-distance runners, serious amateur competitors run with a ferocious pace and steely stare, each competing against each other and their own personal bests. The morning run for them was just a minor part of their relentless weekly training regime and the quest for acknowledgement.

Sam considered the search for acknowledgement an interesting concept in human behaviour, used by many groups in different ways, from your average runner or biker acknowledging you with a nod as one of the group – *"Yes, I know what you are going through"* to handshakes and codes of secret societies as authentication that you are a member. Other groups, such as the armed forces, used signs as part of operations. Something he was very familiar with.

Sam wasn't in some big running clique and wasn't looking for confirmation. He was keeping his fitness levels up and getting his mind alert for the day ahead. He always found that a morning run, as hard as it was to get up and do, set him up for what the day ahead would bring.

Rounding the pinnacle of the Onassis reservoir, Sam was on the home straight down the east side of Central Park, running past the Obelisk, the Central Park Turtle Pond and the first of the hot dog vendors, setting up his stall for the day. His pace began to slow as his energy levels waned.

Finally, as he headed down past the Rambles Shed, he cut left onto 5th Avenue along the sidewalk, looking for a break in the traffic to cross the road. A quick glance over his left shoulder confirmed a gap in the traffic behind him. In the oncoming traffic, there was a gap after a taxi cab. The cab crawled past as if looking for a pickup, forcing him to delay his crossing. Then finally, as the cab passed, he picked up his pace as he crossed the road and began running again along the sidewalk past the synagogue.

Taking a quick glance left and right before crossing East 65th Street, he reached his finish line on East 64th Street. Out of breath, he checked his watch. He cursed under his panting breath when he saw he had somehow missed his best time by twenty seconds. Time lost as he had slowed around the lake and then waited for the cab to cross the street, he thought.

Never mind, not a bad run, he made a promise to himself to go back and buy the biggest loaded hot dog from an early morning vendor when he beat his time. He walked down the sidewalk, wiping the sweat from his brow with his sweatshirt sleeve. He ducked off the sidewalk into Mango's, an independent fast-food coffee shop chain, to get a drink.

As he walked through the door, the girl behind the counter smiled and called out to him in her New York accent, 'Hey Sam, haven't I told you before about coming in here all sweaty? You'll scare off all my customers.' She tossed him a sports drink over the counter, which he caught and started to open. The coffee shop was empty, which was unusual for this time of day.

'Gina, you know I've told you before I'll give free consultations to anyone mad enough to buy anything from you,' he smiled. 'On my tab?' he called out, waving his drink in the air.

'As always. That tab is getting bigger, you know. When are you going to make good on your promise to repay it in beer?' she joked as usual.

Gina and Sam had a routine every time Sam dropped in for his post-run drink. Gina had started Mango's four years earlier and had developed the chain into a successful operation with ten outlets across New York City. She was a petite brunette with her hair worn in a layered bob. Her kind face had laser-focused eyes, much like her ambition, and a wicked smile.

She and Sam had met when she was fitting out the shop on 49th Street and he was setting up his office further down the road. They had used the same delivery firm that had mixed up their delivery.

A clinical psychologist had little use for juicers, espresso machines and stainless steel kitchen equipment in the same way that Gina would have struggled to set up her business with a couple of office desks, computer equipment and a therapy chair.

The confusion had caused them to meet, and they had been

friends ever since, playing out a similar routine whenever Sam visited for a drink and Gina was on site. They shared a mutual appreciation of each other, but neither took it much further.

When they first met, Gina had a long-term boyfriend, which stopped anything happening between her and Sam, but the demands of her business operation caused the relationship to fail after two years. Since then, Gina and Sam had played the flirting game with neither ever really making the first move, yet both enjoying either casual or short-term relationships in their separate social circles.

'I've told you, the next time the Yankees win the World Series, I'll see you down at the Spring Bar on Mulberry Street and take you out for dinner.' Sam replied. He stood holding the door open for two well-dressed ladies entering the shop for their morning coffee takeout. Mango's had built up a good local reputation for quality amongst both New York's elite and the average Joe alike.

'I'll see you later,' he waved as he left through the open door. Gina smiled and waved him out, calling her assistant from out back to serve so that she could get on with her other duties.

Sam strolled down the street, sipping his drink and heading towards his office. It was 7:30am and his diary was free until 10:00am, so he was in no hurry. His thoughts turned to breakfast and back to Gina and their friendship. He tried to reason why he had never actually offered to take her out after all this time.

They had been in the same place within separate circles of

friends on the odd social occasion. When she split up with her boyfriend, he had helped her move some furniture from her apartment, but he had never made good on his promises in their playful role play.

He snapped out of his thoughts when he saw a man standing on the steps of his office building. The man was frantically pressing the buzzer marked Doctor SJ Martin. Clinical Psychologist. He was showing clear signs of motoric restlessness, looking frantically from side to side down the street, searching for someone and anyone, pacing on the spot.

Sam reached the steps to his building. It was typical of this part of town, built in the early twentieth century and primarily used for residences of the wealthy. Over time, many of the buildings had been converted into apartments or high-end consultancy businesses. He looked up to the man standing at the top of the steps.

'Can I help you?'

The man turned to look at him. He was about forty years of age, dressed in a smart business suit but with a dishevelled face and a frantic look in his eyes. Sam guessed he was probably a Wall Street type. Despite his dishevelled demeanour, the man had signs of good grooming, his suit was well cut and he wore a Rolex watch on his left wrist.

'I'm looking for Doctor Martin. Do you know him?' The man asked desperately.

'Yes, I'm Doctor Martin,' Sam replied cautiously. 'Who are you?'

The man bolted down the steps towards Sam. Sam took a step back and braced himself, placing one foot behind him for additional stability, allowing him to counterbalance any attack from the man now heading straight for him.

He had dealt with many people during his career in the military. Military personnel were more susceptible to psychological disorders than most because of the nature of their work. The events they experienced could be horrific, the actions they had to take even more so, and the substances they were exposed to as part of modern warfare caused some to struggle.

Sam's experience had shown him that military conflict has a massive effect on the human mind. He knew that people often needed a lot of help to overcome the mental trauma they had experienced in war. People displayed their suffering in many different ways, and sometimes mental distress manifested in a physical reaction.

Sam's time in the military had taught him how to defend himself. He found this knowledge comforting in civilian life, where there was no on-site support in a privately run clinic, where he might become involved in a physical entanglement with a patient. This could be one of those occasions.

'I'm Miles Branfield,' the man blurted as he reached the bottom of the steps. He grabbed Sam's arms in search of support.

'I'm your ten o'clock appointment. I'm sorry for turning up so early. I couldn't wait any longer. I have been up for three days. I can't sleep, I think I'm going mad. At first I didn't think it was real, but then it got stronger and stronger, more repetitive and more vivid. I feel like I'm about to die! You have got to help me!'

4.Donna Forte

Elisa Giusti sat in the café's cool shade, sipping the last of her Franciacorta. Despite her cool demeanour, her body was tense. She had spent the last two weeks entertaining herself in the splendour of Lake Garda in the summer. But this was no holiday. It was business, a job.

She was due to meet her contact here in Lake Garda. She didn't know exactly where, and she didn't know when. All the voice on the phone had said was that she was to meet in Lake Garda in August. It could be worse, she thought. There are worse places in the world to stay.

She had made herself quite comfortable. Renting a villa just off Viale Guglielmo Marconi, the main street leading down from the train station through Desenzano del Garda to the lakeside. The villa was perfect. It had private gardens, a swimming pool, and a secure gate with an intercom system. Ideal for a woman who wanted to maintain her privacy.

In order to move around easily, she had hired a car, an Alfa Romeo in Giulietta red. She was in Italy after all, so she wanted to blend in, although by her own admission a two-seater sports car was not exactly low-key.

As the days passed, she had ventured the short journey on the train into Milan for some shopping, all on expenses, of course. If they were going to keep her waiting, she was going to make it worth her while.

The first week of waiting for the call had been tense. Elisa had spent the week staying within the confines of the villa, expecting her phone to ring at any time. She always got nervous at the start of a new job. Putting someone to death did not come naturally to her, not anymore anyway, although she had always found a way in the end. She had resented her clients, thinking them cowardly for hiring her to do their dirty work. Despite her resentment, she was wise enough not to take them for granted, for she knew they could easily turn on her.

When the call didn't come in the first week, she had made more of the private holiday maker image she was trying to portray. In her fantasy, the image she had decided upon was that of a wealthy heiress of a rich and powerful dynasty, escaping from the hustle and bustle of the major cities of the world and the constant media attention. Rather than holidaying in the usual destinations of the social elite in the Bahamas and Saint-Tropez, she had decided instead to retreat to the family's secluded private villa in the lakes.

It wasn't one of the family's main residences, of course, which were many, comprising private island retreats, houses and offers to stay in the residences of the rich and famous. All these options were too well known and obvious. She had wanted an authentic Italian experience, something all the money in the world couldn't buy.

She had decided to conceal herself away in a little known family home passed down through the family as a reminder of the more humble beginnings, revelling in the simple things in life, a trip to Milan, a walk to the local café bar, a boat trip to the other towns on the lake and perhaps taking an interest in the local men.

Away from the fantasy, she had decided if they were going to call as agreed, she would get on with the job, for real this time. Her growing resentment towards her clients and her profession had led her to default on her last job, taking her advance but not completing the contract. In her line of work, it was a dangerous action to take, which could have resulted in her own demise if the client had been as dangerous as some of her others.

If they didn't follow-up, she would use the advance wired to her Swiss bank account to live out a brief fantasy and have a good time. By the end of the month, with her reputation restored, she would put the word out that she was back on the market for work.

The call caught her off guard when it finally arrived. It came in the early hours of the morning, which shouldn't have surprised her. In her business, people didn't keep strict business hours. She was however, taken aback by the circumstances she was in when the call came through.

Elisa had taken her guise as a carefree, holidaying socialite too far, beyond what she considered professional, even by her standards. In the preceding evenings she had dined in the various bistros around Desenzano del Garda, sampling the best the little town had to offer. She never stayed long or tried to attract attention to herself. She simply enjoyed the culinary delights before heading back to the villa to continue waiting for the call and considering who or what her next job would entail.

The previous evening she had been sitting in a restaurant 'Bella Luna Ristorante'. Her meal of risotto had been delicious, and she was finishing the evening with an amaretto. Across the room, a man had been dining alone for the last twenty minutes. He appeared to be a local and a regular in the restaurant.

He had shared a joke with the waitress and talked to the restaurant owner at length in the local dialect about something at the bar. The service he received was casual, not the kind given to a new customer, but that of a regular everyone knew.

He was dark, with bright eyes and a friendly smile, sharing a good rapport with the waitress. He was in his late thirties, about six feet tall with dark brown hair, slim through a good diet rather than exercise.

The man wasn't Elisa's usual type. She preferred a more rugged look. He sat at a table for two nearest the window at the front of the restaurant. Positioned next to the window, the table gave him a clear view of the restaurant and easy access to the bar. The restaurant wasn't particularly big, seating around twelve tables in the front section, with additional seating through an alcove in a smaller room that led to the kitchen. The tables were rustic, thick, solid wood, which matched the room's Italian kitchen feel.

Elisa sat at a two-seater table against the wall halfway down the restaurant, just beyond the bar. She faced the front of the restaurant, with the alcove to her left shoulder and the bar in front. The man's table and the front door were in her direct line of sight. She liked the table because it provided a view of the entrance, allowing her to evaluate people as potential threats.

The only attack the man at the table was making was with his smile. She had ignored him at first, but as she finished her starter and began the second half of her bottle of Merlot, the thought of some company that evening grew more appealing. After all, he wasn't unattractive. The chances of being called about her job were the same as any other night in the last two weeks, when the phone had stayed silent. What harm would a bit of fun be?

Over the main course, she had matched his glance with a smile, inviting him to make a move. She had had no particular plans to take him to bed at that point. Only to satisfy her curiosity about him and the heightened desire that she had gained from the wine. She was, after all, far more dangerous than he was should he overstep the mark.

If she decided he didn't like him, it was easy to move on. When the call came, it would prompt her swift departure from Desenzano del Garda, preventing any awkward reunions. When the waitress had brought across the dessert menu, the man made his move.

'Can I make a recommendation?' he said, flashing his friendly smile, now standing alongside her table. His English was good, but his accent betrayed his Italian nationality. Despite her Italian looks, he had taken notice of the fact that she had been conversing with the waitress in English.

'Please do.' she said, returning his smile and handing him the menu.

'My name is Max,' he began, taking the menu slowly from her hand and taking the seat opposite her. 'And yours?'

'Sophia.' She lied. There was no point in being honest with him. She didn't want to blow her cover in case he wasn't a local. Even if he were, it would be safer for him if he didn't know who or what she was.

'It's a beautiful name,' he remarked, 'the same as my cousin's. Greek for wisdom.' He motioned towards the dessert menu. 'I won't need this. What I recommend is not on the menu.'

'Really!?' She tilted her head with intrigue. She knew Italians often used innuendo to make English sound more effective.

'No,' he went on, 'the best dessert is a specialty. Franco, the owner, has a special dessert. Franco!' he called, turning to the man at the bar. 'Bring me the special dessert of the house for the beautiful lady.' Franco acknowledged with a nod and instructed the waitress accordingly in his Italian dialect.

'Franco's passion is cakes. He and his brother have been

making desserts for over thirty years. They owned a delicatessen together until twenty years ago.' He lowered his voice and moved in closer to Elisa, as if he was about to tell her a secret that he didn't want anyone else to hear. 'The two brothers made cakes. When, one day, they fell in love with the same beautiful woman. They each made a cake to impress her. Franco's cake was the best, and the woman became his wife. But it caused a rift between him and his brother. The delicatessen closed down. His brother moved to Milano to set up a business and Franco stayed here and started this place. Now he doesn't put the dessert on the menu.'

Elisa smiled politely, encouraging him to go on. It was a likely tale but amusing nonetheless. 'So how do you know about the dessert if it isn't on the menu?'

'Ah!' he said, holding up his hand. 'Franco is a passionate man. He is sad about the rift with his brother, but he is proud of his creation and his beautiful wife. So he is proud to tell the local men that his cake creation helped find him true love and if the men should want to be as lucky as he, then they should buy his cake for a beautiful woman and they may be as fortunate as him and find true love!'

'And how many women have you bought cakes for?'

'Well…let's just say I'm not lucky in love, but the cake is worth the search,' Max laughed.

As they shared the joke, the waitress approached their table with the "Torta D'Amore." It was a beautifully decorated cake laced with multi-coloured chocolate swirls, ribbons and adorned with fresh fruit. The waitress presented the cake on a beautiful round plate that seemed to be encrusted with jewels. The plate had two forks for sharing. Truly a lover's cake, Elisa thought. It looked like a good choice. Alongside the cake, the waitress placed two small glasses of Frangelico liqueur.

Max handed her a fork. Elisa cautiously lifted a piece of the cake to her mouth, the flavours burst into her mouth with a delicious explosion of sweetness and spice. The cake had a strong chocolate flavour with velvet undertones. It was laced with an alcoholic ingredient that gave it a unique taste. Elisa was impressed. It was one of the finest cakes she had ever tried.

'Buona?' Max asked.

'Yes, it's lovely,' she said 'I can understand why Franco's wife married him.'

'Now you must drink the Frangelico. It will complete the taste in your mouth, and you will think you have gone to heaven!'

Elisa took a sip of the liqueur, the smooth amber liquid coated her tongue. Max was right. The contrasting tastes of the hazelnut and herb liqueur worked to enhance the flavour of the dessert and left a lingering taste in her mouth.

As the meal drew to a close, Elisa warmed to Max's Italian charm. Feeling relaxed from the wine and his easygoing nature, Elisa allowed herself to be swept along with the moment. From Franco's restaurant, Max had suggested a small bar away from the bustle of the main strip of Desenzano del Garda.

The bar, with its intimate size and characteristic rock walls, was bathed in warm golden light, giving it a cosy atmosphere. Over another drink, Elisa had begun to let her guard down. They talked about each other's families, shared experiences and hopes for the future. The evening went by in a romantic haze. In the taxi from the bar back to her villa, Elisa had already decided to invite Max in for a drink. He had initially declined but soon accepted the follow-up offer.

Once inside, they wasted no time on drinks. They tore each other's clothes off as they staggered across the villa in a passionate embrace from the front door, down the hallway and into the bedroom. They made passionate love until the early hours before they had both drifted off to sleep.

It was then in her post-coital slumber that her phone had begun to ring. It had taken her completely by surprise. She had totally let her guard down. She knew immediately that it was her contact, as she had set up a new phone for this job and no one else knew the number.

Startled by the ringtone, she had woken up in disarray, but almost immediately her mind reset and she was focused again. She put the phone on a silent ring as she slipped out of bed quietly so as not to disturb her now unwelcome guest and walked naked into the adjoining bathroom, cursing herself for her carelessness.

Her mind raced as the phone continued to ring and she

considered what her next steps might have to be. Depending on the call, she might have to leave immediately or, worse, get rid of the man now lying in her bed.

Once inside the bathroom, she closed the door and accepted the call.

'Hello,' she said in a low voice.

The man's voice on the other end of the phone replied with a phrase that confirmed the contact's identification.

She had replied with a corresponding pass phrase. The code had been predetermined to ensure her phone had not been compromised.

'Good evening,' the voice replied. 'I trust you are not disturbed?' The man's voice was deep, slow, and assured. It was distinctly American.

'No, not at all,' she replied calmly with a hint of impatience in an attempt to cover up her awkward situation. 'I have been expecting your call for some time. I was beginning to think that the job was going to be cancelled.'

'We do not cancel jobs,' the man replied flatly. 'You are to meet at noon tomorrow at the table reserved for "Silvio" at "Café sul lago" there, you will wait for further instructions. Do you understand?'

'Yes.'

'Good. Do not bring your friend, for his sake and yours.' The phone clicked off as the man ended the call.

'Shit!' she cursed under her breath. She had made a mistake in bringing Max back, and whoever this client was, he was clever. They sounded like a big corporation or government given that they had been monitoring her. She put the phone down and wrapped a towel around her naked body. She needed to prepare for tomorrow. That meant Max had to leave…now.

5.Crazy Talk

Without hesitation, the man had followed Sam up the steps to the main door of the complex. The main entrance, a huge twenty foot double door made of solid wood with attractive architrave details, was finished in a deep dark blue gloss. It was accessorised with original heavy brass knockers and door knob. On the left was the obligatory intercom system that allowed visitors to summon the office of his or her choice. Sam's office was on the ground floor and so his button that the man had been frantically pressing was at the bottom of the list.

Through the main doors and in the lobby, the property developer had maintained many of the original features of the building. The floor was made of marble, chequered with small navy diamonds that led down the hallway and then opened up into a lobby outside the elevator. The lobby provided access to the ground floor offices, and a left turn past the elevator led to the stairs, which retained a heavy, highly polished wooden handrail atop solid brass railings.

Opposite the elevator to the right was a small superintendent's office which was fronted with a cashier style window and a secure door. Square mailboxes, with dark navy cast metal doors, were built into the wall next to the cashier window.

The building manager maintained a rota of superintendents that were employed by a security company which also serviced many other buildings in the area. Whilst they invariably changed as part of a shift pattern, Sam only ever noticed the one man, a fat but solidly built greying man called Harry, who looked like he was in his early fifties. Sam had learned through his infrequent conversations with him that he was a native New Yorker from Brooklyn, retired from the New York Fire Department and now working in security to make a few extra dollars.

Harry spent his time in his office staring at the television, which perpetually broadcast sports, only occasionally looking up. He acknowledged Sam's arrival with a nod, ignoring the frantic man following closely behind him. Sam's office was the first door on the right and was a replica of the building's main entrance.

It had taken Sam ten minutes to calm the man down enough for him take a seat in his office. The man was extremely agitated and close to a panic attack. He was showing classic signs of acute behavioural disturbance. Branfield sat in the main office area, beyond a tiny lobby that led to a kitchenette on the left and a small bathroom down the hall.

Sam's office was positioned at the front of the building as it curved around behind the lobby, occupying the front right portion of the building with a large window that overlooked the street outside. It was light and airy. Dark coloured wooden shelving units, stretching from floor to ceiling, adorned the main wall to the left of Branfield. Each shelf was filled with books ranging from Clinical Psychology to fitness, along with some books Sam had acquired in the military.

Sam's desk stood to the right of the window. It was a wooden desk produced from the same wood as the bookshelves. It was complete with the usual office equipment, PC, a phone, an old fax machine and a large Bird of Paradise indoor plant. He had read somewhere that indoor plants helped create an atmosphere of serenity and calmness. There were two chairs, one for his desk and one he used for talking to clients. The client chair was a large dark green leather chair with wooden armrests.

Branfield sat nervously on the edge of a leather sofa, finished in the same green leather as the desk chairs, that rested against the wall under the window. He was sipping water from a plastic glass that Sam had convinced him to drink. Sam, still dressed in his running gear, was perspiring despite having cooled down. He was taking sips from his own drink and had wrapped a towel around his neck and shoulders so he could mop his brow and soak up his perspiration.

'OK, so start from the beginning. You are safe here. Nothing is going to happen to you,' Sam said to Branfield reassuringly.

Sam waited for Branfield to answer. He already had half an idea of what he was going to say. Whilst Branfield turning up on his door unexpectedly early was a surprise, his general demeanour and agitated state weren't new. Over the last month, Sam had seen his client base swell four hundred per cent. Every day he had a new case contact the office, reporting the same symptoms and desperate to seek clinical help.

These new clients often asked to be committed to a mental health facility to protect themselves from the impending doom they believed was inexorable. The increase was such that he was now turning people away as his practice was being overrun by the same sort of cases.

His peers had reported the same pattern through the New York Psychological Collective forum of which he was a member. Branfield was one of the last of this new breed of client that he had accepted to see.

Branfield finished the dregs of his water and began to explain.

'It all started a couple of weeks ago. At first it was just a one off, nothing out of the ordinary, nothing I hadn't experienced before, but then it started happening more frequently and more vividly.'

'What exactly?' Sam asked, already suspecting the answer.

'Really strong déjà vu.'

'It's perfectly normal, déjà vu is nothing extraordinary. Everybody experiences the feeling of having lived through an experience before from time to time. What was it about your déjà vu that is concerning you? Can you give me an example?'

Sam knew about déjà vu. He understood even more in the last couple of weeks than he did a few months ago. The recent increase in cases reporting déjà vu and delusional disorders had led Sam to research the phenomenon in much greater detail. He had discovered several factors could cause déjà vu and delusional syndromes. Genetic disorders, biological and environmental factors, including drugs and other interventions, were key triggers.

'It started pretty normally. I was walking into my office on Wall St. I had crossed the lobby and had made my way into the elevator on my way up to my office. The elevator stopped at the twenty-third floor. A woman from accounts stepped into the lift. She was about forty-five years old, dressed in a trouser suit. She had short, mousey brown hair. As she reached to press the button for her floor, she dropped all the files she was carrying at my feet. As I bent down to pick them up, it hit me. An overwhelming feeling that I had been there before doing the exact same thing. I paused for a second before helping pick up the folders and handing them to the woman.'

'As I stood back and waited for the elevator door to close and take us on up, I tried to remember why I thought I had been here before. Had I had a dream or premonition? I couldn't remember, so I just shrugged it off as one of those things. Then a couple of days later, it happened again, standing in a queue at the coffee stall. A man asked for a coffee, as he handed over his money it all felt so familiar, that he was paying with a one hundred-dollar bill, the way the coffee stall woman didn't put the plastic top on the cup properly and then as the man went to pick up the cup, the top flew off and he split the coffee all over his shoes.'

'That's not so bad,' Sam said. 'It isn't so uncommon to get a feeling of familiarity in situations we do every day.'

Branfield shifted in his seat. His brow was perspiring and he was rubbing his hands uncontrollably. 'You don't get it Doc, that's how it started, every other week, then every other day, and now several times a day. It's driving me insane, I can't concentrate, I'm on edge, everything I do, it feels like I have done it before, I've seen it before. I tried to use it to my advantage, where I work on Wall Street. I felt everything was familiar. I felt I might be able to predict the markets. I took some risks, thinking I could prompt the feeling of familiarity, thinking I knew the outcome of events. But I didn't. I lost, and I lost big. Millions of dollars. The only thing that was familiar was the feeling after I had made the bet. The feeling that I knew this would happen, I couldn't understand it. But the events kept happening. The future seemed so familiar. I can't sleep at night because of the constant interruptions in my mind.' Branfield became frantic again. His movements became more animated as he was describing what had happened to him.

'This morning I woke up and every step of my day was familiar. No odd feelings of Déjà vu, it just felt like everything I was doing was a memory. It didn't seem new, it just seemed like even though I was doing it, I was just remembering it. Then, in the elevator down to my garage, I had the feeling that there were going to be three men standing on the other side of the elevator door. When the door opened there came three chauffeurs going to their office. It freaked me out. Then I could almost see the future. I felt I could remember what was going to happen. The door of the parking garage getting stuck, which it did. The delivery truck pulling up to the pavement as I drove out of the garage onto the road, the cyclist clipping my car at the lights. I could see it all.' Branfield was visibly shaking. He was staring blankly into the distance as he spoke.

'Then it happened. I had a memory of me in my apartment, in the clothes I am wearing now, stumbling across the floor with severe pains in my chest, clutching and stumbling and then nothing, just blackness.'

Branfield began hyperventilating on the sofa, panic grew in his eyes. Sam quickly poured him another drink of water and tried to calm Branfield down by getting him to breathe deeply. Branfield gulped down the water and attempted to breathe, but he was already too worked up and was heading for a panic attack.

'Miles, keep breathing, there is nothing to worry about.' Sam tried to reassure him. 'I'll give you something to help.'

He had experienced several patients suffer panic attacks over the years to varying degrees. Some had gone into full panic attack mode, which had led to heart palpitations and unconsciousness, but he had no intention of letting Branfield get into that state.

In the army he had been permitted to use beta blockers such as Propranolol or Atenolol and on long-term severely affected patients he had prescribed Benzodiazepines like Alprazolam, Clonazepam or Diazepam. He could also use force where appropriate. Neither was appropriate here and through experience he had found that both drugs and physical restraint only aggravated the patient over the long-term.

In the army, he had the advantage of physical backup. Whilst he was confident Branfield wasn't a threat to him as he had dealt with bigger, stronger and better trained people in the military, it was still important to be cautious. Sam now preferred to use other techniques wherever possible, such as breathing or distraction. Breathing wasn't working, so instead Sam eased Branfield back onto the sofa, encouraging him to breathe.

'Take a seat. I'll give you something that will help,' Sam said calmly.

Sam found that patients often reacted a lot better if they expected some sort of drug to help them. It was the human psyche to believe that something was going to make everything better for them.

Sam took a key from his desk draw and unlocked the cabinet on the wall. Inside was a collection of prescription medicine boxes.

Branfield looked on in expectation. He was already calming down in anticipation of getting a drug to "fix him". Distraction was a key technique in calming patients experiencing panic attacks.

Sam took an official-looking bottle from the draw. He twisted the cap, which came free with a pop. He poured an oblong shaped pill into his hand and handed it to Branfield.

'Take this, it will help calm you down.' Sam handed him the pill, a vitamin supplement. A placebo, unethical but effective. Branfield took the pill eagerly and immediately began to calm down.

Sam watched as Branfield lay back, his breathing slowed and the panic slowly faded from his face. Soon his breathing had returned to normal and he had become lucid again. It never failed to amaze him how the human mind could be duped with a simple pill.

Sam assured Branfield that he was suffering with a temporary mild psychological disorder common to people under stress or duress given his high-pressure job and sent him home with instructions to relax, avoid work, take some exercise and to come back in a couple of days.

As soon as Branfield had left. Sam picked up the phone to the NYPD.

'NYPD, Morgan speaking.' The voice had a thick New York accent.

'It's Sam, I've got another one. He was in total disarray. Something has to be done.'

'That's the least of your worries Sam,' Morgan replied. 'You remember that Spanish kid you said you had in last week?'

'Yeah,' Sam replied pensively. 'I remember. He was extreme. I had him sectioned. He had more than just psychological problems. He was doing drugs and all sorts.'

'Well, he got out.'

'What? How? How do you know?'

'We just found him.'

'Where?'

'Hanging off Queensboro Bridge by a chain! I think you had better come into the precinct and have a chat. That's not all, it's just the tip of the iceberg.'

'What do you mean?'

'Not on the phone. You had better come in, Sam. I'll explain then.'

Sam put down the receiver and started for the door, forgetting he was still in his training gear. It sounded like Morgan might have some information that might help explain what was happening to his patients. He had to get over to the 20th Precinct and find out what the hell was going on.

6. Lake Garda

Elisa was tense. She had made an error of judgement, a poor decision that had almost caught her out. But now she was focused, she had a job to do, one last job she'd promised herself.

She sat at the café table looking out over the lake. The café's outdoor tables were nestled amongst low-rise buildings, painted in understated hues, with balconies and flower baskets adding a touch of charm. Her instructions were to be at "Café sul lago" at noon. She was to order a Ca' Del Bosco Franciacorta rose and wait for further instructions.

Drinking was the last thing on her mind. Despite her moment of weakness, she was a professional, and when on a job, she didn't drink. Getting rid of Max hadn't been that hard after all. He had protested at first but an empty promise to see him again persuaded him to leave. She would be long gone before he came back to see her.

Now she wanted to get the job done and get out of the business alive. This job was getting messy, and she liked things nice and simple. As she sat at the café table, she looked over towards the lake. Its vast expanse shimmered in the bright sunshine, the gentle waves rippled across the surface and lapped against the quayside where the cluster of café's and shops were nestled.

Elisa turned to watch the waiter as he tended the table next to hers. He wore black trousers, a white shirt, a black waistcoat and a tie, all immaculately presented. She saw the pride he took in his work, a pride that only waiters in continental Europe seem to possess. When satisfied that he had captured his diner's requirements, he turned to Elisa table to tend to her.

She ordered a Franciacorta Rose. Franciacorta is a small wine-producing region of northern Italy, famous for its excellent sparkling wines that rivalled the quality of the best French champagne and was a popular choice.

The waiter asked her, "Quale varietà vorrebbe?" she paused for a moment, remembering what she had been instructed and then asked for a 2009 Ca' Del Bosco.

'Certo,' he replied and after ensuring there was nothing else he could provide for her, he retreated proficiently and efficiently into the café to fulfil her request.

As she sat, she wondered how her client would contact her again. Would they travel across the lake by boat and provide her with details face to face as some of her clients liked to do? It wasn't long before she found out. Her phone rang, displaying "Private Number" on the screen.

Elisa picked up the phone from the table and accepted the call.

'Hello.'

'Buongiorno.' The voice on the phone replied. It was the same voice as the night before. 'Listen carefully to what I have to say. You do not have to say anything. To acknowledge, just run your fingers through your hair. Do you understand?'

Elisa did as she was told. This client, wherever he was, could see her, but where was he?

'Good,' the voice said. 'You will receive your full instructions at the Hotel Refersco. A woman with a red briefcase will be in reception and will escort you to a secure area. In there you will find a safe. You'll need to use the code that will be given to you shortly. The package inside contains all the details you need. You must complete the instructions within one week or you will not get paid. Understood?'

Elisa ran her hand through her hair to acknowledge again, as she did, she heard the disconnection as the call was ended.

Elisa remained calm and placed her phone back down before her on the table. She wasn't new to receiving contract instructions unconventionally. Her job was unconventional after all. Her clients had varied motives, ranging from political matters to corporate hostility and even personal vendettas. Many of her clients were uncomfortable with what they were asking to be done, so wanted to remain discreet and anonymous. Others had no concerns, to them it was just a matter of fact, another task to be completed in a long list of chores. To Elisa it was the same, although she had now progressed from being a contracted assassin to being a confidence trickster as she found it to be more lucrative and less risky.

Most of her clients were inexperienced in the world of contract killings. They were not in a position to punish the contractor for not completing the job. They would have had to have taken the time to accumulate the assets to pay for a killing in the first place and the time to develop the emotional courage to ask for such an act to be performed.

They were, therefore, unlikely to have either the additional emotional or financial means to pursue revenge on a contract killer who failed to complete the job. Most people wouldn't risk the hitman turning against them.

Despite this, Elisa had to be careful about which jobs she dishonoured. There was always a risk that she crossed a client who would decide to seek recourse against her for failing to meet her obligation. She had, however, developed an astute sense of client selection. It had become relatively easy for her to identify the dissatisfied spouse wanting the ultimate divorce from their partner or the business partner who wanted to simplify dissolving their business relationship.

These types of clients were often operating out of their comfort zone and were not in a position to put Elisa at risk. They would accept the monetary loss and think themselves foolish for ever considering such a course of action. Then unhappily grind through their situation for the rest of their lives, or use it as a blessing and see things in a better light, an epiphany of sorts, in that fate had saved them from the guilt of a death they would undoubtedly have had to have lived with forever.

Others, naturally, might be pushed to the brink, interpreting it as yet another cruel twist of fate, and resort to desperate measures against themselves to escape the situation. Elisa felt no remorse. It was just life, their choice, their risk. She had her own plan and her own problems to deal with, especially in her line of work and the way she operated.

There was a downside. Domestic clients paid less, and she couldn't always guarantee receiving the full fee because she wasn't always paid in full upfront. They were, however, surprisingly frequent. There were, it seemed, a lot of people in the world who were prepared to take extreme measures to resolve their unhappy circumstances.

The real danger lay in her other clients. Big business, organised crime and well-connected people. In accepting work from this sort of clientele, she had to be careful. Some would act in the same way as her domestic clients and be docile to her deception, but she knew that others, in fact, most would have no reservations in contracting work out on her. They had the means and motivation to do so, and she knew it. Therefore, she had to be selective in the work she accepted and, in some circumstances, she had to fulfil her contract. She wasn't sure about this latest job. She felt uneasy, which was not a good sign.

As she sat facing the water, Elisa felt the rays of the sun on her face and she immersed herself in the warmth that they gave as she considered the instructions she had just received. Around her, the bustle of people on the quayside hummed as they went about their business. The waiter returned and on her left-hand side placed a silver stand next to the table and then in a graceful move placed a shiny wine bucket filled with ice and her bottle of 2009 Ca' Del Bosco securely positioned in amongst the ice cubes upon it.

He then accurately placed a coaster and a champagne goblet on the table before her. The waiter presented the bottle to her and efficiently sliced open the foil at the throat of the bottle before expertly exhuming the cork from the top without any spillage in what appeared to be one elegant movement. He poured the sparkling liquid into the glass and, after pausing briefly to make sure Elisa was happy, pulled an envelope from his waistcoat. He then handed it to her and said, 'Signora, per favore, complimenti della casa.'

Elisa took the envelope and thanked the waiter, he nodded respectfully before moving onto another table to resume his duties. She opened the envelope and pulled the simple card inside out slowly until it revealed a six-digit code printed in plain black letters.

She now had to get to the hotel and the woman who would guide her to the secure location. Elisa was becoming increasingly uneasy, this contract was becoming dubious and her intuition told her that there was something different about this job. She needed to be on high alert if she was to see the job through alive.

7. The Precinct

James Morgan was normally based in NYPD headquarters in One Police Plaza in Lower Manhattan, but he asked Sam to meet him in the 20th precinct where he was based for the day. The 20th precinct of the New York Police Department was on West 82nd Street on the Upper West Side. It was a grey drab looking two-storey building with grubby grey concrete walls and uniform dull looking windows.

The precinct was built in the 1970s and served the area that contained some of New York's most cultural visitor attractions, including the American Museum of Natural History and the New York Historical Society.

Sam's office was close to the 20th precinct, but New York was a big city and he was short on time. He took a cab north up Columbus Avenue, to Theodore Roosevelt Park before stopping short of turning left onto West 82nd Street and walking the rest of the way.

When he arrived at the precinct, he was greeted by the desk sergeant. He was a veteran officer in his early fifties, a no-nonsense kind of guy, polite, but straight down to business. He looked like he needed a holiday. Once Sam had explained why he was there and had gone through the physical security checks, he was allowed to meet Morgan beyond the security barrier and in an area of the building closed to the general public.

James Morgan was in his late thirties. He was a tall man of around six feet two, with a taut face and a chiselled chin. His hair was brown, neatly styled, cut short at the sides, but not close to the skin, with swept back hair crafted neatly on top of his head. He had sharp eyes and a serious-looking face that showed signs of experience or weariness or both. He wore a dark blue suit that, though not tailored, fit his athletic body well. His shirt collar was unbuttoned, and he didn't wear a tie. His badge hung on his jacket pocket for all to see.

When he saw Sam, he smiled and his face lost some of its sternness and transmitted the kind of openness that comes with a genuine recognition of friendship. He reached out his hand, and they shook hands, like the old friends that they were.

'Good to see you again, James.' Sam returned a smile back at Morgan who gave Sam a friendly pat on his shoulder with his free left hand.

'You too Sam, glad you could come over.' Morgan indicated to the corridor behind him and to a pair of elevators in a small lobby. He pressed the button to call the lift and as they waited, Sam took in the hubbub of the office beyond. There was a small reception area with desks manned by police officers tapping away on computer keyboards and staring into screens.

A partition cordoned off the elevator lobby area from the office to give a semblance of privacy. It was perhaps some form of administration or processing area. Sam thought the area's openness and proximity to the main reception made it an unlikely spot for holding criminal suspects, so it wouldn't require any special security.

The elevator arrived, and they took it to the second floor where it opened to a tightly packed office. Rows of workspace, like benches, stretched across the floor, with desks lining either side of a central partition. The paperwork that the officers were working on was piled high on the desks. Around the office there were notice boards laden with memos and posters informing the officers of various information, from codes of conduct to a local fundraising activity. Each wall held a large screen attached as high as the ceiling would allow, displaying yet more information to be observed.

The ceiling in the office was low, with three central lines of fluorescent strip lighting running the length of the office. Despite the illumination, the office felt gloomy. The sheer amount of furniture and people crammed into the space created a claustrophobic feeling in the room, and a sense of overwhelming urgency pervaded the atmosphere as phones rang, keyboards clicked, and various conversations took place. In the far corner, a well-used drinks machine gurgled and spat as it dispensed another serving of coffee into a cup for its willing recipient. In the other corner, a printer dispatched a ream of printouts to its user. The aroma of toner and coffee seemed to have merged and hung in the air.

Morgan directed Sam through the desks to a corner office which was positioned against a partition wall. It was glass fronted on one side with a solid wall on the other with windows looking down onto West 82nd Street. There was a desk and several well-used leather office chairs inside. Filing cabinets were positioned against the wall with various family portraits on. Sam assumed it was a designated office of one of the more senior officers.

'Have a seat, Sam.' Morgan pointed towards one of the chairs and pushed the door shut, whilst he positioned himself in the main chair behind the desk.

'Thanks for seeing me, James,' Sam began in a friendly tone. 'I really am concerned. These cases are becoming more frequent, so I hope you are going to tell me that NYPD has this under control.'

Morgan leant back and rested his arms on the chair, bringing his hands to a point, taking a small breath before starting. He had assumed the pose of a teacher considering a trivial question from a student. 'You are right to be worried, Sam. This is a serious situation. What you are witnessing is the tip of the iceberg. We are seeing an increasing number of psychotic related incidents and deaths across the city. But before we get into that, tell me how you knew that Spanish kid, Garcia, we found on Queensboro Bridge.'

Sam gestured at the room. 'Are we talking officially here, or is this just you and me having a conversation? You're usually down at the Plaza and hard to see during the day, so we have these kinds of conversations over bourbon in the Village. What's going on?'

Morgan adjusted himself in his chair and shrugged. 'There's nothing to worry about, Sam. I just happened to be up this way. The Commanding Officer of this precinct is a friend of mine. He lets me use this office when I need to get away from the main building. Sometimes you need space to think, you know?'

Sam looked around the room at the framed certificates on the wall and the Aglos plant on the desk. He wasn't sure why he felt so apprehensive. He put it down to the episode with Branfield that morning. 'Yes, I suppose so. Sorry. I just think it's strange how many of my clients are experiencing these abnormal episodes. I'm used to seeing people suffering from forms of distress that results in a change in a person's behaviour. I saw a lot of post-traumatic stress disorder from my days back in the forces. Usually, there is a trigger that is personal, which results in that person responding in a way unique to them as a form of a coping mechanism. In the forces, this was often because of seeing a grotesque incident or being blown up. This feels different.'

Morgan repositioned himself in his chair again and leaned forward slightly. His expression remained stern even though he was trying to pull a smile. He lifted his tone in reassurance. 'The situation is serious, Sam, but we are working on it. Tell me, what do you know about Garcia and maybe I can put your mind at rest.'

'Of course.' Sam relaxed a little. He'd known Morgan for long enough to give him the benefit of the doubt, even though his instinct told him something wasn't quite right about the circumstances. 'Garcia has been a client of mine for a number of years. You know I have over one hundred clients on my books, don't you?'

Morgan nodded. 'I'm sure you do. Go on.'

'Initially, a representative of his parents came to me in confidence. He's only in his early twenties. Garcia comes from a prosperous background. His family runs a successful chain of supermarkets that focused on the Hispanic community in New York. The chain has become a multi-million dollar business that has expanded nationally and the family has used the success of the supermarket business to expand into commerce and real estate.'

Morgan nodded again. 'Yes, Garcia does come from a very privileged background. This much we know, but why did he come to you?'

Sam paused before answering. 'There is such a thing as patient confidentiality, so I need to know that this is between just you and me.'

Morgan nodded before saying curtly. 'Sam, I need to know. It's important. I am speaking to you as a friend, but this is a live case. I'm not the only one working on it and I am trying to keep you out of being involved in it officially. If you were, you would have to say anyway and it wouldn't be me you would be telling. Have you heard of Scott Benante?'

Sam thought for a moment before replying. 'Scott Benante of the FBI, the guy who was heading up that counter terrorism job last year on the West Coast?'

'The same,' Morgan confirmed. 'We have the assignment within the NYPD for now, but Benante is sniffing around us. He thinks that the case could be linked to a national operation. We think otherwise, but we need to prove it or else we'll have to hand the case over to the FBI and they will come in all guns blazing and upset the Police Commissioner. He has political aspirations for when he leaves the position and wants to keep a closed shop. He doesn't want the FBI coming in on NYPD business and being seen to come in and save the day. One way or the other, these things get out into the press and he wants to demonstrate his capability for managing crime without help from federal agencies. It wouldn't do his record any good, do you see? If we can put this case to bed, then he gets all the glory and it is something he can shout about when he is running for office. We think the reason for Garcia's death might be the last piece in the puzzle and you may know something that helps us put it into place.'

Sam's brow furrowed in thought. Despite his trust in Morgan, something wasn't quite right. But, he thought, he knew he wasn't going to find out what was really going on unless he shared some information. At which point he might learn something else about what was really going on.

'Fair enough.' Sam shrugged. 'Garcia was first registered with me by a representative of his parents. Despite his upbringing through expensive private schools and given every opportunity to gain executive experience within his families businesses, they felt that even with his relatively junior years, he was not performing as well as he could. They thought he might have some sort of issue that I could help with.'

'What was the issue? He wasn't exactly shy according to the records we have on him.'

'Quite. It was the opposite. He was overconfident, arrogant, and aggressive in some circumstances. Not an attractive trait, but not uncommon amongst the very privileged children of hard-working families who have become very successful. It seems they had given him opportunities across a number of their businesses, a bit like an executive intern. He was working across different parts of the business to build up his skills and learning how the business runs, that sort of thing.'

'OK, so what was his problem?'

'In short. He just wasn't that clever, or very good. He was incapable of engaging with others and working collaboratively, and he didn't share the same strong work ethic as his parents. When his colleagues suggested changes to his business proposals or pointed out poor management decisions, he became aggressive and abusive. Any other intern would probably have failed their probation and been fired. But, since he was the son and heir to the family business, they continued to move him to different business units, trying to find something he was relatively good at, or at least something he wasn't terrible at and didn't irritate the people in the area he was assigned to.

'Sounds like he was a bit of a disappointment then. What treatment did you give him? I didn't know you type of quacks could make people smart.' Morgan quipped.

Sam flinched inside a little. For as much as he liked James Morgan, this sort of comment irritated him, especially coming from his friend, who knew some of his military background. Sam had chosen his new profession when he had left the forces because he could see how some of his fellow personnel had suffered as a result of years of mental and physical trauma and felt that he could help them and people like them out in the real world. A trauma surgeon could recover people physically and he could help people recover mentally. He thought it was karma for the years he had spent physically breaking people in his previous line of work. He was fixing heads now rather than smashing them.

'I started by engaging him through a course of Cognitive Behavioural Therapy. As you say, I couldn't make him any smarter. Deep down, he knew he wasn't the smartest kid on the block, but then, none of us are. Through the CBT, I could at least help him recognise when he was behaving unreasonably, understand where other people were coming from and ultimately give him a coping mechanism to deal with what was ultimately an inferiority complex. The intent was that he would be able to stop his aggressive and unreasonable outbursts and develop enough self confidence that he could become an adequate representative in the family firm and take it from there. The advantage he had over all the other employees was that he never wanted for money and was never actually ever going to get fired because his family owned the business, all he really had to do was become a good enough executive in the firm to make his parents proud.'

'So what happened? Did it work?'

'To a point.' replied Sam curtly.

'What do you mean, to a point?' pressed Morgan.

'He didn't really want to take part in the therapy, but when his family pressured him and they threatened to cut off his allowance, he agreed to participate. His progress was slow at first. He was late for appointments and distracted, but he did eventually engage and I thought he was beginning to commit. Then something changed.'

'What exactly? How do you mean changed?'

'In one session, he started asking about how he might accelerate the course of therapy, whether he could take a prescription to speed things up a little. I detected he was getting impatient in some sessions and he knew that I have a licence to prescribe medication.'

'So what did you do? Can you prescribe medication? I didn't realise that you could.'

Sam flinched inside again. Whilst he didn't expect most people to understand that there was an increasing movement to allow psychologists to have prescriptive authority, it was actually the reason that Sam had first been introduced to Morgan. Sam had gained a certificate from the Department of Defense Psychopharmacology Demonstration Project as he was preparing to leave the military. As a result, he was referred to the NYPD by someone to consult on a case several years ago that Morgan was also working on, and they built a relationship during their work on it. That Morgan had casually overlooked this or had done it deliberately as part of this increasingly abnormal discussion raised more suspicion in Sam's mind, so he reminded him to test his response.

'Well, if you remember, the reason we first worked together on the De Souza case was because NYPD needed a psychologist who could prescribe medication and who also wasn't intimidated to get into a room with a suspected psychotic. I didn't have a problem with it back in the forces and still don't.'

Morgan took a pen from the desk and pointed it toward Sam, waving it up and down like a conductor. 'Yes, of course. Do you prescribe much these days?'

'Occasionally. It's usually by exception. I didn't think prescribing Garcia medication would help him.' Sam paused as if to say more, but decided against it. The reason he was keen to meet was to get information from Morgan, not the other way around. Morgan still hadn't explained what he knew about Garcia and how they had come to find Garcia swinging from Queensboro Bridge. It was time for Morgan to start talking.

8. Trouble

Elisa spent more time than she planned to sitting at the café table. The instructions she had received were clear enough, but the nagging doubt about her situation compelled her to stay at the café longer than she really needed. She couldn't put her finger on it, but something about this job didn't feel right.

She could have left immediately to obtain the next set of instructions, but she considered it was important to think what she was going to do next and how best she was going to do it in the safest way possible.

She thought that by spending more time at the café, she could survey the area and plot her route from where she was to the hotel where she would find the safe and use the code that she had been given. More importantly, she could take the time to identify any observers who might be watching her.

When she had first arrived at the café, its tables had felt open and airy. It had felt like a protective shield because it was so public. However, since the telephone call, the low-rise buildings that once felt free and expansive now felt enclosing and restrictive. The sprawling lake in front of her which once lapped in a sedative manner against the quayside now seemed to be like an aquatic clock ticking away the seconds. Every ripple and splash was like a menacing metronome measuring time slipping away and urging her to move.

The sunshine that once glimmered therapeutically from every angle of the ripples in the water on the lake, reflecting beams of positive energy, now felt like they were projecting piercing laser beams repeatedly stabbing and probing. The lake now seemed to glare rather than glimmer.

Elisa resisted the growing sense of claustrophobia that the plaza was instilling upon her and refocused her mind. She took her bag, a brown leather Hermès with a gold clasp that glinted in the sunshine as she placed it on her lap. As she rummaged inside, her skin brushed against the soft chèvre leather lining before her fingers reached the reassuring feel of the cold hard steel of the Beretta Pico pistol that nestled amongst the other contents.

The Beretta Pico was her preferred choice of self-defence because it was specially designed for easy concealment and a snag-free draw. Its .380 calibre bullet was sufficient to inflict ample damage at short range and its ability to hold seven rounds, six in the magazine and one in the chamber was enough for immediate self-defence in close quarters although it was not her primary weapon for completing work for her clients.

She preferred more subtle, less crude methods than a gunshot, although from time to time she had found that guns and all that they entail were sometimes a necessary evil in her line of work. A similar model, held in a holster on her left thigh, complimented the Beretta in her bag.

Elisa found what she was looking for, a pair of Persol shades, with a brown and black patterned rim. She placed them on and sat back in her chair. The sunglasses helped to avert the glare from the lake and gave Elisa a false sense of camouflage. Whilst the shades did not hide her, they allowed her to study the area casually without appearing to be looking around.

She casually looked to her left and the direction that she must take to the Hotel Refersco. There was an alleyway between the low-slung buildings of the plaza facing the lake that led to the hotel. Flanking the alleyway, there were tables on the plaza from the "Casa sul lago" café. Most were occupied by people who looked like holidaymakers. They were groups of people of mixed ages, families most likely. There was the odd table with couples, but none that appeared to resemble any threat.

It was not possible to see where the caller might have been. Elisa thought the most obvious place for them to be sitting was in one of the building's balconies, hidden by planters or the shade of the building's overhang.

The alleyway that led to the central part of the town was in between the Casa sul lago and Bar Italia. The seats and tables in front of the bar were arranged in uniform rows and occupied similarly to that of Casa sul lago with the waiters bustling around like ants tending to the tables.

There was no obvious threat, so Elisa decided it was time to make her way to the hotel. There was little to gain from being over paranoid. Even though the wine had been compliments of the house, she placed a tip under her glass and gathered her belongings. She kept her bag strung over her left shoulder and the clasp loose so that she could quickly snatch the Beretta if she needed to.

She strode from the table towards the alleyway, glancing to her left and right, in tune with her natural stride. She took in faces and people's movements, remaining on high alert. The clinks of cutlery and lively chatter followed her as she walked. As she neared the alleyway and the low-slung buildings, the sounds faded. The tables nearest the indoor of the café's appeared less popular as they were away from the grandeur of the lake and were partially shaded from the splendour of the sun.

The alleyway was framed with an ancient stone arch that spanned the width between the café and the bar. The window in the arch had traditional shutters in dark wood and, on the roof, there were turrets on either side connected by a railing. The bars of the railing were intertwined with the green stems of the herbs in the planters that had wrapped themselves around the bars and were peering above the rail up towards the sky.

The ancient cobbled stones of the alleyway were laid in a uniform pattern. It was wide enough for a small car to pass through and there were signs of where tyres had run over the cobbles wearing them down. To the left and right of the passageway there were occasional doorways, grand in stature with heavy traditional wooden doors dressed with heavy ironmongery and the occasional metal gate reinforcing the already steadfast doors.

As the passageway progressed, the buildings became taller, some reached up to four storeys, yet the ancient stonework and occasional draping of vines down the walls gave it an intimate rather than intimidating atmosphere. Nevertheless, Elisa's instincts drove her on to get back out in the open as quickly as possible where she felt less vulnerable to being trapped.

The passageway ran straight for fifty yards before leaning left and back right again before opening up to where several other alleyways joined to form a large open piazza. In the centre stood a fountain, which was adorned with bubbling jets and a central ornate statue.

On each corner of the piazza stood a café, gelateria or shop that were adorned with traditional stonework and discreet signage that were welcoming to all and tended to the needs of the locals and tourists. People drifted casually along the pavements whilst the occasional car trundled carefully around the fountain over the cobbles. The sound of Vespa's rasped in the distance as they accelerated and the sound echoed against the walls of the narrow roads.

The Hotel Refersco stood prominently on the piazza. It was a tall building of around ten storeys. It was grand in stature, presented in traditional Roman concrete with heavy Baroque architectural influences. Each of the windows was highly decorative with square lintels and semi-circular arches. Tuscan columns flanked the sides of the window. The perfect proportions of the windows and columns were maintained across the entire facade of the building.

Ornate ledges spanned the width of the building below the windows of each floor. A dome, infused with windows, adorned the roof, creating a grandiose effect of its own.

At ground level at the entrance to the hotel stood a porte-cochère constructed with the same Tuscan style columns as the windows and garnished with decorative plants. It was wide enough to allow the passing of several vehicles side by side.

As Elisa entered the piazza, she glanced behind her into the passageway to check for any familiar faces that may have followed her from the quayside. She orbited the piazza to the right, occasionally glancing into the shop windows, feigning interest to allow her to pause and check her surroundings.

At the entrance of the hotel, a doorman stood next to one of several large grand doors. They were gilded in a golden frame and adorned with highly polished solid gold door furniture. As Elisa approached, the doorman greeted her politely and held the door open. She returned the greeting with a smile and as she passed into the building, removed her shades. As she put the shades back in her bag, she made sure the Beretta was still there.

The lobby of the hotel was large and luxurious. The floor was made of highly polished marble that was arranged in a symmetrical pattern of black and white squares and emblazoned in the centre with a crest inscribed with the words "Vincere est vincere omnia" - *"To Conquer One is to Conquer All"*.

The opulence extended to the ceiling and walls, lavishly adorned with additional gold gilding. The ceiling's discreet lighting and the bold fixtures on the walls worked together to cast a light that emphasised the luxurious design, making the space feel airy and inviting. The lobby was filled with several beautiful pieces of furniture. The chairs and sofas were constructed of the highest quality wood and upholstered in the finest Italian fabrics.

Elisa's instructions had been to liaise with a woman in the hotel lobby who would be working from a laptop with a red leather briefcase open on the table adorned with the hotel crest. The woman in the lobby would guide Elisa to a secure left luggage area of the hotel, where she could use the code to obtain the papers detailing the target. This method of sharing details using physical paper was supposed to help limit the digital trace of activity.

She scanned the lobby, looking for her liaison point. In the distance, she could see the reception desk. Adjacent to the desk, there appeared to be an archway to a private area, which to Elisa, seemed to be the most likely location of the secure luggage area.

To the left of the marble crest on the floor there was a

collection of chairs arranged around an antique table. Upon the table rested a red leather briefcase adorned with the hotel crest. Sat in the chair was a serious-looking lady working on a laptop. She was dressed in a tailored grey suit with a golden coloured cravat. She had long, dark hair and was no more than thirty years old.

As she worked, another hotel worker, a man of around fifty, smartly dressed in a similarly coloured suit, approached her table. As he neared the table, he paused respectfully with his hands behind his back, waiting to be invited to speak. The lady with the golden cravat continued to work for another moment before pausing and granting the man the opportunity to interrupt her. After a short exchange, he nodded, turned on his heel and headed toward the reception desk. Elisa smiled to herself. Whoever this lady was, she held some seniority.

Elisa watched the man for a second as he started his walk towards the reception desk before she began her own walk towards the woman holding court amongst the gilded glamour of the marble and gold hotel lobby surroundings. As she did so, she wondered how this woman would treat her. Would she be expected to wait until invited to speak, standing on point like a naughty schoolgirl?

Elisa presumed her arrival was expected and that her description would have been given to anyone who needed to know. The lady in the lobby might not have known the nature of the business but would, Elisa suspected, be expecting her arrival and would as a result be ready to extend her a level of courtesy that guests of such an establishment expected to command.

She took a couple of purposeful steps in the table's direction and cluster of chairs. As she did so, the woman at the laptop seemed to sense her presence and looked up from her laptop, their eye line met and their eyes locked for a moment.

Without warning, their connection was broken as the woman was thrown forward from her chair as an explosion from the direction of the reception desk engulfed the hotel lobby. The sound of the blast had splintered the air with a thunderous crack and sent a shockwave across the room.

The force of the detonation sent Elisa sprawling to the marble floor, which was now littered with debris. For a moment, she lay still on the ground. The blast had disorientated all her senses, and she needed time for her brain to process what had just happened.

Smoke drifted from the reception area across the lobby. The lights in the ceiling that had once gleamed were now extinguished. Part of the ceiling now hung down, exposing wiring and cracked concrete beams. Beneath the gaping holes above, the floor was littered with fragments of plaster and dust. The splinters of material dispersed across the now cracked marble floor seemed to glisten like dangerous confetti.

Elisa's disorientation subsided as she registered her senses one by one. The blast had caused her to lose her hearing and her head pounded with a throbbing pain caused by the pressure of the explosion.

She staggered to her feet, using a toppled sofa to support her as she tried to regain her sense of balance and orientation. Behind her, the once grand and elegant windows and doors that had adorned the front of the hotel were cracked and shattered. As she turned her head, the smoke drifted over her face and she smelt the acrid burning of plastic and felt the heat of the room on her skin. She coughed as the smoke caught in her breath and then, without warning, her hearing returned.

The wall of sound in her ears was loud and piercing. Between the ringing, she could hear cries of pain and screaming coming from within the smoky mist that engulfed the lobby. She regained her balance and stood tall, checking for her bag as she did so. Miraculously, it had held steadfast on her shoulder despite her fall to the floor.

As her instincts kicked in, she quickly released the clasp on her bag and reached inside to grasp the Berretta from its position nestled next to her sunglasses. She turned to look where the table had once stood with the laptop and briefcase on. The table had been toppled, and she couldn't see the briefcase or laptop through the smoke. There was no sign of the woman that she had glimpsed before the blast had sent them both sprawling.

Now in full survival mode, she turned back towards the entrance to escape. As she did so, she glimpsed the flickers of flames in the distance through the smoke and with them, the carnage of destruction that the blast had inflicted upon the once luxurious lobby.

Through the smoke, she could see silhouettes of people lying on the floor amongst the rubble. A couple, drenched in dust, dishevelled and disorientated, staggered past her. The man, in his fifties, supported a woman as they made their way towards the exit of the building. Both of them had bloodstains on their clothes and had injuries to their faces.

Then, without warning, another figure lurched from the smoke. Elisa recognised him as the man she had seen moments earlier, taking instructions from the woman at the laptop before making his way towards the reception desk and what appeared to be the epicentre of the blast.

The man was no longer smartly dressed. Blood poured down what was left of his face from the top of his skull, which had been damaged in the blast. His right leg was only a bloody stump interlaced with the rags of what had once been his tailored suit trousers. The blast had seared the front of his body, and the remnants of his suit were interwoven with his flesh in a bloody mesh of tissue.

He dragged his stump forward in a last ditch effort to find something, or someone, to help him out of his desperate plight. He tried to raise his bloodied and ragged right arm forward as his natural human instincts of survival drove him forward before he let out a final gruesome cry and collapsed face first down onto the once flawless marble floor. There he lay as the final stillness of death overtook him.

Elisa began coughing again. The ringing in her ears was subsiding. She looked towards the table where the woman with the laptop had been and still couldn't make anything out. She couldn't do anything to help. It was time to leave.

She turned to face back where she came in. She held the Beretta in her hand as she half walked, half crouched towards the doors that she had come through. The glass lay shattered on the floor, with most of the remnants pushed outside on the pavement by the force of the blast. The glass had cut the doorman, who had let her in just a few minutes earlier.

He was still resolute in his professionalism and was helping people to escape from the building via gaps in the glass. Where necessary, he had smashed out the jagged remnants that had remained stuck in the frames to make escape easier and less dangerous.

Elisa carefully hopped through a window frame and hurried through the people gathered outside the entrance. The piazza was a scene of chaos, with the injured stumbling out of the hotel, while others rushed towards them from across the square, desperate to help.

The sound of sirens wailed in the distance as the emergency services made their way towards the scene. Spectators had already gathered on the edges of the piazza to witness the drama as it unfolded, close enough to feel part of the action but far enough away to feel safe.

As Elisa made her way through the crowds, she returned the Beretta back to her bag and put her sunglasses back on. Despite the shock, she had escaped unharmed. Whilst she had witnessed the painful final moments of a man suffering an unholy demise, she wasn't fazed. She had seen death many times before.

She picked up her pace and took the first turning away from the hotel into a street that she knew led to where she had parked her car. She could hear noise all around as people shouted in the air behind her from the hotel. Emergency services were arriving, and good citizens were trying to help those injured in the blast.

A crowd drifted in front of her, heading toward the hotel and the scene of the incident. As they did, she had to weave between them to keep moving. Amongst the mix of sounds, the loud rasp of a Vespa filled the air over her shoulder and her instincts made her turn to face the sound and prepare to take action. The Vespa accelerated towards her, forcing people to jump out of its way.

Elisa reached for the Beretta in her bag and, as she did so, recognised the rider of the bike as the woman with the golden cravat from the hotel. She wasn't wearing a helmet, and as the air rushed past her, it swept her dishevelled hair back, giving her an air of elegance. She stopped in front of Elisa and reached into her suit.

Elisa pointed the Beretta at the woman in readiness. She had no desire to kill in cold blood in an open public space, but given the circumstances, she felt she had no choice. Now that the two women were close to each other, Elisa could read the name badge on the lapel of the woman from the hotel. It read "Daniela". Daniela pulled an envelope from within the inside of her suit.

'Take this!' she said in perfect English, holding out the envelope. 'It is for you. It is what you came to the hotel for today.' She pushed the envelope towards her again, urging Elisa to take it from her.

'I don't understand. What happened back there at the hotel? Who are you?'

'It doesn't matter who I am. I was supposed to give this to you today. I saw you in the hotel lobby before the explosion. It was supposed to be in one of the hotel secure lockers, but I had it removed before you arrived.'

'Why? What made you do that? There was an arrangement in place to use a code.' Elisa shouted above the noise. She put the gun back into her bag.

'Yes, of course, usually it is not a problem, but earlier today we had a problem with the locker security system. I couldn't afford to take the chance that you did not get the package as arranged. The people that supplied it are not to be let down, you understand?' She pushed the envelope towards Elisa again, urging her to take it. She now had a look of desperation on her face.

'As you arrived I had Lorenzo, the man you saw me talking to in the lobby just before…' she paused and began to sob. 'Oh, poor Lorenzo, I asked him to check if the security system was fixed so we could prove the code to you if you didn't want to take the package without it.' She leaned forward and forced the envelope into Elisa's hands. She looked into Elisa's eyes, tears appearing in her own. 'Take this. Whatever you do, don't let them down. They will not forget, I know.'

She got back onto the Vespa and looked again at Elisa. 'Trust me. That explosion was no accident. They didn't care who would be coming today to pick up the package, they just wanted whoever it was dead, which means someone now wants you dead. I've done my bit and I'm in danger now too, but I'd be dead anyway if I didn't get that envelope to you. You understand? I'm leaving now. I suggest you do the same. Whoever you are, whatever you do, I don't care, but don't let them down and watch your back!'

With that Daniela turned and sped off on the Vespa, her long dark hair flowing behind her. To anyone else, she looked like every other erratic scooter rider in an Italian city darting between people in the narrow ancient streets, but Elisa knew she was running for her life. She now had to do the same.

9.Thorny Words

Darko and Marvin watched with interest from within the crowd of onlookers outside the hotel as smoke drifted through the broken windows of the building and up into the sky. They had followed Elisa as she had left the lakeside café and ventured through the narrow streets and to the hotel. They thought she had seen them following her, but she had carried on walking, oblivious to their presence.

When she reached the piazza, they watched as she went into the hotel and then they waited patiently, sitting inside a coffee shop on the edge of the piazza. They sat at the café's raised seating. The seating was setup like a bar at the front window, tall chairs faced outwards, looking across the square to the hotel across the piazza.

They did not have to wait long. The explosion had come as a surprise. For a moment, they had been worried that there would be a problem with the plan, which meant that they themselves might have a problem. It was at that point they had left their Americanos and joined the rest of the onlookers watching events unfold in the cluster of people that had formed at the front of the hotel.

When Elisa had skipped through the broken glass window and

made her way through the bystanders at the hotel entrance, they were relieved. Unlike most, they had noticed the gun she was carrying close to her body as she made her escape and saw her put it back in her bag to avoid causing suspicion or alarm. Knowing her background, they expected her to be armed.

As she made her way through the streets, they drifted away from the cluster of spectators and began their discreet pursuit of her from a distance. They were certain Elisa couldn't have completed her business at the hotel before the explosion and watched on with interest when the girl from the hotel had zipped past them on a Vespa. They had paid her well to facilitate the exchange, so they were keen to see what she would do next.

They watched from afar as the exchange between the two women took place before the girl on the Vespa motored off into the distance. The hotel girl could wait. She could run all she wanted, but they knew they could find her if they really needed to.

When Elisa reached her car, she had driven the red Alfa Romeo with a high degree of skill and urgency to her villa. The black AMG Mercedes they were driving was powerful enough to keep up, and they knew where the villa was, but they had to make sure that she was going there and not to another location. If they lost her and the information in the package she had just received, then they would have a problem. They stayed far enough back from her to avoid her suspicion and drove to avoid any attention from the local Carabinieri.

Now that she was back at her villa with the package, they knew she would soon prepare to leave. With the sun beginning to set and the darkness of dusk laying shadows on the ground, it was time for them to strike.

***

Tension hung thick in the office's air on the second floor of the 20th NYPD precinct. Sam had become tired of answering questions and feeling like he was under some form of interrogation. He had responded to all of his friend's questions and now wanted answers to some of his own.

Morgan had been pushing Sam about the treatment he had recommended for the kid, Garcia, and what medication he had been prescribing. Though Sam was getting bored with answering the questions, Morgan was not and kept pressing for more information.

'So tell me what exactly you prescribed Garcia. I need to know. Garcia was mixed up in some dodgy underground business and I'm trying to work it out. I'm not saying you had anything to do with it, but I need to know what went on between you two.'

Sam was taken aback. In one seemingly innocuous statement, Morgan had accused him, a friend, of both being involved in some sort of drugs business and simultaneously threatened him to get answers. If he thought that this discussion was strange before but wasn't sure, he was certain now that something wasn't quite right.

'Look, I don't know what you are getting at but I don't like how this conversation is heading. I came here because I thought you could help me get some answers about why my list of patients with psychosis is going through the roof, not bust my balls about my practice. What exactly do you think happened to Garcia?'

Morgan threw the pen he had been holding onto the desk in front of him and held his hands up in defence. He looked straight at Sam.

'Sam, I'm going to level with you. I am interested in what went on between you guys. I need to know. Not for me, you understand. I know you and you know me. It is to protect you from the other guys investigating the case who don't know you like I do. If I know what happened, then I can make sure that there is no more heat put in your direction.' Morgan leaned in. 'That's why we are down here, rather than up at the plaza. You would prefer to tell me than have some of the other guys pull you in officially, wouldn't you?'

Sam nodded. He still wasn't convinced. He could smell bullshit a mile off, and Morgan was dishing it out by the truckload.

'I thought so. Look. Tell me about you and Garcia and I'll tell you everything I know about him, how he died and what we think is going on. I promise you, once we've been through it, I'm sure it will all make sense and we'll be back to normal supping bourbon in the Village and arguing about the Mets and the Yankees.'

Sam put on his best smile to feign satisfaction with the crap he had just heard from a friend he thought he could trust. Morgan was playing him and he didn't like it, he felt the rage inside him growing at the betrayal. The last thing he wanted to do now was to share a drink with him. As far as he was concerned, Morgan was lucky Sam hadn't shoved the pen he had been waving about through his face and beaten the truth out of him.

It was one thing to do his job, but he seemed to have forgotten their history together and Sam's past life in the military. He had survived interrogations in Afghan caves with mercenaries and come out the only one alive. If Morgan thought he could intimidate him, he must be delusional. Nevertheless, he knew he had to play the game. He kept his calm and told Morgan what he wanted to know, or at least what he needed to know for now.

'Like I said,' Sam began. 'We started with a course of CBT, but Garcia was impatient. He didn't want to take the time to work it through, he wanted faster results.'

Morgan listened though he didn't take notes, nor was he on the edge of his seat.

'It was innocent enough at first.' Sam began. 'He framed the question about medication speeding up the CBT course, but then he just started asking if there was anything I could prescribe to fix him up, like a performance enhancing supplement. It's easy to find out I am authorised to prescribe medication as I am registered with the American Psychological Association, as you probably know.'

Sam couldn't help having a sly dig at his "friend" given his earlier comment.

'His family probably knew this as well before they decided on whom to provide treatment. Given their business acumen, I'm sure they did their research, and as I operate at the premium end of the market, they will no doubt have checked my credentials before getting in contact. I'm not intimidated easily. I just advised him that he didn't require medication and that he should follow the course as agreed.'

'Do you prescribe medication to many of your clients?' Morgan asked flatly.

'No,' Sam replied equally to the point.

'So what did he do? How come he ended up mixed up in drugs?' Morgan asked, finally giving over some information about what might have happened to Garcia and what this was all about.

'What do you mean? Mixed up in drugs?' Sam said. Morgan shifted uncomfortably in his chair as if he had said something he shouldn't. He paused for a second before replying. His face was filled with concentration, as if he were trying to work out exactly what to say or how to say it.

'We found Garcia was involved with a…' he paused before continuing '…drugs organisation,' he finished. 'That's why we are so interested in what he had been saying to you. It could be important.'

A drug "organisation" was a strange choice of words, Sam

thought. What the hell was a drug organisation? He couldn't have meant a gang because he thought Morgan would have just said gang. Perhaps he meant a company, he wasn't sure. He made a mental note of it and continued to explain about Garcia's treatment.

'After I refused him a prescription, he seemed to accept my decision. We carried on with the course of CBT for several weeks, but over time, I detected a change in his behaviour. At first I thought he was responding to the therapy, but I could tell that there was something more. His therapy should have just made him more confident, less self-doubting and to have learned several coping strategies in order to lead a team without being overly aggressive and to continue his family's business legacy.'

'What do you mean, something more?' Morgan said.

'Well, he seemed to become more…intelligent, like he had just had a brain transplant or had suddenly read a million books on everything. It was like talking to a different person. Within our conversations, he began reeling off obscure and highly detailed facts in great depths on a varied number of complex topics, such as chemistry, mathematics and physics. He could talk extensively and often did throughout the whole of our appointment. It was quite unnerving to see this sudden change.'

'That's interesting, and unexpected I guess, so what did you do?'

'I listened, but he was talking about things I didn't really understand, so I recorded some of our sessions and did some of my own research on what he was saying.'

'Sounds like a good idea, what did your research tell you?' Morgan shifted in his seat again and leaned forward slightly, as if to listen more intently.

'When I played back one session he was talking about Planck mass, quarks and bosons and that he had worked out how to calculate the value of dimensionless physical constants and that he could tell me how to work it out if I wanted, although I would have to pay him. Naturally, I declined. not really understanding what he was talking about. However, when I researched what he actually meant, I was amazed.'

'Well, what *was* he on about? It doesn't make any sense to me.' Morgan was now on the edge of his seat, listening hard.

'When I looked it up, it turns out that dimensionless physical contacts is an element of quantum physics of which there are many unanswered questions and he seemed to think he had worked some of it out.'

Morgan shook his head, trying to absorb what he had just heard. His forehead was frowned in deep thought. He leaned back in his chair before responding.

'And did he say anything else? What about your other sessions with him?'

'Well, that's where it becomes even stranger. We had one or two more sessions where he would recite the most fantastic details of things I had never heard of and then nothing.'

'What do you mean, nothing?'

'He just stopped. He came to the sessions and he could barely string two sentences together. He struggled to speak, to think, almost like he was suffering some sort of mental illness, just like the others.'

'Remind me, how many people have you seen like this?'

'Well, I have several hundred clients on the books, but I would say this has been affecting around twenty, the latest being Miles Branfield, a well-respected and very rich Wall Street financier, I can't see him being involved with a drugs organisation though.'

Morgan harrumphed in disagreement. 'I think you probably know that Wall Street and respect are a matter of opinion, especially after the financial crash. There are lots of people on Wall Street who take drugs.'

'I agree, many do. I just can't see Branfield being involved in a drugs organisation in the same way that you are suggesting a young man like Garcia was. It doesn't explain the others as well. Are you saying they are all in on this drugs organisation?'

'No, no, no.' Morgan held up his hands. 'You're getting the wrong end of the stick. That's not what I am saying at all. It's just strange that a lot of these episodes are happening with your clients.'

'I'm not sure what you mean by that.' Sam's tone was much more aggressive now. He was getting frustrated again. 'I've seen this in some of my clients and I've talked to some of my peers and they have had the odd instance too.' He stared at Morgan. 'If you read the news, there are people having issues all the time. How many are drugs related? I don't know, but they don't all come through my door.'

Morgan smiled, trying to calm the atmosphere. 'I know, I know, so what do you think is going on?'

Sam was ready to explode. He came to his friend to find out what was happening, not to be interrogated about his practice.

'I don't know, James, as far as the pattern goes with my clients, I am treating them all for various degrees of psychological disorders that are well within the boundaries of treatment. If I were to hazard a guess, I wouldn't be surprised that drugs of some sort might be involved, certainly in Garcia's case, but the varied nature of my clients experiencing these issues doesn't all paint the same picture. Are you trying to tell me that Iris Helmsley, a near eighty-year-old woman who is part of a wealthy New York family suffering from terminal cancer, is mixed up in the same business as Garcia? Now cut with the crap and tell me what I came here for. What do you think happened to Garcia and how did he end up hanging from Queensboro Bridge?'

Morgan stirred in his chair uncomfortably before beginning to talk.

'Alright Sam, I'll tell you, but I think you are going to be disappointed. We don't know that much.'

***

Two hours later, Sam sat in his office on the Upper East Side, thinking over what Morgan had finally revealed. The conversation with Morgan hadn't exactly gone as he had expected and he was happy to have left the grey, drab building of the police precinct behind.

In contrast to the office in the precinct, Sam's own office was light and airy. He kept a separate space to the room which he used for clients. The office had a high ceiling and there was a large window that filled one wall and looked out onto New York. He had a mahogany desk that was over seventy inches wide and over fifty inches deep. The surface was finished with black hide writing leather, made from a single piece.

He had salvaged the desk from a shop in the Bronx. The desk had been in a room at the New York State Library and was damaged in the 1911 fire. It then spent years slowly deteriorating, unloved by its various owners over the years. Sam had bought it for a hundred dollars and spent many more having it restored to its former glory. It was now the centrepiece of his office.

Sam took a sip of coffee. He didn't mind admitting he was a coffee snob. He liked his coffee to be full-bodied in its purest form, made from freshly ground beans with no milk or sugar. He felt a sense of calm as the coffee's familiar taste hit his tongue.

Taking a large gulp of the dark liquid he went over in his mind what Morgan had told him about Garcia.

'*Mixed up with a bad bunch of drug dealers from The Bronx, up to his eyeballs on God knows what.*' Is what Morgan has said. '*Had probably been high as a kite when he was coming to see you, which would explain his strange behaviour. Nothing for you to worry about. We have it all under control.*'

But Sam was worried. The story didn't stack up to him. Garcia was an intelligent kid from a wealthy background. Why would he get mixed up in the New York underworld? It didn't make sense. It also didn't explain why he was seeing similar behaviour in some of his other clients. Was Morgan trying to say they, too, were getting mixed up in some drug ring?

If that wasn't enough, it was the last thing that Morgan had said to him as he left that really didn't add up. Morgan had meant it to sound like some sort of olive branch after their somewhat thorny conversation, but it came across loud and clear as a threat.

'*You know, Sam, I saved you a lot of trouble with the Feds by doing this. They thought that because of your connection to Garcia that you were acting as some kind of high-class drug dealer, serving the Upper East Side's finest. They could still think it, if I told 'em so. So I would steer clear of the Garcia case. I would also think twice about those other clients of yours who are acting funny. Do you really want to keep them on? You don't want the Feds knocking on your door, do you?*'

Sam swallowed the last of his coffee. Its taste gave him a sense of satisfaction, unlike Morgan's words still ringing in his head. There was no doubt in his mind that there was more to it than Morgan was letting on and he had no intention of giving up any of his clients which meant that if his old friend wouldn't tell him the truth, he would just have to find it out for himself.

10. Villa of Death

Elisa felt the drive from Desenzano del Garda had taken a long time. She had been eager to leave after receiving the envelope with the job details during her encounter with Daniela. Every turn in the road had felt like an effort and despite the power and speed of the Alfa Romeo, it seemed as if the traffic had always been against her, slowing her down.

Unusually, the explosion in the hotel had unnerved her setting her on edge. Now above anything else, she felt an urgency to leave. Even worse, her frame of mind meant that she had not kept her discipline and followed the procedures that she normally followed so meticulously.

She hadn't checked her mirrors when driving for any signs that she was being followed. She hadn't taken an indirect route back to the villa to mislead anybody that might try to follow her and now upon arriving at the villa she had not checked for any signs that anybody may have entered the villa while she had been away.

Before leaving, she had carefully set several motion-activated cameras at key entry points around the villa which she could view through her phone. She did this wherever she stayed, whether it was a luxury villa or a budget hotel to give her a first line of defence. Even though she herself was not usually a target, her paranoid protection routine had, to date, kept her on track to get out of this business alive.

Pulling up to the villa, exiting the car, and walking up the short drive, she missed the icon on her phone showing the motion-activated cameras had been triggered and that a recording was available.

She rushed up the drive, clutching her bag from the passenger seat, which held the Beretta and the envelope she'd been given. The villa Elisa had rented was a single storey building with a double door entrance at the front. It was painted white in a classic Mediterranean style and had a terracotta tiled roof. A small, open porch with square columns framed the double doors at the front. One of which was adorned with a plaque displaying the villa's name "Villa Angelo". The grounds were well maintained, showcasing a colourful mix of plants and the occasional cypress tree strategically placed to create a classic Mediterranean landscape.

As she hurried from the car, the scent of lavender lingered in the air from the garden. Ignoring the main entrance, she followed the path from the driveway to the side of the building where a large iron gate adorned with a decorative floral pattern stood. It was secured with a digital lock that was controlled by a keypad hidden in the adjacent brickwork.

Elisa tapped in the access code to release the lock and pushed the gate open and made her way alongside the villa, allowing the gate's spring return mechanism to close itself and for the lock to reengage with a sturdy click.

The side passage opened up to an expansive outdoor dining area, alongside a spacious swimming pool that shimmered in the evening light, with the pool lights now illuminated both in and around the water.

She took the keys from her bag, ignoring the gun and fumbling, used them to open the heavy, wooden framed glazed double doors into the villa. Locking the doors behind her, she rushed through the kitchen and headed towards the bedroom to collect her belongings and to make her escape.

Once in the bedroom, she took a leather wrapped Louis Vuitton case from the cupboard and threw her clothes from the wardrobe into it. She collected her accessories from the adjoining bathroom and placed them into the matching holdall on the dresser.

She began feeling paranoid as she packed, pausing now and then when she imagined a sound inside the villa, before shaking it off and going back to what she was doing.

As she emptied the last of her clothes from the drawers, she zipped the larger holdall up and clicked the lock shut and pulled out the handle to move the bag onto the bed. As she did so, a man's voice spoke to her from behind.

'Going somewhere?' he asked.

Acting on instinct and using all her strength, she gripped the handle with both hands, turned, and swung the case from the bed lunging it toward the voice behind her. As the bag left her grip, she reached for the concealed Berretta under her skirt on her left thigh and assumed a shooting position with her legs spread for balance, gripping the small gun with both hands in readiness to shoot.

The holdall sailed across the air and hit the man in the chest, knocking him off balance, forcing him to fall backwards into the bedroom doorway.

Lying on his back and looking up from the floor in surprise, the man cursed. 'Cazzo di inferno! What are you doing? It's me, Max!' He pushed the case to one side and sat up, steadying himself with his arms behind him and looking up to face the barrel of the gun now pointed in his direction.

'What are you doing? What did you do that for? Is that a real gun?' he blurted out in a panic. 'I'm sorry. I didn't mean to frighten you, don't shoot!' he cried as he turned his head and tried to cover his face with his arms in a vain attempt to protect himself from the potential gun shot.

'What are you doing in here?' Elisa screamed, still holding the gun, pointing directly at him. 'How did you get in here?'

The adrenaline surged through her veins and her heart pounded in her chest. Upon seeing Max she felt relieved, but she was equally annoyed that she had let him creep up on her without noticing.

'I'm sorry, I'm sorry. After last night when I had to leave so quickly, I wanted to see you again before you left. I know the family that rent out this villa and told them I wanted to give you a nice surprise. They gave me a key so I could get in. What is this all about? Why have you got a gun?'

'You stupid idiot, you shouldn't have come here.'

She didn't have time for this. Last night she had told him that her holiday was over and that she had to leave. Elisa's composure returned after the initial surprise of Max's untimely and unexpected arrival. She became aware that she was still holding the gun towards Max and that he was cowering stricken on the floor like a rabbit caught in a set of headlights.

With the danger averted, she lowered the Beretta and quickly stuffed it into the holdall on the dresser with her bathroom accessories. She held out a hand to help Max to his feet. He paused momentarily before accepting it, and then took it, pulling himself up to his feet. He stood back, straightened his shirt and ran his hand through his hair before smiling gingerly at her, trying to reassert himself.

'Pass me the case off the floor, will you?' she instructed, pointing to the case that was now resting on the floor half in, half out of the bedroom. He did as he was told, silently turning to pick up the case before placing it on the bed and sitting upright beside it.

'I have to leave,' she said as she leant over the bed to reach her handbag, placing it over her shoulder and then grasping the holdall.

'What is going on? Are you in trouble? Was that a real gun?'

'Look,' she began before pausing and starting again less aggressively and with more patience. 'You shocked me, that was all. It's not a real gun, it's one of those self-defence gadgets. It would have given you a nasty shock and a bad headache at worst,' she lied. 'You shouldn't have sneaked up on me like that.'

Max relaxed, letting his shoulders slide.

'I'm sorry. I just wanted to see you again.' He reached for her hand with his. She ignored it and stood back, with a serious look on her face, holdall in hand, ready to leave. He went to reach for her again when the sound of a window being smashed came from the direction of the kitchen.

They turned instinctively towards it before turning back to face each other. Max looked bewildered, while Elisa's face remained serious, but now with a focused gaze and a glimmer of zeal in her eyes. They remained momentarily frozen as they listened to the sounds coming from the kitchen.

The sound of glass cracking as a metal crowbar struck the kitchen door forcing the reinforced window to shatter echoed across the villa. The crashing sounds continued as fragments of glass fell onto the floor tiles and the sound of someone hitting the window repeatedly until a powerful final hammer blow forced a large segment of the glass through the door and onto the floor.

As the crashing sounds travelled from the kitchen to the bedroom, Max stood up from the bed and looked back at Elisa. He then began to scan the room as if searching for something before remembering the "self-defence gadget".

'Give me the gun,' he said as he held out his hand. 'I'll see what's going on. Whoever it is, they won't be expecting to see me and as soon as they see the gun, they will get scared and run.'

Elisa's mind raced. She knew that whoever was breaking into the villa was unlikely to be an opportunist burglar, as Max suspected. Elisa was sure that the assailants were connected to the day's earlier events and had come to the villa after her and the envelope she had received. She cursed herself for not being more careful on her drive back from the town.

As Max held out his hand, waiting for the gun, Elisa quickly considered her options. What was she to do? If she let Max confront the invader, he was likely to be badly hurt or worse. Whoever it was or whoever they were, they were likely to be trained or at least experienced assailants. Her priority was to take care of herself and the envelope and make her escape. But did she do so by putting herself in the firing line ahead of a casual acquaintance or use him as a shield to allow her more time, however short, to assess the situation and find a way out alive?

Within a second, she had decided, she unzipped the leather Louis Vuitton holdall and retrieved the Beretta and placed it in Max's outreached hand. He took it gleefully and, without taking the time to examine the "self-defence gadget" in any detail, held it with both hands up close to his head pointed at the ceiling like a detective on an American TV show. He took a step towards the bedroom doorway before turning back to Elisa.

'I'm sure as soon as they see me and the "gun" whoever it is, they will make a run for it, but it might be worth phoning the police in case there is trouble.'

Elisa nodded and moved towards her handbag as if to reach for her phone. Max leaned forward and kissed her on the forehead, giving her a reassuring smile before heading into the hallway towards the kitchen. The bedroom was in the middle of the hallway. To the left, the hallway stretched out for around ten yards before opening up to a small reception area behind the main entrance doors to the villa. To the right, the hallway extended for a similar distance, becoming increasingly wider as it neared the kitchen and the poolside area.

Despite its length, it was light and airy, with large floor to ceiling windows on the outside wall to provide maximum light. High archways in the ceiling sat upon columns along the length of the hallway and heavy metal chandeliers hung between each archway, suspended from the ceiling, out of reach.

The floor was made from natural stone tiles, which extended throughout the villa, but in the hallways, solid wood flooring was used with the stone tiles inset within it. The walls were light in colour with clean lines adorned with the occasional original painting so that the smooth appearance was maintained throughout the hallway.

Max made his way slowly towards the kitchen trying to stop his shoes from making a sound as he stepped along the solid floor. The crashing of shattering glass had stopped, replaced by the sound of clicking as the doors were unlocked and the sound of footsteps crunched the fragments of glass against the tiled floor as the perpetrator or perpetrators entered the villa.

As he made his way along the hallway and neared where it opened up into the kitchen, Max thought about what he was going to do. He remembered from the previous night that the hallway opened up to the right of the kitchen, so he knew that until he rounded the corner, the intruder would not be able to see him.

He decided that surprise was his best tactic and that when the intruder was faced with a man holding a "gun" when they were only expecting a woman alone, if anyone at all, the encounter would be all but over in seconds, with the invaders being scared and running for their lives.

Max shimmied along the hallway with his back against the wall and the Berretta held up in front of him. He paused for a second, listening to the crunch of footsteps in the distance before using his back to push himself off the wall and launch himself out from the hallway and into the kitchen. He held the gun up with both hands and shouted, 'Stop what you are doing! I've got a gun and the police are on the way!'

Before he had even finished his sentence, he knew he had made a mistake as he saw the stranger standing before him. Darko Vidic stood across the kitchen twenty feet away, his face chiselled and calm. Dressed all in black, wearing gloves and holding a two-foot crowbar in his hands that he had just used to smash the door window in.

In the confinement of the room, he looked taller than his six foot four inches. Max noticed the holster around the man's waist. He was no expert in guns but knew straight away that he was in trouble and that this was not an ordinary burglar.

Ignoring the gun pointed at him, Darko began walking towards Max.

'Where's the girl?' he asked. His accent was thick Eastern European and his tone gruff and direct. He held Max's gaze directly with his own.

'Don't come any closer, or I'll shoot!' Max shouted. His arms trembled in trepidation as his finger began to squeeze the trigger. He feared the "gun" wouldn't be enough to deter the advancing man and began to wonder what would happen if it didn't.

Darko saw fear in Max's hesitation, a reaction he knew well from past experiences in the military. Max, afraid to shoot, took a step backwards to prolong the need to fire and, as he did so, glanced down again at Darko's holster.

In that moment Darko seized his opportunity and lurched forward and upwards with the crowbar in his left hand attacking the gun Max held in his right. The crowbar struck the bone of his forearm, lifting the arm and the gun upwards. As Darko approached Max pulled the trigger, but the momentum of the crowbar forced the shot wide and the Beretta out of Max's grip, causing it to spin through the air and land on the floor, sliding towards the sink.

Darko moved in quickly, dropping the crowbar on the floor and grabbing Max with both arms, pulling him closer and with his own forward momentum, delivered a vicious head butt that caused Max's nose to split and blood to gush down over his mouth. Max screamed in pain as the blow landed and stooped forward, bringing his hands up to his face. As he did so, Darko brought his knee up hard into the man's face, jolting Max's head back and forcing him back upright.

Using the power and weight of his body, he grabbed the scruff of Max's neck and pushed him from behind across the floor towards the sink, forcing his head to crash against the tap. With blood now dripping from a cut on his forehead and blood streaming from his nose, Max screamed for mercy.

'Stop! Please!' he cried through the blood dripping over his lips.

Darko span him around and leant him back against the sink and grabbed his shirt. 'Where's the girl?'

Max blubbed. He lay back against the sink, feeling disorientated and confused. Who was this man and what did he want? His right arm was screaming in pain and his head was throbbing. He could only muster up a muted response

'Mmph, huh I...I,' garbled Max. Before he could finish Darko grabbed him again slamming him back against the sink like a rag doll and screamed in his face.

'Where's the girl?'

'I don't know,' Max lied, panting through the blood still dripping over his lips. Enraged, Darko slammed him against the sink again.

'Tell me or I'll kill you!'

Dishevelled and beaten, Max pleaded for his life. 'Please…no!' He tried to push Darko away with his good arm, but Darko was too strong and forced him back against the sink.

Darko, fuelled by rage and with the expertise of a close-combat expert, quickly forced Max's injured arm upward, He then spun Max around to face the sink, pushing his right arm deep into the garbage disposal. The pain in Max's injured arm pierced through his body as the bigger man squeezed his forearm tightly, holding it down the hole.

'Tell me where the girl is now!' Darko snarled. 'Or I'll turn it on.' Darko used his free hand to move towards the switch on the wall behind the tap that operated the garbage disposal unit whilst using his right arm to squeeze Max's injured arm and keep it forced in the disposal unit.

Max, now delirious, couldn't think clearly. The pain up his arm was excruciating and seemed to reverberate throughout his body. Blood dripped from his forehead, obscuring his vision and as he glanced back over his shoulder at the granite face and the soulless eyes that seemed to want to penetrate his skull, he knew that this man would not stop until he was dead.

In desperation, he balled his left hand into a fist and swung it with all his strength at the man's head. The blow landed against the side of his body, but the angle of the punch and his debilitated strength meant that Darko barely registered the impact and the attempt at retaliation only seemed to fuel his rage.

Defeated, Max pleaded again, 'No! Pleaaasseee!'

His plea turned to a sickening scream as Darko flicked the switch on the wall. The rumbling sound of machinery began, and the sink vibrated as the metal impeller plate began to spin and grind against flesh and bone.

Blood bubbled within the grinders as Max's fingers were mangled and torn. The pain was too much for him and he passed out. As he did, he slumped forward onto the sink, lifeless and forlorn.

As Max went limp, Darko flicked the switch to stop the mechanism. Max's arm disengaged from the mechanism and his listless body slumped to the floor, a trail of flesh and blood from Max's mangled hand smearing its path. Blood seeped from the injury and began to pool as his body lay still on the ground.

Darko stood back from the sink, standing over the body,

looking for signs that Max was feigning unconsciousness. Satisfied that he was no longer a threat, he turned to search the rest of the villa for the woman.

The speed and ferociousness of the steel crowbar took Darko by surprise. The cold metal struck his temple and sent him reeling backwards. His arms flailed in the air as his instinct sought support to prevent his fall. As he stumbled backwards, his boots caught Max's dishevelled body on the floor, unbalancing him further.

As Darko floundered, another blow from the hard steel hand tool struck the side of his head. The force of the second blow and momentum from the first drove his body to collide with the kitchen unit behind him before he collapsed unconscious on the cold floor. He landed with his back propped up against the cupboard and his long legs splayed over Max. His head lolled downwards onto his chest as if he were snoozing on a long car journey.

Elisa stood poised in the middle of the kitchen, crowbar in hand, alert and ready to strike again. She paused momentarily, composing herself as she looked down at the two men slumped on the floor in front of her. Her heart was beating fast, and the adrenaline was coursing through the veins in her body. She had only just made it in time. If Darko had turned around even a second earlier, he might have seen her approach and blocked her attack.

She gave Darko's leg a hard kick to check he was unconscious.

The solid mass of a leg moved, but he remained still. Lying beside him, Max was still alive. She could detect the slight movements in his torso as he breathed in and out.

The face she had found so alluring was now battered and stained with drying blood. She could see the grotesque deformation of his hand and the pool of blood that had formed around it on the floor and felt a tinge of guilt. She was responsible for letting him unwittingly confront the slab of a man who now lay partially on top of him and who she had known was more than just an ordinary intruder.

Elisa quickly pushed her feelings to one side, telling herself that Max had been nothing more than a convenient romantic acquaintance in a rare moment of misjudgement and that she had to refocus. She'd not asked him to find her, and there was nothing more she could do for him without putting herself at risk.

Still gripping the crow bar, she picked up the Berretta from the floor next to Max. As she bent down, she caught sight of the gun holster on the side of the large man slumped next to him. Placing the crowbar down, she readied the Berretta and leaned over and unclipped the gun from the man's holster. She held the Berretta firm, ready to fire in the event the man woke up.

Struggling because of the angle, she retrieved the gun and stepped back to give herself space from the two men and to inspect the weapon. She recognised it immediately as Heckler & Koch VP9, a gun she had used in the past. A 9mm semi-automatic handgun used by police forces the world over for its ease of use and significant stopping power. However, she doubted that the man lying slumped against the kitchen units was a member of any law enforcement organisation.

Standing in the kitchen with the Heckler & Koch, she heard a voice calling out in the distance. It came from the same side of the villa where she had entered. The voice rang out again, louder this time. A man's voice, urgent but trying to stay hushed.

'Darko. Darko, you there? Have you found the bitch yet? I heard noises.' The voice was American with a southern drawl. He called out again. 'I'm comin' in. I've got something for her.' His voice sounded much closer this time.

A man came into view through the window over the sink that overlooked the outside dining area. He was of medium build with short cropped hair. He walked with a swagger as he rounded the villa into the pool area and towards the now open kitchen double doors.

Elisa stood still and watched as he walked around the building, unaware that she was watching him from the kitchen. As he passed the windows and reached the double doors, she could see he was casually holding a gun in his right hand. He glanced at the broken window, before looking up straight at Elisa.

'Wha? What you doing, bitch?' he asked with a confused look on his face. He began to speak again, but before he could, Elisa had dispatched a shot from the VP9 into his chest. His face changed from a look of confusion to shock as he stumbled backwards towards the pool. He tried to raise his own weapon, but he was too slow. Elisa fired two more shots into his chest, forcing him back even further. Dark blood stains appeared on his shirt and flickers of blood splattered to the ground around him.

As the now stricken man staggered backwards, Elisa fired a final shot, hitting him directly in the face, sending blood and fractures of skull airborne. When the bullet struck, his body seemed to lift off the ground before plummeting, arms flayed into the pool behind him. Shockwaves spiralled across the water as the impact broke the stillness of the surface. As the body drifted on the water, blood seeped from its wounds and turned the illuminated water a crimson red.

Emotionless, Elisa turned to check that the man on the floor was still unconscious before quickly heading back into the villa to collect her belongings and leave. This time, she had been lucky, her carelessness had almost cost her life. She could not afford to be as careless again. The events in the town had told her that this job was going to be different, but was she ready for what was to come? She had always planned that this would be her last job, but it might not be for the reason she had thought. This time, she might not finish it alive.

11. Investigations

Two days had passed since meeting Morgan at the 20th Precinct. Sam had spent the previous day seeing clients as normal, trying not to think too much about the meeting with his old friend. To say that the meeting was a disappointment was an understatement. He had trusted Morgan, and still did to a certain extent, even though he had been treated with a certain level of unexpected disdain. Morgan's accusations did not sit well with him, and he couldn't help but think that all was not as it seemed.

Could Morgan actually be trying to help protect him by warning him off? Was Morgan under pressure from someone or something else that was forcing him to act the way he did? Sam wasn't sure either way. He knew one thing for certain, he was going to find out.

Sam had spent the morning calling around several colleagues who also worked in the psychotherapeutic field. He was not a regular on the professional circuit and did not attend professional seminars, instead, concentrating on his own work and a trusted network of associates. One of his measures of assurance he used flippantly, yet seemed to hold a high degree of accuracy, was whether he would go for a drink with any of the people he liaised with in professional circles. If they passed the "beer test" then it was more often than not the case that they were likely to work well together, or at least not annoy the hell out of each other. It was a measure that worked both ways. Sam hadn't always seen eye to eye with other practitioners in his chosen field.

His military past had left him with little patience for people he felt were being deliberately obfuscating, either through choice or a lack of the ability to consider alternatives to the consensus on a topic being driven by the professional community.

Sam met individuals at seminars who, when discovering his military past before becoming a psychotherapist, considered him and other non-traditional practitioners as inferior. He and some of his peers had also faced prejudice because he had not come from a family of practitioners within the medical field or attended any of the most prestigious institutions to study his field.

Whilst he and others like him had not attended Harvard, Stanford or Oxford or any of the other elite institutions, he was a qualified professional. Besides his study, he had first-hand experience of intense psychological circumstances in the Middle East, Asia and Eastern Europe that would have the Upper East Side's psychological elite crying into their cosmopolitans and retreating to the Hamptons for their own psychological wellbeing.

During a seminar in Singapore, he had encountered a psychologist who asserted that his ground-breaking techniques for managing Post Traumatic Stress Disorder were unparalleled and would revolutionise the treatment of those afflicted with the disorder.

Sam had recognised the man through sheer coincidence from a small article in the Wall Street Journal. The piece was not about the doctor directly. He was photographed in the paper with his brother, who was a member of the US Senate. The doctor, hailing from Massachusetts, had just delivered a thirty-minute lecture to an audience of nearly a thousand delegates in which he spent most of the time criticising many of the methods employed around the globe. His new methods lacked any clinical examples, or data to back his criticism, even though many charities had used established techniques to improve the lives of countless patients.

His lecture had finished with a five-minute sales pitch to the audience to invest in his new methods so that he could grow his new institute and extend the use of these new techniques around the world. Sam had felt that he had been watching a sales pitch for a fast-food franchise.

He was introduced to the man, Doctor Scott Silver MD, shortly after the lecture as an affiliate of the New York Psychological Collective or NYPC. Upon introductions and learning that Sam had a military background, Doctor Silver had quickly overlooked Sam's professional credentials and tried to use him as an example to sell his new techniques and institute that he was establishing. He went as far as advocating that Sam would be a prime candidate to invest in his new institute and may not only help others through his learning but help himself.

Sam had considered a throat punch to shut him up, instead when Silver had paused for questions and was expecting adoration from his audience, Sam asked him why he needed more investment when he had just secured $200 million from the Pentagons military medical research fund. The article in the Wall Street Journal had been celebrating the investment and the actions by Senator Silver to secure the funding, tipping the new company as a potential investment.

Sam's sharp probing had turned Doctor Silver's Perma-smile into a frown which then turned into a scowl when Sam had gone onto ask whether his brother was going to be on the board of directors and if the staff and patients from the seventeen not-for-profit organisations that were closing down because of the diversion of funds were likely to be transferred to the new institute. This information had not been declared in the newspaper. Sam had learned of the connection from an industry magazine. The only reason he had remembered it particularly was because one of the clinics affected was near to his practice in New York City and had been successfully helping emergency service first responders with their conditions.

Silver was not given the chance to respond as his team ushered him on to the next group of regional specialists to which he could continue his pitch. As he did so, his Perma-smile returned to his face as he began his introductions to his new audience. As Silver left the group, the president of the NYPC had ambled up to him.

'You really got him there Sam, but why do you have to be so direct about it? We may have been able to use his group to promote our own.'

'He was only interested in establishing more funding for his own institute. He doesn't care about anyone else,' Sam had retorted.

'Well, next time just smile and shake his hand, eh?'

'Yeah, sure,' he had replied unconvincingly as the NYPC president scampered off towards Doctor Silver to make amends.

Despite his somewhat curt approach to his wider professional peers, he seemed to command a level of respect from them, even if it was probably more of a reluctant respect out of courtesy and a response to his more direct approach.

During the day, he had spoken with a dozen of his more hesitant contacts within the NYPC. Despite their reluctant respect or disdain they may have harboured for him when he asked them about any patterns of new or concerning behaviour they might have observed in their clients, new or old, they were, after some comforting small talk, quite open to discuss matters of professional concern.

Sam found most professionals are keen to do their best for their patients, and psychotherapists were no different. If there was the possibility of improving their patients' lives (and their own pockets) then they were keen to work with others in their field. Some patient behaviours could also be alarming and from purely a self-defence point of view, practitioners were keen to share information discreetly about conditions and sometimes individual cases that could help them avoid potentially challenging or even dangerous situations.

During each of the conversations, the pattern had been the same. Initial shock and reluctance to talk, followed by a slow thawing of the ice as Sam had launched into a somewhat less than direct and distinctly unconventional charm offensive during which he explained his concerns about his own patients. He did so without sharing the details of his engagement with the federal authorities but did include his fear for the community in the city during which he could sense the shift in receptiveness in most (but not all) of those he had spoken to.

After his explanation, he was met with a brief pause before the voice on the other end of the line began slowly opening up about one or more clients that they were treating that had begun to cause them concern. It was often prefaced with a statement that they were only sharing the information because they were concerned about the wellbeing of their clients and seeking reassurance that any information shared would be treated in the strictest confidence and in line with the professional code of conduct.

Following sufficient reassurance from Sam, who maintained a professional demeanour despite his impatience, they detailed client behaviours consistent with his own professional experience. One such description from Doctor Meadows, an aloof character when it had come to Sam in the past, who ran a practice upstate and had done so for nearly forty years, was surprisingly keen to discuss what he was seeing.

Doctor Francis Meadows was not a man to mince his words. If he had something to say, he would say it. To whom he liked and how he liked. Doctor Meadows was a man in his mid-sixties, with thinning white hair and a trim white beard. He was overweight and almost appeared to waddle as he walked. Despite his abrupt demeanour, he was very well respected within the profession, both in New York and across the country. Until the last five years he was a regular on the international lecture circuit until the point where in his own words he'd "eaten enough hotel food, spent enough time in airport lounges and spoken to enough people who thought they knew best and didn't listen anyway" and so had retired from the circuit and focused his time between his own practice downtown and his place in the Hamptons where he courted wealthy widows with his intellectual tales and basked in the memory of his short-lived national fame.

He had, in the past, commanded a handsome fee for his efforts, most notably for his involvement in working with the police to identify and convict a serial killer that slaughtered lone female night workers across the mid-west, twenty-five years prior. He had appeared in the pictures of the TV newscasts and had stood with the chief of police as he had updated the press on the progress of investigations in the case. From time to time, he had addressed the press directly in the pleas for information regarding possible suspects based on his psychological analysis of the patterns of behaviour.

At first, he had been mocked for his analysis and had been a source of ridicule in the media for his so-called insights. The media were convinced that the murderer was most likely a lone male, a bum with no job, most likely a Mexican or a black man. This theory was supported and stoked by various TV psychologists and ex-cop turned TV hosts who had claimed the behaviour was consistent with that of previous cases and had then gone onto host TV specials describing how this new killer was copying those that had come before him.

When the killer had turned out to be as Doctor Meadows had described, a wealthy white woman using hired hands to seek revenge against her husband for marital misdemeanours, Doctor Meadows was hailed a hero and had courted a period of media fame before the attention inevitably turned to the next big story.

The relationship between Doctor Meadows and Sam dated back over five years. When Sam had opened his practice, Doctor Meadows was one of the first of his peers in New York to welcome him into the fold and to offer his advice. Now many years later he was still following that advice, "if you smell a rat then there probably is one".

'Noticed any strange behaviour in my clients?' Meadows had balked with a hearty laugh at the question. 'Most of the clients in this business have strange behaviours. That's what makes them clients. I thought you would have worked that one out by now!' Meadows had teased.

Sam smiled down the telephone receiver refusing to bite, he knew Meadows liked to toy with his peers, in fact he liked to toy with anyone he talked to, it was his way of working out what the other person knew and what kind of state of mind they might be in.

'True, but as you have always said, it is our job to understand and to help not to mock or pass judgement,' Sam had retorted tongue in cheek. Meadows had once said this to him when Sam had expressed anger in a seminar about one of his clients who had refused to help in a police investigation, citing their delicate psychological state. Sam thought that his client's knowledge could have helped the police identify the suspects in the case. It wasn't his psychological state (he was being treated for a minor obsessive compulsive disorder). He was just too chicken shit to help.

Meadows laughed again. 'Very true and very wise words might I say'. Meadows paused before continuing. His tone had shifted and Sam knew that playtime was over.

'Particularly erratic behaviour, you say? It's not exactly uncommon in our profession, as you are already aware. There are many circumstances and psychological triggers that prompt erratic behaviour. It is often the body's natural coping mechanism to the situation it finds itself in. It is our job to help clients identify what these triggers might be, may they be economic, physical or any other trigger that might cause the body to respond. Once we have done this, we must help our clients control this behaviour through the various tools that we have at our disposal, cognitive behavioural therapy etc.' Meadows breathed hard in between sentences, it sounded like he was impatient to get through the detail.

'Anyway,' Meadows went on, 'to answer your question, I did attend a recent meeting of the NYPC where several members of the group had highlighted that they had been seeing an upturn in cases of particularly disruptive and psycho psychotic behaviour.'

'Did anybody have an explanation for it or identify any patterns?' Sam asked.

Meadows paused before responding. 'Yes, and no. Did you ever meet a Doctor Riggs practising out of Brooklyn?'

'No, not that I recall,' Sam replied after pausing for thought. 'Why do you mention him in particular?'

'Well, Doctor Riggs is quite a character. He is a very successful man, both inside and outside of our field. Quite an entrepreneur, you might say. He has expanded his psychotherapy practice beyond pure psychotherapy. His practice is now much more of a medical centre employing a number of doctors in various fields, from your regular MD to dermatologists and pharmacy dispensation. I understand he may even have expanded out onto the west coast and have several successful medical centres out there too.'

'He sounds very successful, but what has that got to do with the upturn in patients with erratic behaviour?'

'It doesn't directly, but what if I were to tell you that in our meeting of fifteen members representing hundreds if not thousands of patients across the state, every single one of those doctors, many with decades of experience in the field and some who have published works to their name, agreed that there was a new and concerning pattern of behaviour from new and existing clients displaying the same symptoms as you describe, extreme paranoid psychosis.'

'I am sorry to say that your example of the young man committing suicide on the Queensboro Bridge is not an isolated occurrence. Half of the members of the group had patients who had killed themselves, as a result, it would seem of their distressed state, though not conducted quite as publicly as your own case. These were patients of varying ages and of relatively affluent backgrounds. Even colleagues who hadn't personally encountered such extreme cases knew of others who had. This series of events is unprecedented. Every single member agreed that this was not a normal pattern and that we should, as a professional community, report it to the medical and legal authorities as a cause for concern. Everybody except one.'

'Riggs?'

'Yes exactly, Riggs!' Meadows exclaimed, banging the desk so hard Sam could hear the thud of his fist on wood down the phone line. Meadows was now breathing even more intensely down the other end of the phone.

'Did he give a reason for not wanting to report it?' Sam asked impassively. He could sense his old friend getting worked up and imagined him getting pink in the face.

'Yes, he did,' grumbled Meadows. 'Have you heard of the Medical Research Group?'

'Vaguely,' Sam replied. 'I think I've had a call or an email from then inviting me to join. I don't think I paid them much attention and dismissed them as some sort of scam organisation. I seem to recall them being quite persistent, though. They were offering some sort of financial reward and guaranteed clients for joining them just as long as I gave them a priority commitment of my time over my own client base. In the end, I lost patience with them and told them in no uncertain terms (he stopped himself from using the exact language he had used) that I wasn't interested. It felt like joining them would strip me of my independence as a practitioner. I took enough orders in the military. I wasn't about to sign up to take orders again anytime soon.'

Meadows harrumphed on the other end of the line. 'You may well have made the right call there. The Medical Research Group, or MRG as Riggs called it, is the parent group of his burgeoning medical empire. He was keen to raise the pattern of increasing extreme psychotic episodes in the state and wider area with them before going to the authorities. He said that we might be able to use their wider resources to help provide a solution.'

'What did the others say?' Sam queried, although he thought he already knew the answer.

'Initially there was some reluctance from one or two members of the group who were keen to report it as soon as possible, as was I, but Riggs was quite insistent. As he made his case, a number of the group backed him up, before eventually the group agreed to let Riggs refer it to the MRG before reporting it to the normal medical authorities.'

'Why do you think they agreed to his proposal? It doesn't seem entirely in line with professional ethics,' Sam asked.

'Quite. I was absolutely furious that the group would agree to do such a thing. We need to maintain our independent integrity as an organisation, not to pander to unaccountable corporate entities,' Meadows replied angrily.

'So what did you do?'

'I argued against the decision, but it was pointless. Most of the group were supportive of the MRG proposal and were happy for Riggs to take the issue forward,' Meadows retorted. 'God damn fools!' Meadows breathing was becoming alarming now. 'The meeting ended with Riggs agreeing to come back with an update from the MRG findings in our next meeting or before if he learnt anything significant.'

'And has he come back with anything?'

'No, and I wouldn't trust anything he came back with, anyway. This needs a proper investigation by the correct authorities, not by some two bit drug store chain. I wasn't going to wait to see what he came up with.'

'What do you mean?'

'Well, I stewed on it for a couple of days, trying to understand why the group would want to use this MRG organisation rather than the usual route for these kinds of concerns. Then, whilst browsing through the business section of the New York Times, I saw them.'

'Saw who?'

'The whole goddamn lot of them, that's who!'

'Sorry, who are you talking about? I'm not following.'

'Castle, Wolfe, Stolberg, Hansen, the whole goddamn lot of them. All fifteen of them,' Meadows said with a growl as he reeled off the names.

'The NYPC? Where did you see them?'

'In the paper, all standing together with Riggs in a group of about thirty people, celebrating the opening of the latest MRG medical centre in New Jersey. The lot of them are members of the goddamn MRG!' bellowed Meadows.

'No wonder they all sided with Riggs in your meeting,' said Sam. 'And you didn't know they were signed up MRG members?'

'Of course I didn't know!' yelled Meadows down the phone. 'I knew they probably would have been asked, just like both you and I have been. But I didn't know they had signed up. As members of the NYPC, they have a duty to declare any interests and not a single one has. They've all been bought, the bastards!'

'So what can you do?' asked Sam. 'Expel them from the group?'

'No, that would be pointless. There's no rule against having outside interests, it's just wrong to not declare them. They are good people too. I wouldn't want to lose them. Anyway, I've already done what I can.'

'What's that?'

'I've done what we should've done in the first place instead of referring it to the MRG. I've reported it to the correct authorities.'

'And? Any luck?'

'Disappointingly, no, not much progress. I was promised a call back within a couple of days. A couple of weeks later, I had a call from a guy at the 20th precinct, telling me it was on their radar and they would look into it. I'm not holding my breath. So, maybe the MRG might be our best route after all. Perhaps if they are a big enough organisation and they want to, it might get the right level of attention.'

'Thanks Doctor Meadows, can you keep me informed of any developments please? I need to get to the bottom of this.'

'Yes, of course. What's your plan?'

'I'm not sure yet, but you have helped to confirm my suspicion that something is happening in the city and it needs to be fixed before more people die!'

Three hours and several calls later, Sam was sitting at his desk in his office. The day was drawing to an end and the sun from the New York sky cast a shadow across the room as it shone through the window and across the room. Sam was feeling jaded. He had brewed a cup of strong black Hawaiian Kona coffee. He took a sip as he lay back in his leather office chair, closed his eyes and savoured the smooth flavour. He felt the warmth of the evening sun through the windows as it drifted over him. His mind began to wander and as he took another sip, still with his eyes closed, he thought of Gina in the coffee shop and how he would like to take her out on a date.

He should call her and began to think about where he could take her out. He had heard good things about Bené's on West 55th Street, a taste of France in the heart of New York, or so he had been told. He took another sip of coffee and began to consider what might be on the menu. He was debating fillet mignon or Dover sole over in his mind as the sound of his phone ringing broke his train of thought.

It was Morgan. He sounded stern and stressed.

'Sam,' he grumbled down the phone.

'How are you?' Sam replied jauntily.

'Not good, I've just spent the last half hour on the phone to the Fed's. I told you to be careful.'

'Now wait just a...' Sam interrupted before Morgan interjected again.

'No, God dammit! You listen! They want to talk to you about Garcia and the drugs. They want me to bring you in. I'll pick you up in thirty minutes. Don't go anywhere.'

'OK, I'm...'

'I know where you are. Don't go anywhere, or it won't be someone as friendly as me picking you up!' Morgan snarled and hung up.

Sam threw his phone nonchalantly onto his desk, put his feet up, sipped his coffee and waited for the ride off his old friend.

12. Dead Men Tell No Tales

It was rare for anyone to get the better of Darko. In a war zone, you had to be alert at all times, and Darko had developed a habit of maintaining high levels of concentration. If you lost your focus in the heat of the battle, then you could end up dead. He had learned his lesson the hard way and was lucky to be alive.

In his case, a scar on the right side of his abdomen from a knife wound served as a constant reminder. He had been careless then, allowing himself to be blindsided by an attack during a close quarter military operation in an assault on an enemy installation. The knife had deflected off his body armour missing any internal organs as it had pierced into his flesh. He had bled badly and had never forgotten the pain of the knife as it had entered his body. On that day, he was lucky, his assailant had been shot dead by another member of his team.

Although not now in a combat zone, he was again fortunate. As he regained consciousness from his position, slumped on the kitchen floor of the villa, he felt the dried blood down the side of his face and the throbbing pain in his skull.

As his senses returned, he noticed the man sprawled next to

him. The man's mangled hand lay in a pool of blood that had gathered around his severed limb. His body was contorted, his face turned towards Darko, cheek pressed against the ground, his lifeless eyes staring into nothingness. He was dead.

Darko felt no remorse. He had no intention of killing the man when he had come to find the woman, but it was inevitable when the man had confronted him that it would not end well for him.

He pushed the man's body aside and stood up, pausing for a second to rest against the kitchen counter as he felt dizzy. When the light headiness had passed, he assessed his surroundings. He patted himself down, checking for his gun, which he realised was now missing. Pausing, he listened for sounds of anyone in the villa. Nothing. There was a stillness in the air as if a thunderstorm had just passed.

He pulled the kitchen drawers open, searching for a weapon, before noticing the knife block near the sink. He took a large knife from the wooden holder and then scanned the room for another armament. He saw the metal bar lying on the floor tiles and he had a flashback to the face of the woman as she had caught him off guard and knocked him unconscious.

"Bitch!" he thought as he reached down and picked up the bar. "She should have killed me." With the knife tucked in his belt and the metal bar to hand, he quickly searched the villa, looking for people or clues to the woman's whereabouts.

Most of the property was undisturbed, as if unoccupied. Not

unsurprising, if it was just a bolt hole. When he reached the bedroom, he found signs of existence and a hurried exit. In the ensuite, scattered toiletries surrounded the sink, and towels were left hanging over the bath.

Darko worked his way through the drawers and wardrobes. Empty. He stood staring at the bed, cursing himself for being so careless. If he had to report that he'd lost her, he might not get paid. Not the end of the world, but he didn't like to fail.

As he turned to leave, he saw the flash of white in the corner of his eye next to the bedside cabinet. Moving closer, he saw it was a piece of paper, wedged down the back of the cabinet against the wall. He pulled the cabinet aside. There he found a pen, a ring and a piece of paper that he examined. It was two pieces of paper folded together.

One was a receipt of two days ago from a restaurant in Desenzano del Garda and on the other, written in pen was an address in Milan. The date on the receipt convinced him that this belonged to the woman. It must have fallen behind the cabinet and either the woman had not noticed or missed it because she had been in a rush to leave. Darko put the paper in his pocket knowing that it could be nothing. In a fit of rage and frustration he put his foot through the night stand.

He then made his way through the villa back to the kitchen, taking a last scan of the room for any weapons or anything he might have dropped before frisking the dead man's body. He found car keys, a wallet and a phone. The phone was showing several missed calls but had a PIN code, so he tossed it aside. The wallet contained around two hundred euros in cash, which he took and various other cards he left behind.

Crunching over the glass from the broken door, he made his way out into the garden and the poolside where he saw Marvin's blood-soaked body bobbing in the pool. Darko was about to turn to leave when he had second thoughts. He knew Marvin was careless and may have something on him that might tie both Marvin and the job they were working on back to him when the police and forensic team searched his body. He may also still have his gun on him, which would come in useful.

Darko circled the perimeter until he reached a storage unit on the far side of the water next to the pool house. Inside, amongst the various maintenance equipment was a long hook. He used it to catch Marvin's shirt and drag his heavy body across to the poolside.

He worked quickly, routing through Marvin's pockets, trying to avoid getting any blood on himself. Marvin's skull was no longer intact, but the grisly nature of his injuries didn't faze Darko. He had seen many gruesome injuries during combat and could mentally block out any negative thoughts. That he had a severe dislike for the man almost brought a smile to his face.

He found Marvin's phone and wallet and put them in his own pocket. Marvin still clasped a gun in his right hand. Darko prised the gun from the stiff, cold, wet, death ridden flesh of his former colleague and put it in his own gun holster. Despite the water, he knew the weapon would still operate if had to use it.

Satisfied there was nothing incriminating left on Marvin's body, Darko pushed his sodden corpse back into the pool and strode to the side gate through which he had come some hours earlier.

He wasn't exactly sure how long he had been unconscious, but it must have been at least two hours. It was getting dark and the sound of crickets could be heard as they began their evening chorus. The looming darkness pleased Darko, as it would help him leave undetected. Less pleasing was letting the woman get away. Frustrated at his own shortcomings, he was keen to resume the pursuit and determined to let nothing else get in his way.

He hit the electronic release pad to the side of the gate and dragged it open. As he did, a set of car lights rounded the corner and pulled into the drive. The engine gave a final throaty roar as the driver pulled the car up close to the villa. Darko was not a car enthusiast, but he knew the iconic shape of a Porsche 911. The driver climbed out of the vehicle, adjusting his expensive-looking suit as he stood tall. He smoothed his dark black hair back to ensure everything was perfect before heading to the villa.

With an air of confidence the man knocked the front door. He surveyed the garden as he waited. He knocked again, harder this time. He waited briefly before calling out in Italian, *"Ms Giusti, are you there? Max, where are you?"*

Darko watched as the man knocked on the door again without waiting for an answer and impatiently turning to head back to his car, muttering under his breath. The man rounded the vehicle and instead of getting back in, opened the passenger door and rummaged through a box before producing a set of keys. Darko cursed as he realised the man must be some sort of estate agent.

He now had a decision to make. If the man went into the villa and found the dead body in the kitchen and Marvin floating in the pool, he would alert the police. This was something that Darko wished to avoid. It would likely mean police being put on high alert, with the possibility of roadblocks if the police identified either the woman or himself as a suspect and started a manhunt. Darko was going to have to deal with the man to stop this from happening. He quietly closed the gate and dashed around the rear of the building and entered the villa through the kitchen doors.

Once inside, he crept silently down the hallway and positioned himself beside the front door to remain hidden when it opened. As he waited, Darko considered his next steps. He could take out the man as he entered the villa, snapping his neck to kill him instantly. Whilst this would be quick and easy, based on the look of the man, Darko did not consider that he would be any danger to him so there might be another option.

As the man on the outside negotiated the lock on the door with a key, Darko made a decision. He wouldn't kill him straight away, he would disable him and see what information he could get about the woman. If nothing else, he would take the man's Porsche.

13. Meeting the FBI

Morgan arrived at Sam's office well within the thirty minutes he had predicted. Given the time of day and New York traffic, that was pretty impressive, which made Sam think Morgan either couldn't have been too far away or was already on his way when he called. Either way, he was interested to hear what Morgan had to say and even more interested to hear what exactly the FBI was going to say about Garcia and the reason they felt they could pull him in. This was about to get interesting.

Morgan buzzed on the intercom to Sam's office with three long, hard presses. Sam pushed himself away from his desk, stood up, and slowly left his office, walking across the room to the intercom in the reception area. The intercom had both an audio and video link. He paused momentarily to watch Morgan on the doorstep of the building via the video feed.

Standing in his regulation suit, one hand in his pocket, his body facing the intercom while his head turned back and forth, gazing up and down the street, Morgan looked like a schoolboy up to no good, waiting to be let in and out of sight. He appeared agitated, so Sam waited and watched. There was no harm in winding him up a little more, he thought.

No more than ten seconds passed and Morgan, now facing the intercom and staring into the camera, pressed the buzzer, long and hard, another three times. Sam counted to ten in his head before pressing the audio button to respond.

'I'll be right there,' he said abruptly and cut off the connection before Morgan had a chance to reply. He left the door locked to make him wait on the doorstep. He would normally have let his old friend in, but on this occasion he wanted to keep control of the situation because as soon as he was in the FBI's office, he sure as hell wasn't going to be.

Sam pulled his Tom Ford Harrington jacket from the small office closet, putting it on and zipping it up three quarters of the way. He turned his phone off and placed it on the small slot shelf in the closet. He didn't think he would need it and wanted to avoid the FBI taking it from him. He knew ultimately if they really wanted it, and he couldn't think why they would, then they would find a way to obtain it, but he saw no sense in making it easy for them. Locking the solid wooden door behind him, he headed into the lobby to meet Morgan on the doorstep.

As Sam exited the building, Morgan stood facing the street. When the door opened, he turned, saw Sam, and then, with a grunt of 'C'mon!' went down the steps and onto the sidewalk, without looking back.

Morgan's car was a dark coloured Ford Taurus, free from

police livery but marked with a scratch down the left wing. Either Morgan had pulled a pool car from the lot or his ranking wasn't worthy of anything more luxurious.

Morgan jumped into the car, slamming the door before starting the engine. Sam followed Morgan's lead and sat beside him up front in the passenger seat. The interior of the car was worn and the dash and centre console were littered with various communications and computer equipment not found on a regular car, suggesting that Morgan had taken the first vehicle from the police fleet rather than his own. Morgan slipped the transmission into drive and sped off into the New York City traffic.

The traffic was normal for New York, busy with cars, vans, trucks and taxis all battling their way along the road. Cyclists weaved between vehicles and pedestrians crossed at allotted cross walks, making the traffic come to a stop when the lights turned red. The sound of the traffic was relentless, car horns beeped and engines revved, yet the noises seemed to combine to make a blanket of sound that was part of the character of the city.

The two men sat in silence as Morgan negotiated the city traffic until Morgan cursed at a van that pulled out of a junction and into their path. He blasted the horn, holding it for a second before beating it again, letting the two loud honks join the cacophony of traffic noise in a futile sign of his disapproval, which would ultimately melt away with the rest of the sounds of the city. He cursed under his breath again before adjusting himself in his seat, sighing as he did so as he regained his composure.

Seeing Morgan's agitation, Sam provoked him for another reaction.

'You need to calm down. I'm not sure this piece of junk can take that kind of abuse and it isn't good for your blood pressure, either.'

'God dammit Sam. This isn't a joke, you could really be up for it and so could I…' Morgan trailed off as he swerved a pothole in the road before turning to look at Sam for the first time. 'They mean it Sam, don't bullshit around with them or they'll send us both down.' He turned to face the traffic again, settling in his seat and focusing on the traffic ahead.

Sam wasn't sure who or what Morgan meant. He had done nothing wrong. Had Morgan got himself into trouble and needed help to get out of it? If he did, he was going about it the wrong way for his liking. But, for now, there was nothing he could do, so he made himself comfortable for the rest of the ride. He would find out soon enough when they got to wherever it was they were going.

Thirty minutes of stop-start traffic later, Morgan pulled the car across the road towards an underground garage of the Jacob K. Javits Federal office building in Central Plaza of Lower Manhattan, the home of the FBI in New York City. Sam peered up through the car's window at the forty-one story building and its chequerboard pattern of Alabama limestone, black Minnesota granite panels and glass and wondered what "game" he was about to be entered.

The car bellied as it crossed the road and over the dip on the sidewalk and onto the spiralling ramp of the parking garage. The ramp swept around clockwise before circling back in the other direction and reaching a barrier and a security post tended to by a tall man in a police uniform. Morgan flashed his badge to the guard, who then briefly checked his notes before nodding subtly and activating the release on the barrier.

The barrier sprung upright and Morgan pulled the car forward, screeching the tyres on the smooth painted pavement as he did so. He pulled the car around to the left and into an empty parking bay next to an elevator reception area.

He cut the engine and turned to face Sam. 'Whatever you do, don't bullshit these guys. As soon as we get into that building, I won't be able to help. You'll be on your own.'

'I've got nothing to hide. This whole thing is crazy. How can they even think I'm involved in anything?'

'They have their ways, trust me, just know that whatever you think you know or think they don't know, they probably know everything and more.'

Sam knew about the FBI's powers of intelligence, but he still couldn't understand why he could be accused of something. He was starting to think he was being set up. He would have to be on his guard.

The two men exited the car, the door slams echoing in the cavernous parking garage. Even though the car park was secure, Morgan activated the car's remote lock, its sharp beep cutting through the silence.

They walked towards a glass-walled reception area with a security door at the entrance. Morgan held up a pass to the security panel, which beeped, turning the light on the panel from red to green and allowed the door to be opened. Once inside, the two men were greeted by another security officer at a desk ahead of a set of elevators. Morgan showed his ID and explained to the guard who he was and the purpose of their visit. After a brief exchange, he handed Sam a red-coloured pass that he clipped to his jacket. Morgan produced a similar pass from his own pocket that he promptly clipped to the breast pocket of his suit jacket. Sam noticed that the colour of Morgan's pass was the same as the security guards, which suggested he must be a frequent visitor.

The guard ushered them to elevator number five and watched as Morgan used his pass to activate the call button. Once inside, Morgan used his pass on the elevator control panel to select the twenty-third floor. The guard watched as the doors slid shut before returning to his desk and turning his attention to a screen on his desk which showed Morgan and Sam in the lift.

After a few moments the doors opened onto an anonymous lobby area. A military-standard shine covered the neutral-coloured tiled floor, and unidentifiable artwork decorated the plain walls.

Security desks and a row of several barrier gates guarded both directions from the elevators. Morgan led the way east out of the elevator lobby and used his pass on the barrier security pad. The barrier beeped and the glass door swung open to allow entry. Sam followed the same procedure and followed Morgan down the hall. A security guard, a squat man of around fifty, with narrow eyes, watched as they passed.

Routinely spaced office doors lined the corridor and as they walked, Sam predicted the door that they were due to enter. Twenty yards ahead on the right, where a man in a dark suit stood guard to room 23C. As Morgan and Sam approached, he nodded to Morgan and knocked on the door. A voice from behind the door called 'Come.' in a calm, authoritative tone.

The door opened into an expansive office full of light from the external windows. There was a large desk adjacent to the windows facing into the office. The walls were plain, bar a centre piece picture of the president on the main wall behind the desk. In each corner of the room dark-suited men sat, each with the dull stare of a security detail. A man in an expensive-looking suit with a thick set of hair sat behind the desk. The name plate on the desk read "Bob Keating". Bob stood up as the pair approached and motioned to the two buttoned leather chairs. 'Please gentlemen, have a seat.'

Bob Keating was a slim but solid looking man. Sam guessed he was around six feet tall and, despite his healthy head of hair, he estimated he was about sixty years of age. His face was still relatively taut, but the pallor of his skin and the few lines he had on his face, combined with his somewhat scraggy neck, indicated an age beyond his relatively youthful aura.

Keating didn't offer a handshake. He took his seat, resting his arms on the table around his paper work watching as Sam and Morgan sat in the two leather office chairs facing his desk.

'Thank you for coming, Mr Martin.' Keating began in a no-nonsense tone. 'I appreciate you taking the time out to come and see us.'

'Did I have a choice?' Sam retorted. Morgan shot him a look before turning back to face Keating.

Ignoring his comment, Keating continued. 'Let me introduce myself. I am the director of special narcotic operations here in the FBI. I head up the department that investigates and shuts down illegal domestic narcotic operations and, where necessary, my department supports international investigations of similar illegal activity.' His voice was gravelly, and it reminded Sam of Tom Bosely from the TV show "Happy Days", though he suspected he was more likely to get thumb screws rather than a thumbs up from Keating.

'No doubt you will be curious about your invitation, but I'm sure that you'll be glad you accepted. Mr Morgan here, who I believe you know well, is one of our special operatives within the NYPD, something I suspect you were less familiar with. He and others like him are our eyes and ears on the ground and are key to our success in investigating and stopping illicit crime. He is sworn to secrecy and so could not discuss any details of the operation we are conducting with you.'

'If you have Morgan and half the NYPD helping you, what the hell do you need me for?'

'Let me explain, but before I do, let me reassure you in case you had any doubt that we are aware of your military past and are confident that because of your service to this great nation of ours that you can be trusted to be discreet. In fact, that is one of the reasons we chose you.'

'I'm in a new profession now. I'm sure you know that too, and I happen to be a busy man, so perhaps we can get to the point.'

Keating shifted in his chair and a look of irritation flashed across his eyes.

'Mr Martin, it will be no surprise to you that we are tracking a narcotic operation here in New York City. I understand you have had conversations with Morgan here about your worries surrounding increased psychotic behaviour in the city. You were right to be concerned.'

Sam glanced at Morgan, who returned his look with a shrug of his shoulders as if to say, 'What do you expect me to say?'

'I don't believe you just brought me here to tell me that. He could have just told me that when I saw him last,' Sam retorted.

'You are quite right, Mr Martin. We didn't and Morgan here was under obligation not to share any information given the nature of the investigation, but I am. We believe that the psychotic behaviour you have witnessed in your practice and that some of your other colleagues have witnessed is because of a defective batch of medication being distributed.'

'How widespread is it?'

'Unfortunately, we believe it has been distributed nationwide by someone.'

'So what do you need me for? If you know there is a defective drug on the market, just pull the plug on it and withdraw it from sale.'

'I'm afraid it's not quite that simple, and we need your help. We have stopped the manufacturer of the drug, but we know that the remaining drugs are being distributed by unscrupulous medical professionals who have obtained the batches at next to no cost, as the recall has refunded the original purchase. We also believe that a sub-contractor may be continuing to produce the defective drug because of the low cost of manufacture and corresponding high demand. What we have not been able to do is to penetrate the professional medical circles to establish the connection and put a stop to it.'

'So you want me to be a mole? Where exactly?'

'We understand the NYPC group you are a member of is potentially linked to one of the sub-contractors. What we need from you is to identify the connection. Then we can do the rest.'

Sam took a moment to take in the details Keating had shared.

Drug operations were nothing new, but using him as a mole in one of the most respected organisations, at least until now, seemed unusual.

'Why me and why would I do this? I'm just a psychotherapist.'

'The reality is, even with our extensive resources, some organisations are difficult to penetrate. We need evidence of who is illegally manufacturing the defective drug and then we can use our resources to close them down. And why you? I thought it would have been obvious, despite your new career, you have significant experience in military surveillance and investigation, which makes you a prime candidate for the role.'

'Maybe, but my investigative experience is a little more hands-on than I think you might be expecting. Anyway, let's just say I decline your offer, then what?'

'We are well aware of your hands-on skills. You may need them, there are some dubious characters out there and people will do whatever it takes to protect their interests, so we think, therefore, you would be good for the role. You are unlikely to get yourself into too much trouble and if you do, then you have the tools to get yourself out of the situation. We will, of course, support you in times of trouble, but we expect you would need less help than one of your less able colleagues in the NYPC, wouldn't you agree?'

Keating didn't wait for Sam to reply. 'And as for your acceptance of this offer, I think you would be wise to accept it.

Who says that it is not you who is the corrupt party here? Who says it is not you distributing these drugs amongst your community and profiting from them? Who says it is not you who is responsible for the deaths of those who have fallen victim to the effects of the drug? After all, you are the only person publicly declaring your patients have been struck by the effects of this drug. Perhaps your concern is no more than an attempt to cover up your own involvement, driven by a guilty conscience, a cry for help even. Maybe you've got yourself in over your head and you want out and realise that you can't for fear that you will be the next victim. What do you think, Mr Martin? Do you think we should bring you in and investigate your role in all this, just to be sure? Maybe even open up that military file of yours that you hope is now a closed book, gathering dust on a shelf in some government archive. Perhaps we could do a bit of digging into events of the past to see if there might be a connection. What do you say?'

Sam jumped to his feet and banged the desk with his fist and was about to launch into a tirade against Keating when the two security guards sprang to their feet. Morgan patted him on the back and encouraged him back into his chair, nodding to the two security guards who returned to their seated positions.

'A wise move, Mr Martin. I knew you had good judgement. Now what do you say? Do we have a deal?'

Sam composed himself, he was in a no-win situation, say yes and he would become a slave to the FBI machine, say no and his past would be dragged up and his business was likely to go down the pan or worse. Whatever fake accusations and connections they were likely to concoct, he could be locked up for who knows how long. He had no choice.

'Deal.' He replied through gritted teeth.

Sam spent the next hour being briefed by Keating on who he should investigate, how he should report back on progress and what to do if he found himself in trouble. The briefing avoided the consequences of what would happen if he didn't comply. When finished, Keating stood offering his hand, which Sam took begrudgingly and with the meeting over he was duly escorted out of the building.

He thought to himself that for all the hype Keating had built up in the briefing, he should have had a ticker tape parade down the main atrium of the building with rapturous applause from hundreds of onlookers wishing him well on his quest for truth and justice.

In the end, they escorted him out the same way he had entered, and when he handed in his security pass, the guard told him he would issue him his own pass for his next visit. A sure sign he was now part of the family.

Morgan and Sam sat in silence for the journey back across town. When they reached the brown stone fronted building that served as Sam's office, Morgan turned to Sam.

'I'm sorry about this. There was nothing I could do. For what it's worth, I know you wouldn't be involved in this drugs racquet, but if they want to use you, they will. If there is anything I can do to help, let me know. OK?'

'I know.'

'Just one thing. What was Keating was talking about when he was saying about bringing up your military past? What did he mean by that? What did you do?'

'Nothing. It's not worth talking about. It's best left in the past.'

'It must be something…'Morgan went on. Sam turned and looked him in the eyes.

'It's nothing. Trust me, you don't want to know. The only thing you need to know is that it is as relevant as it is likely that I am involved in all this drugs crap and you have already said that you don't believe I am involved in it.'

'OK, I get the message. Like I said, call me if you need me.'

Sam stepped out of the car onto the sidewalk and, before Morgan could drive away, he leaned into the window.

'How do I know you aren't in on all this? How do I know which side you are on?'

'I guess you never really will know whatever I say. Sometimes it's best if you don't know. There's no harm in being paranoid in this business.'

Sam leaned off the car and Morgan pulled away, screeching the tyres and headed back into the city traffic. As the car sped away, Sam turned and took the steps back up to the entrance of his office. He trudged through the main door and into the shared lobby area before lumbering past the security desk to his front door.

Once inside, he slumped down onto the couch in the reception area. He was jaded and angry, he had been let down by Morgan and felt violated by the FBI. Keating's lecture was like a mix of a dressing down as a naughty schoolboy and a sermon from a corrupt TV evangelist promising wonders that could only be delivered on condition he did what they said.

Keating had told him to attend all future NYPC meetings, something Sam deliberately kept to a minimum, and to try to identify which member or members might be linked to unauthorised medical bodies. Keating had provided a list of names that they had been investigating and wanted Sam to get closer to them under the pretence that he was looking for a new more affordable supplier of medication for his practice.

He thought the cover was feeble and unlikely to persuade anyone given the limited quantities that would be required for a private practice, so they had agreed that he should say instead that he was looking to set up a new pharmacy chain which would demand much higher quantities of medication.

Keating's list was curious as there were only three names on it. Pretty poor, he thought, for a federal investigation. One was a Doctor Slater practising out of Connecticut, but who had previously practised out of New York City, Doctor Günthardt, a well-respected practitioner of over thirty years, and a certain Doctor Francis Meadows. This last name seemed too coincidental to be true, but he knew people did desperate things when their personal circumstances forced them to. A failed marriage, a gambling addiction, you never really knew what went on behind closed doors and motivated people.

If Keating's theory really was true and that one of these well-respected doctors could be a mule between the legal and the illicit drug markets, there could be a whole host of reasons for it. He decided Meadows would be his first port of call, this time in person.

14. New York, New York

Elisa eased her foot off the accelerator as she noticed the speedometer touch the 160 kph mark. The Alfa Romeo with its powerful engine could manage the speed comfortably and to Elisa, it did not feel that the car was moving that fast. However, the E70 autostrada's speed limit was 130 kph, so she was passing other cars at pace and she did not want to draw attention from the Carabinieri.

She had been travelling for around thirty minutes and felt that she had put enough distance between her and the villa in Desenzano del Garda to pause and gather her thoughts. Because of Max's unannounced arrival, her planned departure was delayed, and the subsequent confrontation and hurried exit kept her from looking at the envelope and deciding what she had to do next.

Slowing down to a legal speed, she moved the car to the right lane and looked for signs indicating a rest area. She didn't have to wait long and took the next exit to the Calcinato service area. It was now dark and the lights of the service area were strangely appealing. There was a fuelling area with a café and a large car park.

The intensity of the events at the villa had left her feeling drained yet she resisted the allure of the café. A cup of coffee, or perhaps something stronger, would be a welcome relief after the events of the last couple of hours. Instead, after finding a secluded area in the car park, she reached for the holdall in the rear seat where she had hastily stowed the envelope she had received outside the hotel.

Elisa carefully opened the envelope by slicing it neatly at one end and extracting the documents within. The papers contained several photos of four different men shot from a long lensed camera. Alongside the photos were pictures of one of the men in a newspaper article in the New York Times. The article described a Doctor Slater of the Medical Research Group based in New York. The only other artefact in the package was a receipt for a left luggage location in Grand Central Station, where she could collect her fee upon completion of her contract.

It was clear to Elisa where she had to go next. She did not know why these men were targets, nor did she care. She was more concerned about why the men in the villa had wanted to kill her and the reason for the hotel bomb. Could it have been an attempt to prevent her from receiving the information? She suddenly felt exhausted. The adrenaline from the hotel incident had kept her going until the villa confrontation; only now, having a moment to herself, did it catch up with her.

Following the unplanned disturbance at the villa, she wanted to leave the country immediately to avoid police or airport staff stopping her if the authorities had begun an investigation.

Elisa was confident that she had left little evidence to trace her, but there was never a guarantee. Given enough time, the police could identify potential suspects through CCTV witnesses to the hotel event that could lead to a description of her or the car being issued and, as a manhunt being launched. Worse still, the attackers from the villa may have friends that could look to finish whatever they originally had in mind for her before their plans had been disrupted.

However, there was little else she could do tonight. A quick search on her phone confirmed that there were no more flights to New York this evening. She booked a flight for the next morning and decided to spend the night in a hotel near to the airport.

She plotted a route to her destination, Milan Malpensa airport, along the E70 passing Brescia before joining the A35 autostrada to head due west towards Milan and the airport. She was confident that she could locate a hotel for the night nearby, where she could rest.

Elisa had learned that no action was without consequence and that she had to ensure that following the confrontation at the villa, she came out on top. The only way she could do this was to complete the job as quick as possible and finish the contract. She had fled her last job in Milan, a simple domestic assignment to eliminate an unfaithful husband, there was little chance of recourse for not completing it, but whatever she had become embroiled in this time was more complicated and there was no escaping what she had to do.

Elisa woke up early the next morning. Despite a deep sleep, the events at the villa haunted her dreams, she was terrified by the big man from the villa chasing her, and she felt the guilt of Max's death in the pit of her stomach.

After dropping the Alfa off at the Malpensa Airport rental return she headed over to the departure lounge where amongst the obscurity of the crowds she had a strong coffee and a Danish pastry.

Feeling refreshed and more relaxed, she boarded the KLM morning flight to New York JFK airport. She had chosen the flight as it had an overnight stop in Amsterdam which with its land and air connections gave her several options to alter her travel plans if she thought she was being followed or just felt the need to do so.

In the end, she did not feel the need to change her plans. After a quiet night in an Amsterdam airport hotel where she ordered room service, took a relaxing bath and an early night, she arrived at JFK airport in the early evening the following day.

She liked the hustle and bustle of JFK airport. The swarms of people intermingling, rushing in different directions or simply standing or sitting around gave her a sense of protection and anonymity from anyone that might be in pursuit.

Just over two hours later, Elisa had checked into the Mandarin

Oriental hotel in New York City. The hotel was located on the corner of Central Park, in between the upper floors of One Columbus Circle.

Elisa's room was on the upper floors and lived up to the hotel's reputation for luxury. It was spacious and comfortable, tastefully decorated in cream and black. The bathroom featured marble, limestone and solid gold taps. Every aspect of the room oozed luxury, but the real showpiece was the view from the window. The floor to ceiling windows that stretched most of the width of the bedroom gave a breath-taking view of Central Park and the New York skyline.

With the sky becoming darker as the day was coming to an end, the lights from the buildings shone like thousands of surface bound stars reaching for the sky. The street lights from Fifth Avenue and Central Park West that bordered the famous urban common seemed to shine brighter as the darkness of the night took over.

They formed a border around the park, their hue of blue light radiating from the pathways, lake and reservoir. The way the light rose from the ground seemed to create a cauldron in the heart of the city.

For a moment, Elisa daydreamed as she gazed at the cityscape before her. The ping of her mobile broke her enchantment. She snatched the device from the bed and read the newly delivered message.

It was from an American-based "friend." Her client had promised her a contact to help with the job. She wasn't sure if this was a genuine offer of help or a way to keep track of her to ensure she finished the job. Either way it made her nervous. The text message was short, but straight to the point "Rocco's restaurant midday. Booking for Drake." She threw the phone back on the nightstand, undressed and took a hot shower before getting into bed. Tomorrow was going to be tough.

***

As the door to the villa had opened, Darko sprung from his position. He slammed the door shut, preventing an exit route, and simultaneously pushed the man into the wall. The man stumbled back in surprise before steadying his footing and recomposing himself. He stood up straight, puffing his chest out and readjusting his expensive suit. The man demanded an answer from Darko, but by the end, he would be begging for mercy.

'Who the hell are you?'

Darko stood unresponsive, staring dead eyed at the man, like a lion observing his prey.

'Who are you, what are you doing here?' the man tried again, this time in English.

'Where is the girl?' Darko asked as he took a step forward.

'I don't know, and I don't care. Get out of here before I phone the police!' His voice wavered a little as his confidence faltered. As Darko edged closer, the estate agent realised the extent of what he was up against. The looming colossus of a man with the chiselled war torn face and death like stare in his eyes was in no mood for negotiation.

Darko moved closer to the increasing forlorn estate agent and repeated his question. 'Where is the girl?'

'Honestly, I don't know.' The estate agent stuttered in nervous broken English, taking a step backwards down the hallway towards the kitchen. 'I'm sure that whatever the problem is, I can help you sort it out.'

Darko took several steps towards the estate agent, who impulsively stumbled backwards and continued to edge away as Darko stalked him through the house until they emerged in the kitchen.

'Where's the girl?' Darko asked once more.

The estate agent, panicking now, scanned the kitchen for some sort of weapon when his eyes fell on the sodden body of his friend slumped in a pool of blood on the floor against the kitchen cabinets. He swore under his breath for the last time, realising that his fate was sealed. He turned to the big man intending to plead for his life but it was already too late.

Darko's patience had run out. As the estate agent turned his head, Darko grabbed the man by his neck, plunging him back towards the marble worktop. In one lethal swoop, he smashed the man's head against the counter, cracking his skull and killing him instantly.

As Darko pulled away from the villa in the estate agent's Porsche, he cursed under his breath. Marvin was dead, the girl's lover was dead and now the only other lead he had was dead. He was stuck. He had lost the girl and knew that his employer would not be happy. He had no choice. He would have to check in and get a lead on her whereabouts.

His employer had a global spider web of contacts, he didn't really understand them or how they'd been acquired. He only knew that his employer was an extremely powerful man. He just hoped that he had patience with Darko or else he might as well be dead on the villa's kitchen floor too. As the Porsche hit 200 kph, he made the call on his mobile phone and prayed that it would not be his last.

15. Rocco's

Rocco's Italian restaurant was on the corner of East 114th street and Pleasant Avenue. Large trees lined either side of the street, their branches reaching high and over the road towards each other like long outstretched arms. Some branches interwove, creating a natural archway, while others met in the middle of the sky in a horticultural handshake.

A railing lined one side of East 114th Street, enclosing the adjacent Thomas Jefferson Park. The park was a mix of climbing frames, football pitches and basketball courts neatly segregated into their own self-contained compartments. Interspersed between the play areas, there were picnic tables and tall shade trees and a neat set of pavements.

Elisa walked from the hotel to the 59th Street–Columbus Circle station and took the D train to 42nd Street–Bryant Park/Fifth Avenue, changing onto the seven train to Grand Central before riding the sixth train to the park. She strolled through the grounds, taking in her surroundings as she went. The early afternoon sunshine was warm and there was a pleasant breeze blowing through the trees, making the leaves rustle and the branches appear to wave as she walked among them.

The sound of children's laughter and shrieks of delight from the play areas were mixed with the shouts of players on the football fields and basketball courts. As she neared the end of the path, she checked her watch for the time and took a quick scan of the people around her. It was nearly impossible to detect anybody suspicious, but her paranoia made her do it all the same. There were families, teenagers, groups of people walking, standing and idling around, all blending in with each other, and she looked as inconspicuous.

It was just before midday as she hurried across the crosswalk of 114th street and onto the corner where Rocco's entrance waited offset down from the pavement. She pushed through the red painted doors and a smartly dressed Italian-looking maître d' greeted her almost immediately. She confirmed the name of the booking as "Drake". The maître d' nodded and said that her table was ready but that her other guest hadn't arrived.

The maître d' led her past the busy bar and through to a comfortable booth around the corner of the main entrance. The restaurant's interior was filled with dark wood furniture and the walls adorned with pictures of celebrity guests. She ordered a red wine and sat intently at the table as she waited for her meet to arrive. Strangely for her, she felt butterflies in her stomach. Normally, she wasn't nervous about jobs, but this one was different. She wondered what this contact would be like. She hoped the meet would be brief and that she could go on and get the job over and done with.

A mix of clientele occupied most tables in the busy restaurant. An old couple enjoying a late lunch, a group of tourists sharing pictures and loudly discussing where to visit next and at the far end of the restaurant, a large table of what looked like work colleagues celebrating some sort of achievement.

The men wore suits, though their ties were loosened and collars undone, the women still dressed smartly although a number had changed into more glamourous attire to see out the evening or had not joined straight from the office. They were laughing and joking loudly, champagne bottles popped and they kept the waiters busy with their drinks orders.

Elisa felt a touch of envy as she watched them smile and laugh. It looked like a sense of belonging. She imagined they were all celebrating hitting some sort of sales target or project completion and were expecting a bonus with which they would buy a new car or add a swimming pool to their place in the Hamptons. Belonging was something she never felt in her line of work.

The waiter brought Elisa's wine, snapping her back to the present. She smiled politely as he placed the glass in front of her before moving onto another table. She cursed herself for losing concentration and at what she considered her weakness in wanting to belong. Elisa had grown tired of her way of life and wanted out of the "business". She had stopped the killing, but that could not go on forever. She had known eventually it would catch up with her and that was why she was where she was now. This had to be her last job!

The red front door of the restaurant flew open, with only the hydraulic door hinges preventing it from slamming into the adjacent window. The maître d' looked up from his stand where he was scribbling some notes in a diary. Standing in front of him was a man dressed in a well-worn suit. His eyes darted beyond the maître d' scanning the restaurant and he seemed to shuffle impatiently on the spot.

'Can I hel...' began the maître d' before the man cut him off.

'Table for Drake.' The words spat out from his lips.

'Of course, sir, please follow me.' The maître d' maintained his composure as he took a menu from his pedestal and led the way to the table where Elisa was waiting. As he did so, he glanced towards the bar at the barman and nodded. The barman returned the gesture in acknowledgement.

As they reached the table where Elisa was sitting, the man plunged himself down in the seat opposite Elisa and waved away the offer of a menu and ordered a bourbon. The maître d' nodded courteously before turning away. As he walked away, he muttered 'fuckin' cops' under his breath.

'You seem agitated.' Elisa began sipping her drink. She had recomposed herself and had assumed the appearance of the calm and collected contractor she was, or at least used to be.

James Morgan drew in a deep breath, almost snarling as he did so. 'You could say that.' He was holding back, trying to keep his own self-control. He let out his breath as if he was exhaling a cigarette. As he did, the waiter delivered his whiskey to the table. Morgan nodded to the waiter and took a long swig, savouring the taste of potent liquid and its warmth as it passed down his throat and into his stomach.

Elisa took another sip of her wine to fill the silence, licking the residue of the liquid from her lips. Morgan took another short swig of his bourbon, allowing his shoulders to relax and his body to slump into his seat momentarily before sitting upright again.

'Any problems getting here?' he asked.

'No, none,' Elisa replied confidently.

'You sure no one followed you?' Morgan muttered under his breath as he leaned forward into Elisa's face.

'Of course I was careful.'

In the back of her mind, she remembered the fight at the villa and wondered what he would make of the events. News travels fast these days, she thought, but it should be at least a week before anyone would discover the bloody mess at the villa. No one would be missing the two gorillas that attacked her, and she had paid the rent up front for the week, so it was unlikely there would be any visits from the estate agent or local authorities in the next day or so.

'Just be careful, OK?' Morgan mumbled. He took another swig

of his bourbon and tapped the table impatiently. Elisa pulled the brown envelope from her bag, placed it on the table and slid it across to Morgan. Snatching the envelope, he pulled out four 6" x 4" photographs and slid them across the table facedown to Elisa one by one. 'This first guy,' he began in a lowered tone, leaning in again, 'is a Doctor Slater. He is your target.' Elisa picked up the photograph and studied it. The man in the photo looked like a geography teacher. All hairy faced with a tweed like jacket over a patterned sweater.

Morgan slid over the second photo, weaving between the condiments on the table. 'This is Doctor Günthardt. He is also your target.' Elisa studied the photo of the man. He was not too dissimilar from the first, teacher like, but this time with protruding teeth, tufts of hair above each ear and a gleaming bald head, a bit like a mad professor.

The photo of the third target showed an older man with balding white hair and a neat white beard. He was overweight with a round head. To Elisa, he looked like the kind of guy who would dress up as Santa Claus in a supermarket at Christmas time. 'Doctor Meadows.' Morgan informed Elisa.

Morgan slid the fourth photo across the table. As Elisa went to pick it up, Morgan held it down firmly on the table with his fingers. 'This guy is not your target. I repeat, is not your target, but you need to be very careful around him. Whatever you do, try to avoid engagement with him at all costs.' Morgan released his fingers from the photo and Elisa studied the picture.

This picture looked different from the rest. The others looked like they had been taken in an open setting. This one looked as if it had been taken for a security pass. It showed the head and shoulders of the man. He looked fit, chiselled and younger than the other men. His shoulders, from what she could see of them, looked broad and muscular. His face looked stern as you would on a security pass photo, but not unattractive. She was drawn to his eyes, that looked deep and open. He definitely didn't look like he fit in with the other three guys.

'What's this guy's name?' she asked.

'Sam Martin,' Morgan muttered. 'Be careful around him. Whilst he hangs around with these professor types now, he has a military background, so he knows a thing or two about death. That's why your usual tools aren't required for this job. We've left you an alternative.'

'Wait a minute.' Elisa began. She could feel the tension building up inside her. This was another complication of the job, which made her feel even more anxious. 'I decide how I get the job done. That's always how it works. That's what I get paid to do.'

'Yes, except you haven't been getting the job done, have you?' Morgan retorted. 'Don't think your little misdemeanours have gone unnoticed. You're lucky you are getting this opportunity to redeem yourself. Working for anyone else pulling off the stunt you did would have seen things turn out very different, if you know what I mean. In the end, it worked in our favour that you didn't complete your last job, quite fortunate for you, but don't think that your luck can't change in an instant.'

Morgan snapped his fingers to hammer the point home. His face was now so close to hers that she could smell the whiskey on his breath. 'You just get this done as instructed and you might find yourself alive at the end of it.'

Who on earth was this guy and who had she got herself involved with? How the hell did they know so much about her? For the first time in a long time she felt afraid. Could she go through with this? She forced herself to hide her emotions.

Morgan continued snarling under his breath. 'Just count yourself lucky that I like you. I would have thought you might be a little more grateful.' His left hand had ventured under the table and he began to run it up and down Elisa's right leg. Elisa held her posture and his stare, but her skin crawled at his touch. Her fear quickly disappeared, replaced by disgust and she thought maybe she had another job in her after all.

The moment was disrupted by the waiter arriving at the table. Morgan pulled back his hand from Elisa's leg and signalled for another round of drinks. The waiter nodded and went on to his next table before heading back to the bar. The interruption gave Elisa the chance to regain her composure.

'Let's get down to business then. So what is it you want me to do exactly?' Elisa asked, tapping the photos on the table. She was now in even more of a hurry to get out of the restaurant and get this job out of the way.

'It's simple. Those four guys are all part of the NYPC.'

Elisa looked puzzled.

'New York Psychological Collective, a kind of club for clinical psychologists. You know, doctors for nut jobs.' He tapped the side of his head with fingers to illustrate the point. 'They meet monthly at the New York Hilton, Midtown. Your job is to make sure that the three targets don't make the next convention. Your friend there,' Morgan tapped the picture of Sam Martin, 'is about to get real friendly with these three guys, so I want you to follow him and after he meets them, that's where you come in. Understand?'

'Yeah, I get it. You want this guy framed? A bit obvious, isn't it?'

'That's none of your business. All that matters is that you get the job done. They may look harmless but they are part of a corporate drug ring.'

'What if he meets them all at once? You want me to finish them all off at the same time?'

'That won't happen. The guy is ex-military and will want to see them one at a time. You will be supplied with some equipment that is subtle enough go unnoticed. Your job will be to make sure it is administered without anyone noticing. I don't need to tell you what will happen if you don't do as I say.'

'There is a package waiting for you with everything you need at a pickup point on 57th Street. Here is a burner phone with the details. Make sure you lose it when you are done.' Morgan leaned in again. Elisa could smell the whiskey fumes again. 'When you are finished, I'll have another package waiting for you as your reward.'

Morgan stood up to leave, downed the rest of his drink, and staring back down at her grumbled a warning 'Don't fuck it up. If there are problems, then you know how to contact me.' As he turned to leave, the maître d' appeared.

'Leaving sir, everything satisfactory?' he enquired politely in his thick Italian American accent.

'That depends. How would you like the tab settled?'

'That won't be necessary sir, your "company" has good credit here,' the maître d' smiled.

'Very good, great doing business with you,' Morgan replied, patting the man on the shoulder as he passed him on the way to the exit. As he left, the hydraulic door hinges were put to work again as he yanked the door open before jumping into a grey Chevrolet saloon parked on the kerbside and pulled away into the city.

16. The Last Kill

'I'm afraid I can't help you anymore, Sam.' Doctor Meadows chuntered as he fidgeted nervously in his seat. 'There is nothing more to say. I've told you all I know. Now if you'll excuse me, the conference is over and I really must leave as I have a flight to catch.' He stood up tentatively, as if almost waiting for permission to do so.

'Of course Doctor, thank you for your help.' Sam stood and held out his hand. The doctor took it and shook it meekly. 'I'm leaving myself. I'll walk out with you.'

The hotel foyer exited onto Sixth Avenue. Traffic jostled on the road in an organised chaos with taxi cabs queued in the taxi lane, anticipating fares from the hotel guests.

The two men strolled across the pavement before pausing. 'Thanks again doctor,' Sam said, trying to sound like he meant it. 'Have a safe flight.'

Doctor Meadows nodded and turned, grateful to be finally free of his interrogator. He shuffled quickly towards the taxi rank, eyes focused on the waiting cars. Sam stood back on the sidewalk watching as Doctor Meadows made his way, contemplating what he had heard from the man and tried to determine how much of it was true.

***

Elisa stamped hard on the accelerator pedal of the rental car as she pulled out of the underground parking lot of the hotel. The big Chevrolet lurched forward under the power of the engine. As she drove the big car, she cursed under her breath. It was all supposed to be so easy. The temporary job as a waitress at the conference had been setup as perfect cover. Or at least that's what she had been told by Morgan. She'd had her doubts from the beginning.

Five minutes earlier she had stood as one of many uniformed servers among the hubbub of the NYPC event, indistinguishable from all the others. She wore a simple white blouse paired with a black skirt and apron. As she walked, the skirt's rough texture irritated her leg, and the polyester blouse made her hot and bothered. She couldn't wait to get changed.

The package she had picked up after her meeting at the restaurant included ricin in a discreet container that was to be applied liberally to the Doctor's meals. It would have caused death within days, with almost zero chance of tracing the source. Ricin was a particularly effective poison, a relic of the cold war and popular with the KGB in the past, not something Elisa had used before. Her methods had always been cruder. Critically, she would not be using it or any other method of assassination in the future. She was done, she couldn't do it anymore.

She had stood in the corridor off the main hotel kitchen away from prying eyes with the container of powdered substance in her hand ready to douse the meal with the lethal substance, but her conscience wouldn't let her. She'd changed, this wasn't her anymore.

Doctor Meadows was ready and waiting, sat at the table with the man she recognised as the untouchable Martin, just as Morgan had said they would. It was easy, but something inside stopped her. She realised it would be never ending. This job would lead to another, and then another after that. There would always be one more to fulfil her obligation, but she knew irrespective of the client, government or gangster (was there a difference?) it would never stop. She had to get out of the cycle.

For a second she had even contemplated using the ricin on herself. Perhaps that was the only way out of this rut. She could wait for someone else to finish her off. Surely that was imminent, or she could choose her own fate and go out on her own terms. She stood there, gazing at the ricin, her eyes glazed over, as if in a dream, uncertain which path to take, until a nudge from a passing server broke the spell.

She quickly packaged her dark thoughts away. Going down that route was a guaranteed no-win situation, the biggest loss of all. If she was taken out whilst fighting, she might at least be able to do some damage to those who would harm her. She might even do some good along the way. She may no longer have it in her to kill on demand, but she still had the strength of will and character to never give up.

There would never be a perfect time to change, so now was as good as ever and she might be able to use this situation to her advantage. Only time would tell. She had thrown the ricin in the trash and headed out to the parking garage.

***

She weaved the Chevrolet around a parked delivery truck and stomped on the accelerator again, cursing New York's one-way system. She knew they would be leaving via the front entrance soon and wanted to intercept them.

Driving as fast as she could in the city's dense traffic, she turned onto Eighth Avenue before turning onto West 54th Street. A taxi cab blared its horn as she cut in front of it. She turned onto Sixth Avenue, dodging the oncoming traffic of the one-way system. Horns blared as she veered across the traffic and into the path of a standing taxi cab, coming to a halt inches in front of Doctor Meadows standing on the sidewalk.

The car's near miss caused Meadows to lurch up in surprise. His heart beat wildly in his chest and his feet felt rooted in the ground, unable to move. The world around him seemed to move in slow motion as he regaled from the shock. After a few seconds, though it felt like time had frozen, he regained his senses and grasped what was happening.

The near fatal miss that had set his pulse racing had not impacted others on the street in the same way. Disgruntled taxi cab drivers, angry at the intruding car in their domain, honked their horns in frustration as Elisa's car blocked their path.

Meadow's stumbled backwards before regaining his footing. He peered at the car that was now inches from him. The passenger side window was wound down, and a woman leant across the front of the cabin calling to him to get into the car. Still shaken by the incident and disorientated by the shock and the blasting of the surrounding horns. He stood there transfixed, not knowing what to do.

Sam had watched on the sidewalk as the whole scenario unfolded. The sound of the horns as the car veered the wrong way down the street, the screech of the tyres as the car veered toward the taxi rank and finally when the car pulled to a stop in front of Meadows. It all appeared to happen in slow motion and in those moments, he knew that there was nothing he could do but watch.

As the car swerved, he had projected the trajectory, and knew that it was heading in Meadows' direction. He was too far from Meadows to intervene, and even if he tried, they'd probably both be hit. The moment the car stopped, he rushed forward.

Doctor Meadows still stood transfixed. As the shock wore off, he heard Elisa shouting at him from the car, 'Get in!' With Elisa focused on Doctor Meadows, Sam slipped between the taxis and into the passenger side of the Chevrolet. The sight of Elisa in the driver's seat surprised him; he had expected some sort of crazed maniac. He took the keys from the ignition and began to get out of the car.

When the engine shut off, Elisa turned her attention from Doctor Meadows and back into the car. She grabbed at Sam, catching him off balance, and he slunk back into the seat. They sat momentarily in a strange standoff, the world outside temporarily suspended.

'Give me the keys!' Elisa demanded, trying to keep her voice under control.

'Why, in a rush?' said Sam. He now had control of the situation and wanted find out what was going on.

Elisa panicked for a moment, this wasn't going to plan, but then again she was acting on impulse. She looked up at his face and into his eyes. She didn't know if she could trust this guy, but she felt she had no other choice.

'I know about the drugs!' Elisa cried out, keeping her frustration under control and trying desperately not to reach for the gun taped on the front of the seat.

'What?'

'The drugs, I know about them, I was sent here to kill Meadows, look, I haven't got time to explain you have to trust me,

I'm putting my life on the line to do this and if they get me, they'll get you too. We have to go now!'

Sam paused for a second, analysing what the woman had just said. He had to make a decision quickly before the situation drew any unwanted attention. She looked composed but the urgency in her eyes told a different story. Could she really know what was going on?

'Drugs?' He said.

'Yes, drugs!' She said, a hint of desperation beginning to creep into her voice. 'Quickly, tell your friend to get in the car. We don't have much time.'

'How do you know?' Sam squeezed the car keys tightly in his hand.

'The FBI! A guy from the FBI told me where to find you. He told me all about your friend out there and the others like him. I can tell you more later, but we have to go now.' she pleaded.

The mention of the FBI made Sam's blood run cold. The picture wasn't clear yet, but the mention of the Bureau and its involvement clicked pieces of the puzzle together in his head. All the strange behaviour, his summoning to Keating, it was starting to make sense. Could all this all be related? He had to find out more, and maybe this was the way.

'OK,' he said. 'Don't move.' Sam sprung out of the car and slid around the back of the big sedan to where Doctor Meadow's was standing. The on-looking crowd had crept around him looking to assist.

'This way Doctor Meadows.' Sam pulled the man by his hand and ushered him into the back of the waiting car, slamming the door behind him amongst grumblings of protest from the old man. He rounded the car again, back to the passenger seat, and handed the keys back to Elisa.

'OK, over to you, get us out of here.'

Elisa slotted the car into gear and navigated through the creeping onlookers and queuing taxi cabs, pulling the car onto Sixth Avenue and back into the city traffic. As she entered the traffic flow, the sound of horns from the disgruntled taxi cabs waiting line echoed in their wake.

'OK,' said Sam turning to Elisa. 'You'd better start talking.'

17. Tea for Three

From Sixth Avenue, Elisa drove north towards Central Park. The roads were thick with traffic, so progress was slow, but there had been no signs of any repercussions following her traffic violation outside the hotel.

The journey had been steeped with tension, Sam wanted to talk but Elisa was reluctant.

'Who are you?' he asked.

Elisa's eyes flickered as she scanned the road and tried to concentrate as she negotiated the dense city traffic.

'My name is Elisa Guisti.'

Sam found her Italian accent alluring and found himself distracted by the sway of her long brown hair when she turned her head. He forced himself to refocus. 'This is Doctor Meadows and I am…'

'I know who you are. I was briefed when I arrived here,' she interrupted. 'Now's not the time to talk. Do you have somewhere we can go away from here?'

'My office, it's not too far.' Doctor Meadows interjected from the back seat. 'I'll give you directions.'

An hour later, they arrived at Doctor Meadows' office. Elisa parked the car on the side street next to a black Cadillac.

Meadow's office was like walking into a time warp from the nineteen fifties full of beige and green, with wood panelling and thick carpets. There were built-in bookshelves that were filled with hundreds of books. The smell of stale pipe smoke hung in the air.

Upon arrival Elisa unzipped her overcoat revealing her servers outfit.

'Is there anywhere I can change?' she asked, holdall in hand. Doctor Meadows directed her to a private room where a few minutes later she appeared wearing a tight fitting casual top and trousers. Sam was distracted by her once again, quickly refocusing, turning his attention to Doctor Meadows.

'Could you get us some drinks Doctor Meadows?'

Doctor Meadows poured himself a large brandy, Sam and Elisa both drank coffee. After a tentative start Elisa had told her story. Doctor Meadows and Sam sat in stunned silence as she described her journey to New York and then onto to the hotel where they had met. When she had finished, a hush fell over the room before Sam began replaying her story to make sure he had heard it right.

'Let me get this straight. You were sent here to kill Doctor Meadows and his two colleagues and someone you thought was an FBI agent set you up in the hotel to do the job, but now you've changed your mind?'

The air was thick with tension as they talked. They were still unsure about trusting each other. Sam thought that if what she was saying was true, then she really was in trouble and this was likely a desperate plea for help, but he was alert to her every move.

'It's my job. It's what I do, or at least what I did. I want out.' She stood up from where she was sitting and paced the length of the office before turning to face Sam and Doctor Meadows again trying to gauge their reaction. Her face had reddened and her eyes had become teary. 'This was to be my last job. I stopped the killing a while ago. I just used to take the money.'

'And now you're worried that you're not going to get away with it this time?' Sam asked.

Elisa put her hands up to her face, wiping her eyes and regaining some self-control. 'No one ever came after me when I didn't finish my last assignments, but there is something about this job, this client that is different. I had to go through with it, but I sensed that even if I did, it wouldn't be over. I had to do something.'

Recalling the villa incident, she felt tense again. As she sat down, she turned to face Sam. His strong, athletic build hinted at his military background, but it was his gaze that captured her attention. She wasn't sure she trusted him yet and didn't know what she'd do if he couldn't help. She would likely be on the run forever, but there was a sincerity and resolve in his eyes that drew her to him.

'What do you mean, they came after you? What happened

exactly?' Sam asked.

'I was attacked. I had a rented villa, and before I could leave, two men broke in, I managed to get away. But it must be to do with this job, what else could it be?'

Doctor Meadows looked across at Sam who paused for a second thinking over this latest information before asking. 'And why do you think I could help you?'

'I don't know.' Elisa shook her head. 'It was just something he said about you. He didn't want you killed but he wanted me to know that you were dangerous. It was just a hunch, maybe if they didn't want you killed there was a reason and for the same reason you might be able to help me. I couldn't exactly go to the police.' Elisa paused, casting a glance towards Sam. 'What are you anyway?'

'He's a clinical psychologist now. He's left his past behind.' Meadows declared above his brandy.

Sam glared at Meadows across the room before turning back to look at Elisa.

'What does he mean by your past?' Elisa said.

'I used to be a member of the army, nothing more. It was a long time ago.'

'Special Forces, Ranger Regiment, specialising in hostile territory until…'

'Thank you Doctor.' Sam cut him off. 'Like I said, it was a long time ago.'

'Maybe that's it. He wants to use you for something, or perhaps he's scared of you.' Elisa declared.

'Perhaps, tell me more about this man you met. What did he say to you and what exactly do you know about the drugs?'

'My client put me in contact with him. I was instructed to come to New York to meet him and get further information on the job.'

'What exactly did he say?'

'He explained the three targets were involved in a corporate drug ring and that they had to be removed. They had your picture too, but I was told to leave you alone. Then, when I saw you at the hotel, I knew I had to talk to you.'

'Didn't you ask why they wanted me left alone?'

'I wasn't interested. I had all I needed to know. I had my targets and my method. I just wanted to be done.'

Sam paused and thought. The silence in the room hung heavily in the air.

'Do you still have the pictures?'

Elisa rifled through her handbag, retrieved the envelope and handed it over to Sam. He flipped through the photos, pausing briefly at his own as he wondered where the photo had been taken, then leaned across to Meadows and handed him the pictures.

'Who are these two other men?' Sam asked.

Meadows slurped the rest of his brandy and looked around for a place to put down his glass. Unable to find anywhere at arm's length, he swapped the glass for the envelope and asked Sam for a top up. Relenting, Sam took the glass and crossed the room to the sideboard where the brandy bottle stood, now half empty. Meadows began sifting through the photos as Sam poured him another drink. Meadows mumbled to himself incoherently as he thumbed past his own picture and then Sam's before reaching the final two photos when he proclaimed his appraisal to the room.

'That's Günthardt and Slater. Well, I never.'

'You know them then?' Sam handed the glass of brandy to Doctor Meadows, who took a deep slug as he continued to gaze at the photos.

'Yes, they were just at the conference. I was speaking to them before you, er, wanted to have a chat.'

'I was to lace their meals with ricin.' Elisa interjected. 'Yours too,' she said, looking at Meadows.

Doctor Meadows' face flushed, and he took another gulp of his brandy, thrusting the photos back towards Sam, keen to be rid of them.

Sam snatched the photos back. 'So you do know more than you were letting on earlier. I think you had better tell us what you know. Looks like your life might be on the line. You may have got away with it this time, but who knows who they will send next once they find out you are still alive.'

Meadows shifted in his seat and cleared his throat.

'How do we know we can trust her?' he said, pointing at Elisa.

'I'm not sure we can, but as you're still alive and she wants my help, I reckon we've got nothing to lose. Now, what about Slater and Günthardt? And what have you got to do with all this?'

Meadows swirled the rest of his brandy around in the glass, staring into the liquid as it spun in a vortex before downing the last of the golden liquor. He felt the burn as it travelled down his throat, knowing that it would take something a lot stronger than brandy to take the sting out of this situation.

'Well,' Meadows began. He cleared his throat again, leaning forward in his seat. 'Do you remember when we spoke on the phone and we discussed Riggs and the MRG?'

'MRG?' Elisa queried.

'The Medical Research Group,' Meadows said, 'A man called Riggs heads it up; he is the corporate face of the organisation, but it has a number of silent investors and senior scientific backers. Some would say that these investors have questionable scientific and medical ambitions,' Meadows said, his tone gruffer because of the interruption. 'Have you heard of a man called Doctor William Willoughby?'

Sam shook his head. 'No, can't say I have.'

'He's a biotech super industrialist who has developed revolutionary medications and methods of delivering treatments. Slater and Günthardt were part of his close research team who know the secret details of those drugs and their applications.'

'OK, so a case of industrial espionage. Why would they want you dead?'

'Do you remember I told you about my invitation to join the MRG?'

'Yes.'

'Well, the MRG has close ties back to Willoughby, it's a front for his industrial medical manufacturing, distributing his own medications and drugs produced under licence. But it's more than just a pharmaceutical producer. Whilst the pharmaceutical industry has always undertaken testing, sometimes controversially, Willoughby's organisation is harbouring a darker secret of unethical proportions. Their invite to join the MRG was their attempt to buy my silence.'

'But how do you know what they are doing is unethical?' Elisa asked.

'I went to college with Slater. He voiced his and some of the research team's concerns about Willoughby's work to me. They know my connection to him both personally and professionally, but they needn't have worried, my silence can't be bought. I'm not stupid enough to tell either, but now something has happened that has caused someone to want to kill anyone who knows the truth.'

'This sounds like something that should involve the police.' Sam said.

'No,' Elisa cried, leaping to her feet. 'No police, that's why I came to you.'

'It's OK, I know someone, a friend who might be able to help. I can trust him. Now what about this guy who gave you the briefing? Did he tell you his name?'

'No,' Elisa said, shaking her head, 'You don't share names in my business, but I found it out. He was a slime ball, and he was careless. We met in a restaurant that I think he uses a lot. The restaurant staff don't like him. When I went to pay the bill, they refused to take my money. They said it's free for the local law enforcement.'

'Local law enforcement?' Sam exclaimed.

'Yes, they said it was complimentary for the local law enforcement and their friends. Especially their good friend, James Morgan.'

18. An Uninvited Guest

Sam wasted no time in calling Morgan. Elisa's revelation had set his mind racing, and he needed answers. Why was Morgan involved in the enlisting of a hitman when there was an FBI investigation ongoing? It fed his suspicion that Morgan was not being truthful with him about the drug deaths and manic psychosis incidents across the city. He decided he could no longer trust his old friend and the leeway that he had afforded him to this point was now used up.

The call with Morgan was cordial, but direct. Morgan had sounded under pressure on the call, but was doing his best to sound friendly. He didn't sound concerned that Sam, Elisa and Doctor Meadows were together following the conference and seemed pleased that, following their meeting with Keating in the FBI offices, Sam's investigations had already made significant progress. Or at least that's what he said, though the tone of his voice implied otherwise. For the first time, an undercurrent of anxiety tinged his usually brash New York accent.

Morgan agreed to meet at Sam's office, because it wasn't safe to talk on the phone and he didn't trust that Doctor Meadows' practice was secure. He told Sam not to worry and said he would explain everything when they met, including the situation with Elisa. Morgan's tone sat uneasily with Sam and he decided that the meeting was the last chance Morgan had to give him the truth.

At first Elisa was reluctant to go, concerned that meeting Morgan again would put her in danger.

'We don't have much choice,' explained Sam. 'Morgan is my only contact in the FBI. If he is as corrupt as you think he might be, then he has all the resources at his disposal to make us disappear. If we try to report him, without some form of evidence, he could manipulate the situation against us, regardless.'

Elisa looked across at Doctor Meadows and back to Sam. 'Are you sure about this?'

'Yes, I think you might be right. He needs us, or me, for something, and the only way to find out is to face it head on and call his bluff. He won't try anything unless he no longer has a use for us and I don't think we are there yet.'

'I don't know if I can, how can I trust you? You might be just as bad as him.' Elisa said.

Sam paused before answering, in reality there was nothing he could really say other than the truth.

'You're right and if you'd have asked me a few days ago, I probably wouldn't have had an answer for you. But, the fact is that there is something going on in this city, a strange psychosis, I've seen it myself. Sure, James Morgan is in involved but the FBI are threatening to frame me and if I don't help, then I'm in as much trouble as you. I've known Morgan a long time and I'm sure he must have a reason why he's got tangled up in this. I promise I won't let him do anything to you.'

Reluctantly, Elisa agreed to go ahead with the meet on the condition that she could be armed. She wasn't sure about the plan, but saw little option, but knowing that she had a weapon would gave her some reassurance that if things got messy, she would go out fighting.

They left Doctor Meadows' office shortly after the phone call in order to have enough time to negotiate the New York traffic and get to Sam's office at the agreed time. Doctor Meadows' office was located in a block of large New York town houses converted to form an office complex over four floors. Each floor comprised several individual offices of various sizes available for rent.

A large central expanse dominated each floor, spanning the building's middle and serving as atrium and main lobby. The offices surrounding the perimeter of the atrium on each floor created a mass of empty open space flooded with light from the glass ceiling above. Each floor's corner contained elevators, while a central staircase provided an alternative route directly to the open lobby below. There was a smooth modern white finish to the walls, and glass panels formed the banisters on each floor.

As the evening began to draw in and the occupants of the offices headed for home, the atrium echoed with emptiness and the artificial lights of the lamps hidden in the ceiling began to take over from the natural light of the glass ceiling as the sky became darker.

Sam, Meadows and Elisa took the elevator down to the ground floor. They stood in silence as the lift made its way down. The doors opened as it reached the ground floor and Meadows was first to exit, waddling into the atrium followed closely by Elisa.

From nowhere, someone grabbed Elisa's arm, swinging her with enormous force across the floor and sending her sprawling against the wall. Meadows, alerted to the danger behind him, shuffled as fast as he could towards the security desk and the exit.

Sam reacted quickly, watching the events unfold in front of him, but there was no way he could have intervened, given the speed at which they developed. He watched Elisa get flung like a rag doll against the wall. She now lay dazed, shocked, and semi-conscious on the floor.

The attacker watched Doctor Meadows as he scurried towards the security desk but seemed unfazed. His lack of concern was explained when Meadows reached the desk. Meadows' expression changed from alarm to panic as he saw the security guard slumped lifelessly behind the desk, blood trickling from his forehead. He turned back to face Sam, looking lost and uncertain what to do.

Darko stood staring as Sam stepped out of the elevator. They were similarly built, though Darko stood slightly taller and sported a recent head wound. They stood for a moment, sizing each other up.

Unarmed, Sam was at a disadvantage as he was certain the man that stood before him had a weapon. He edged forward, knowing that if the man was armed, his only chance was to be as close to him as possible.

'What do you want?' he asked, stalling for time and hoping to distract him.

Darko stood resolute, unmoved, then, at lightning speed stepped forward and swung a fist at Sam. Pre-empting the attack, Sam stepped in, dodging the oncoming attack whilst rotating his hips and body anticlockwise, shifting his weight onto his rear foot to launch a counter punch into the man's face followed by a second punch into the man's rib cage. It felt like he was hitting a solid dead weight, but the big man staggered backwards, reeling from the blows, blood seeping from the old wound on his forehead.

Sam moved in again but was caught by a powerful right hand. Reeling from the hit, Sam shifted his body and caught Darko with a right uppercut as he came in for another attack and followed up with another punch to the head, sending the man crashing to the floor.

Physically beaten, Darko staggered onto his knees, reaching into his coat for a gun. Sam looked for cover, but in the open space of the atrium, there was none. As Darko pulled the weapon up and readied to fire, Elisa, now conscious struck him from behind with a security barrier post. The blow sent blood spurting from Darko's head and knocked him to the floor, the gun spinning away across the tiles.

Sam rushed to Elisa. 'Where's your gun?'

'In the car.'

'C'mon then, let's go.' He grabbed her hand and together they ran across the atrium to the exit, leaving Darko unresponsive on the floor. Doctor Meadows stood open-mouthed, transfixed by events, not knowing which way to turn. Elisa and Sam ushered him out of the building and into the cold air outside.

They hurried around the building, across the road and into the Chevrolet Elisa had parked up several hours earlier. Wasting no time, with Sam driving, he launched the car into drive and pulled out into the road.

'That was him!' Elisa cried as the car pulled forward. 'The man in Italy who tried to kill me.'

'Are you sure?' Sam said.

'Yes, of course, it was definitely him, I couldn't forget.'

Sam was sure that he must be dead. The blow to his head had sent more blood gushing from his wound. At the very least, the injury would render the man unconscious and in need of hospitalisation. Yet, unbelievably, in the corner of his eye, he saw Darko standing across the road at the top of the steps at the entrance of Doctor Meadow's office complex. His coat was bloodstained and his head battered, but he stood tall, gun in hand, aiming across the street at them.

Darko let off a burst of shots, missing the car but hitting two pedestrians on the sidewalk behind them who crashed to the ground. At the sound of gunshots, screams erupted in the evening air as the people on the street dived for cover.

Darko kept shooting as he ran down the stairs and into the street, repeatedly firing at the approaching Chevrolet. Sam floored the accelerator, and as bullets ricocheted off the car, he swerved blindly towards the man, catching him with the wing and sending him sprawling on the asphalt as the car flew on down the road.

Reeling from the impact, Darko stood up slowly and brushed himself off. Screams could be heard across the street as passers-by saw the blood-soaked bodies strewn on the pavement. Ignoring the cries, he took his mobile from his pocket, wiped his bleeding forehead with his coat sleeve, and punched a number on his phone as he walked away.

The call was answered in seconds, the sound of the screams in the background echoing down the microphone.

'What the hell is going on there?'

'There was some trouble. A few people died.'

'Oh, for God's sake, OK. I'll get onto the NYPD to smooth it over.'

'They are on their way to you.'

'All of them?'

'Yes, all three.'

'Son of a...'

'Do you have a problem?'

'No, no…not at all, I just thought, if you had got the old man at least…never mind, it doesn't change things. I'll sort it. I suggest you get away from there before anyone sees you.'

The phone went silent as the call was terminated.

Darko slipped the phone back into his pocket and turned to head down the side street where he had parked his car. As he turned the corner, a man called from behind 'Hey, you, did you see what happened here?'

The man chased Darko around the corner. He was dressed in an expensive-looking suit, was around fifty years of age, and spoke with a pompous sense of authority.

'Hey, you!'

Darko turned to face the man. Their eyes met, and the man took a step back, taking in Darko's face.

'You can't just leave. The police will be here soon. You'll need to answer some questions.' The pomposity in his voice tailed off with the end of his sentence as he realised his mistake.

'No. I don't.' Darko fired at point blank range into the man's chest, sending him crashing to the ground. He calmly placed his gun back into its holster inside his jacket and walked away, leaving behind the terrified shouts and the faint sound of approaching police sirens.

PART TWO

And whoever lives by believing in me will never die.
Do you believe this?

John 11:26

19. Voyage of the Damned

Sam's temper was frayed. The journey across the city had been fraught with traffic and delays. He was furious with Meadows for holding back on him and he was angry that they had been attacked and nearly killed by the man who had followed Elisa from Italy. Most of all he was infuriated that his friend seemed to be setting him up.

When they arrived, Morgan was waiting outside Sam's office door, Harry, the building superintendent had made him wait outside which Sam was pleased about.

As soon as everyone had gathered in Sam's office, Morgan held up his hands to apologise. He looked at each of them as he spoke. 'Look, I know what you're thinking but it really isn't. It was all a charade, we knew you were coming,' he said turning to face Elisa before continuing. 'The FBI thought that if we let you go through with the plan, then we could draw out who was behind it all.'

'But I could have been killed,' said Doctor Meadows.

'Not really, the ricin was fake, you would've just had a long nap. It was an FBI setup, we wanted to bring in Elisa and draw out any connections that might help identify any more leads, but because it wasn't carried through, we've lost our chance this time.'

'You better not be bullshitting me,' Sam said staring at Morgan.

'Look Sam, we are in this together, you know how the FBI are, you saw it first-hand. If they want something done, then you've gotta do it.'

Sam looked across at Meadows and then to Elisa to gauge a reaction. They remained stone faced. He didn't totally buy Morgan's story but he felt he had to give him another chance.

'OK, I believe you but no more secrets, we need to work together on this for all our sakes.'

The tension in the room lifted a little, and they sat down in the small reception area to talk. Sam immediately started questioning Morgan about Willoughby, his operations and his involvement in the whole affair. After ten minutes of waffle, Morgan began to give some straight answers.

'He has facilities across the globe, two in the States alone.'

'Where?' said Sam, keen to get to the detail.

'One in California and one here on the east coast. We've been monitoring his east coast facility the closest, as he now seems to spend most of his time there.'

'Tell us more about this east coast facility. Where is it exactly?'

'It's upstate New York, a couple of hours drive out of the city. All of his facilities are out of town. They are marketed as palliative care centres, though we suspect there is more to it than that. By being out of town and far enough away, patients become out of sight and out of mind, relatives simply forget about them. It works because it means they are left alone. Once they are taken, they never come back. They call the one upstate the "Castle on the Hill". The irony is that someone originally built it as a health resort, genuinely exploring ways to improve the health of those suffering from physical and mental disorders. It served rich and poor alike, helping soldiers returning from war and those who lived in such poverty that they were susceptible to disease. It shut down decades ago before Willoughby bought and converted it. When it reopened, the locals were pleased. It was seen as a force for good. We suspect otherwise.'

'And what do the locals think now?' Sam queried.

'Not much, small town mind set, they keep themselves to themselves and they don't talk about the "Castle", a few have jobs there or rely on it for their businesses supplying provisions, materials, etc. If you attempt to talk to the locals about it, you get shut down.'

'What's this town called?' Sam pushed.

'Rooksville. Population of no more than a couple of thousand. It's got a main street, a hotel and a couple of bars and shops, that's about it. Actually, that's not quite true. It has its own airport.'

'A small town with its own airport, how did that happen?' Sam asked.

'A hangover from the old days. In theory, it is a municipal airport, owned by the city. It was used during the Second World War to train pilots.'

'And now?'

'It is still owned by the city, but just like the town, it's a closed shop. It's almost a private airport now. It's rare for any non "Castle" related business to fly out of there.'

'OK, now we know about the townsfolk. How do we get into the Castle?' Sam asked.

'The security is tight, like industrially tight. They check everyone in and out, so it won't be easy, but I think I know of a way.'

'How?' Sam's patience was wearing thin, and he felt that time was running out. It would only be a matter of time before they were tracked down again, and this time, it might not just be the one man.

'Each of the facilities has to have a way to get supplies in and out, right?'

'Go on.' Sam nodded.

'More than that, each facility has to have a way to receive patients, yes?' Morgan went on. 'If we can make use of the patient transfer facility, you can make it inside. It is the easiest way to bypass the security checks. When you get inside, it is over to you what you do next.'

'So basically you are saying we pretend to be patients?' Doctor Meadows snorted. Elisa looked across at Sam and then to Morgan as she considered the plan. It was a long shot, but it's all they had.

'Not you Doctor Meadows,' she said. 'If we are going to pull this off, we are going to need a doctor's referral. You can help verify the admission and then leave. I don't think there is a need for you to accompany us into the facility. You are best placed to be on the outside. Would that work?' Elisa turned to Morgan.

'Yes I think it would.'

Doctor Meadows shifted in his seat. He visibly relaxed, relieved to know he wouldn't have to go into the facility, though he seemed less happy about still having to participate in the plan. He muttered under his breath before grumbling aloud, 'Yes, yes, I suppose you're right.'

'It's settled then. That's what we will do. We are going to need some help to make the patient admission look genuine.' Sam turned to look at Morgan. 'How can you help?'

Morgan shifted in his seat. 'You know that isn't going to be easy for me to arrange.' He protested. 'I'm already taking a risk talking to you guys. I shouldn't be here at all.'

'That's one thing you've got right. You shouldn't be here at all.' Sam said, raising his voice. 'You're only alive because I want you to be.'

'OK, OK, I get it.' Morgan protested. 'But you are going to have to let me outta here if you want me to arrange some paperwork to help get you in the Castle. A few phone calls ain't gonna cut it. I'm gonna need some time to arrange things.'

'You've got twenty-four hours. You can go, but Elisa will watch you every step of the way. Any tricks and we won't need to fake your condition for admission to the Castle.'

***

Twenty-four hours later, Sam, Morgan, Elisa and Doctor Meadows were gathered in the lounge of Sam's practice office. Outside, the weather was changing from bright and sunny to overcast and windy. Clouds had begun to dominate the sky over Manhattan, they moved in swiftly from the south bringing rain showers and gusts of wind. As the clouds drifted in and the occasional beam of sunlight broke the stratus blanket in the sky, the light in the lounge shifted casting a pattern of shadows across the room. The shadows moved as if they were performing a ghostly belly dance, being ushered on by the light before the next dancer arrived to cast its silhouette for all to see.

Thunder rumbled in the sky and splashes of rain hammered the window momentarily before relenting, almost teasing what was about to come. The mood in the room reflected the volatility in the sky above. Intensity followed by a period of calmness, nerves were on edge as a combination of knowing and not knowing what was approaching created an atmosphere of tension.

Sam was holding court, running through the details for a second time. His years in the military taught him that there was no substitute for preparing, planning and practising, however small the exercise was or who was involved, and this was no exception.

Morgan had upheld his part of the bargain trouble free, either through guilt or self-preservation, Sam assumed the latter. As his gaze switched from each person in the room, he reflected on how, in a few short days, his relationship with Morgan had changed beyond comparison. A man he once saw as a trusted confidant, a man he thought he could depend on for his life now appeared to him as a deceitful, deadly, double crossing bastard enslaved by the system such that his moral core was now twisted beyond that of what he once knew. Yet, despite this change, his life and the life of Elisa and Doctor Meadows rested in part on them trusting Morgan and the arrangements that he had made and the hope that the corrupt element of the FBI would not betray them.

The plan was straightforward if nothing else. Morgan had arranged a rendezvous with contacts in Rooksville. Doctor Meadows would pose as a palliative care doctor escorting Sam to Rooksville before admission to the Castle. Elisa would pose as the doting wife accompanying her husband for the final time to the facility where her husband had chosen to donate his earthly body to medical science in return for the receipt of the finest respite care in the land.

Morgan had arranged the necessary transfer paperwork from a city hospital. All that was left was to meet the reception party in Rooksville and the facility's medical staff would transfer them into the facility like any other patient. A Trojan horse into the Castle.

***

As the light faded from the sky, they were ready to leave. Each had a holdall carrying a small number of supplies and a change of clothes. They didn't really know what to prepare as they did not know what they would find once they were inside the Castle. The possibility that they might not return had crossed both Elisa's and Sam's mind. Doctor Meadows was less concerned. Now he knew that his part in the plan was limited, his demeanour had become almost upbeat and with it, his contemptuous and cantankerous nature had returned.

Sam agreed to let Morgan stay in the city because he'd arranged things as agreed. If they needed emergency help, he was their only option. Morgan had promised to arrange reinforcements from the FBI to be on standby. It would be best if Morgan went about his business as normal and be called upon if required, doing anything else might raise the alarm. Ultimately, there was no other choice.

Morgan left Sam's office around dusk. Sam, Elisa and Doctor

Meadows climbed into the rental car. Elisa in the driver's seat, Sam riding shotgun and Doctor Meadows slouched in the back seat, already preparing for a snooze.

They headed North West out of Manhattan towards the Hudson River and joined the West Side highway. The traffic moved steadily for the time of day, only occasionally causing them to slow down. Trees and bushes obscured the view of the Hudson River on their left. Foliage also obscured the city side of the highway, but as dusk turned to night, the high-rise buildings on their right illuminated their windows, commanding a presence like a concrete guardrail that seemed to creep forward and hem them in.

They eventually reached the off ramp for the George Washington Bridge, which led them over the river and out of the city, joining the I95 and then I80 express upstate towards Rooksville. The rental car satellite navigation estimated a two-hour drive. Half an hour into the journey, Doctor Meadows, slumped across the back seat, was already asleep, his hands resting on his chest as his enormous belly rose up and down with each breath. Given the man's size, Sam was surprised that he didn't snore.

The radio had landed on an easy listening station that flittered between soft rock and country. The Eagles, Simon and Garfunkel and John Denver, each had their turn. Neither Elisa nor Sam were really listening, both of their minds were focussed on what was to come when they arrived at Rooksville. They sat in silence until

Elisa broke the silence.

'Do you really think this is going to work?' she asked above the harmony of a Dr Hook song.

'I don't know.' Sam replied. Dr Hook played on in the background singing about "stayin' up to greet the sun." 'It really depends on what we find when we get in there.'

'Do you trust Morgan?' Elisa asked.

'No, not anymore.' Elisa was pleased with Sam's response. She didn't trust Morgan either. It made her think that she and Sam were on the same side and that whatever happened they would look out for each other.

'What do you think we will find when we get in there?'

Sam paused before answering. 'Probably a hidden drug manufacturing facility like the FBI suspect. We just need to collect enough evidence for the FBI to shut them down and get out. That's what I agreed to do and whatever Morgan is up to, it will no longer matter. I'll be free to get on with my life.'

The car rumbled on down the highway. Fleetwood Mac had started on the radio. Cars passed them on the outside lanes, their red tail lights illuminating the way forward. They kept to the speed limit, cruising on the inside lane in order to remain inconspicuous and partly as a subconscious reluctance to arrive at their destination any sooner than they had to.

'I need Willoughby dead or I might as well be. He doesn't forget,' Elisa announced, breaking the silence again. 'He'll just send someone else to get me.'

'I know,' said Sam, turning to face her. 'We're in this together now, I won't let you down.' Elisa's face was shrouded in the dark of the night. As another car passed, her face was lit up momentarily before being cast back into the darkness. It was then, in the moment, that Sam was captivated by her beauty. He felt himself staring and turned away quickly to face the road again.

'Do you think we will make it out alive?'

Sam thought before answering. 'I don't know for sure, but I'm not planning on this being a one-way ticket out of town.'

He reached across with his left hand to hers, which was resting down on the centre console, and squeezed her hand. She responded by interlocking her fingers with his and for a moment, there were no more words to say.

***

The traffic dwindled the further they drove upstate. An occasional car passed them from their cruising position in the inside lane, with just the odd truck the only other vehicle on the road.

Ten miles out from their exit, Doctor Meadows began to stir from the back seat. He began with a grunt followed by an undecipherable murmuring before he leaned forward from his position in the back seat and in between the two front seats. He glanced out of the windows on both sides of the car before muttering wearily 'Can't too long now, there isn't anything this far upstate other than lakes, mountains and wildlife, and I'm not talking about the animals. Anyone who would live this far out from the city and civilisation must be some kinda hick!'

'We'll be pulling off the highway soon and heading down into the town, so won't be long. Why don't you go back to sleep and we'll wake you when we arrive?' Elisa replied.

'No thank you, you need to keep your wits about you on the back roads. You'll have to watch out for animals and hicks. No telling what's out there or which is worse.' Meadows grumbled. 'I'll keep my eyes open until we make it into town.'

Sam and Elisa exchanged a glance of mutual understanding. Doctor Meadows was becoming more troublesome than they had expected. It was something else they would have to look out for when they made it into town and met the townsfolk. It wouldn't do for Doctor Meadows to disrupt the operation with one of his characteristic rants about his views on upstate folk in front of the locals, the last thing they need now was a public scene that drew attention to them.

Twenty minutes from the highway, the first signs of Rooksville came into sight. The road was relatively wide and well maintained, with one lane going in each direction. There was no other traffic and hadn't been since they had turned off at the exit. They passed an occasional house but everything seemed eerily quiet, even at this late hour. A sidewalk ran the length of the road and even where there was only shrubland and woods, the path was immaculately maintained.

They cruised down the road, the big Chevrolet's engine purring effortlessly as they idled along. As they entered Rooksville, a sign greeted them, picturing a happy family enjoying themselves. As they continued down the main road towards the centre of town, more buildings began to appear.

On the right-hand side, a gas station lingered in semi darkness. The forecourt was lit by a lone gas pump, and the store's lights shone brightly, with a neon "open" sign standing out against the dark surroundings. Large glass windows at the front of the store displayed the usual array of gas station products. At the cash register, a well-dressed attendant in a shirt and tie watched intently as they cruised past. Sam caught his eye, but the attendant continued to stare.

When they had passed out of sight, the gas station attendant picked up the phone on the countertop, calmly pushing a well-used speed dial button. He didn't wait for a reply when the call was answered. He simply stated dryly, 'They've arrived.' Then replaced the receiver in the cradle and returned to his game of cards and began humming a nursery rhyme to himself.

Beyond the gas station, the road continued into the centre of town. Every so often, a side road appeared, though they vanished, seemingly swallowed by darkness, as the main road was the only one with streetlights.

As they continued down Main Street, they could see a cluster of buildings in the distance. The area became more populated as they approached the centre. A café, a deli, both closed for the night. A bar with lights on and a neon sign in the window inviting clientele in, but looking short of takers. To the left, a small supermarket stood amid its parking lot, closed for the night, but the store sign dimly lit above the doors.

On the right-hand side of the road stood a grand looking authoritarian building with pillars and steps leading up to the entrance. Sam guessed it might have been a council building. The trio continued cruising along the road to the main intersection without passing another car or seeing anybody walking on the sidewalk. The town felt unnervingly quiet.

'What was the name of the hotel that fella said we had bookings in?' Meadows asked from the back seat. 'This place looks like it's on life support. Can't imagine anything will be open this late.'

'The Blackbird Motel,' Sam replied. 'He said it was just beyond the centre of town. We couldn't miss it as it was the only place in town to stay.'

'A motel...' began Meadows before trailing off into his thoughts and muttering to himself incoherently.

'There it is, up ahead on the left.' Elisa pointed towards a building offset from the main road with a prominent sign on the roadside showing the way. As they neared the motel, the building came into view.

A large sign with a white illuminated background and the name Blackbird Motel in black neat letters stood prominently on the edge of the grounds. The motel was not as they had expected. The car park was freshly tarmacked with well-maintained shrubbery in planters strategically placed to break up the dullness of the space. The main building was a three-storey structure with the rooms on the ground floor accessible directly from the car park.

The white building with smooth walls and solid, expensive-looking doors and windows were a far cry from the regular wooden slat fronted motels that are found on many highways across America. The reception area was well lit with marble floors and a wide large reception desk. It was more akin to a boutique hotel than a small town motel.

Elisa parked the Chevrolet in a parking space close to the reception. There was plenty of choice, because there were only three other cars in the parking lot. Sam, Elisa and Doctor Meadows approached the desk of the motel. A woman wearing a smart suit smiled at them as they approached. She wore her hair tied back and full makeup. It felt as though they were checking into a five-star establishment.

'Mr and Mrs Sterling, I believe, and Doctor Fields?'

'Yes, that's right, we're staying the night before my husband attends the Castle. Do you know it?'

The receptionist smiled politely, ignoring the question.

She produced two key cards and handed them to Elisa and Doctor Meadows.

'Both your rooms are on the first floor. They are accessible internally. One for you, Mr and Mrs Sterling, and one for you, Doctor Fields. There is an elevator around the corner. If you need anything at all, please let me know.'

They took the key cards and thanked the receptionist.

Sam, Elisa and Doctor Meadows took the lift to the first floor. The thickly carpeted corridors of the motel felt luxurious underfoot, the walls were adorned with large, ornate pictures and warm, glowing wall lamps. The two rooms were towards the end of a long straight corridor, which Sam calculated ran the length of the car park outside. He explored the end of the corridor, which went off to the left and the right. The subsequent corridors had several unmarked doors and to the right of the main corridor, there was a large service elevator. Nothing it would seem out of the ordinary.

Doctor Meadows found his room, number 1012, and used the key card to enter. 'I'll see you both in the morning.' he declared as he waddled into the plush room muttering to himself about finding the mini bar and getting back to the city. He left the door to close behind him. Sam caught the door and instructed the old man that they would call for him at 8 a.m. sharp. Doctor Meadows muttered an acknowledgement and waved him away as he bent over to explore the mini bar fridge. 'Yes, yes dear boy, see you in the morning.' Sam let the door close. As it did, the lock clacked shut.

Elisa clicked open the room next door. It was as opulently decorated as the rest of the motel. Elisa deadlocked the door as Sam placed their bags next to the large bed. He turned to face her. Without the need to speak, they were drawn to each other, holding each other in their arms.

'Elisa,' Sam began.

She placed a finger on his lips to stop him from talking and, taking his hand, led him to the bed. She began to undress him and he in return her. They fell into bed naked and for an hour or two it was is if there was no one in the world other than themselves. Exhausted and satisfied, they spent the night wrapped in the solace of each other's arms, disregarding what lay ahead of them in the morning.

20. Knock Knock

At 8a.m. Sam knocked on Doctor Meadows' door. There was no response. Elisa, who had been collecting their bags, joined him at the door.

'No answer?' she asked. 'The old fool probably drunk the mini bar dry and passed out and now can't get up.'

Sam knocked on the door again, harder this time. 'Doctor Meadows, answer the door plea…'

A tall, thickset man in white clinical attire opened the door, cutting off Sam mid-sentence.

'I'm afraid Doctor Meadows will not be getting up today,' he smiled.

From nowhere, two other men dressed in similar clothing appeared either side of Sam and Elisa in the corridor, preventing any escape.

'There is no point in trying to run. We have you surrounded. You would miss your appointment at the Castle, and you wouldn't want to do that now would you?' the tall man sneered. 'We are your new reception party, Mr and Mrs Sterling.'

'What have you done with Doctor Meadows?' demanded Sam.

'See for yourself. You don't need to worry about him. He won't be any trouble.'

The tall man gave way, allowing Sam to pass into the room. There were two more men dressed in white clinical uniforms. Their bulk and rotundness gave their true vocation away. More "heavies" in the party. They had just finished loading a body bag onto a trolley. Sam approached the trolley and one of the two thugs moved towards him. The tall man waved him away, and he stood back. Sam unzipped the body bag, revealing Doctor Meadows looking peacefully asleep. He unzipped the bag a little further and touched the hand of the man he had once thought of as a mentor. The hand was still relatively warm, and there were no signs of injury or struggle in the room. He probably wasn't aware of what happened. He zipped the bag back up.

'There was no need to kill him. He is innocent in all this. What did you do to him?'

'We are all sinners, Mr Sterling,' the tall man replied. 'Just a simple injection, preserving his body and mind but unfortunately not his soul. Now if you don't mind, my colleagues have work to do.'

The two thugs manoeuvred the trolley out of the room and around the corner of the corridor towards the service elevator.

'If you would just like to follow my colleague around to the elevator, please.'

Sam and Elisa did as they were instructed, the tall man and the second man dressed as a clinician followed them. Sam and Elisa exchanged glances as they headed towards the service elevator. It was fronted with a folding concertina door that was closed manually by pulling the door from once side to the other. It was twice the width of a normal elevator. The leading corridor thug opened the stainless steel door, which was painted a soft pastel colour to match the surroundings. Because of its size and weight, the door required two tugs to open completely.

After the first pull, the gap was wide enough for a person to pass through. As the thug repositioned himself to pull on the door for the second time, Elisa took the initiative, she launched herself towards him, pushing him into the elevator and once inside as he stumbled forward, used his momentum to push his head hard into the wall of the elevator and knock him out.

Sam used his size and strength advantage on the second thug to push him into the tall man. The manoeuvre took them by surprise and the thug stumbled backwards, sending the tall man who was following close behind sprawling to the floor. The move bought Sam enough time to close the elevator door and lock it into position.

'Up or down?' Elisa asked, her hand hovering over the elevator controls. The thugs rattled the door on the outside, trying to open it.

'Up to the second floor, chances are there won't be many people up there and we can work out a way back down. It's our best chance.'

Elisa engaged the mechanism and the elevator sprung to life, edging up to the top floor of the motel.

'When we get to the floor, we won't have much time. I'll pull the door open and we will have to make a run for cover as quick as we can.'

Elisa nodded in acknowledgement as the elevator shunted onto the second floor and the light illuminated, showing it was safe to open the door. Sam pulled the door to the side wide enough for them to squeeze through but narrow enough so that it could be closed quickly. They squeezed through the gap and turned the corner from the service lift, looking for an unlocked exit. Sam left the lift open to prevent it being called from any other floor.

As they rounded the corner, they stopped in surprise. The luxurious hallway on the lower level was gone, replaced by an epoxy floor that was as sterile and smooth as that in a hospital. Instead of a series of hotel room doors, there was an open space covering almost the entire floor. Spanning the far side of the room appeared to be dozens of large stainless steel cabinet doors.

'What sort of motel is this? It's so cold up here. Where are the rooms and what is with all the kitchen units?' Elisa said.

They moved closer to the cabinets. A strange chemical smell hung in the air. As they neared the first block of cabinets, Sam stopped and held out his arm to stop Elisa.

'I don't think they are kitchen units.'

'What do you mean?'

Sam examined them carefully before opening one. It was empty, but its long coffin-like structure confirmed his suspicions.

'They are mortuary cabinets. They are storing dead bodies up here.'

'But this is a motel, why would they have a mortuary?' Elisa asked.

'I don't know, it maybe something to do with the Castle. Either way we can't hang around, come on, let's get out of here.'

They scanned the room for options. There were double doors on the far side of the room which appeared to rejoin the main corridor, leading to the elevator and reception area below. Instead of risking running into more enemies, they doubled back towards the service elevator to search for another way out. They went left at the corridor near the elevator after noticing a green light above a fire escape.

They ran towards the exit, pausing briefly at the door for signs of anyone ascending the stairs before launching into the stairwell. It was a standard emergency exit, with grey walls and metal steps. They made the first two sections of the staircase and as they rounded the next corner, they ran into the second thug making his way up. As they came into view, he snarled and charged towards them. Sam accelerated, using his speed and elevated position to deliver a brutal kick to the man's head. The attack caught the thug off guard, causing him to fall backwards, landing awkwardly snapping his neck on the cold steel. Sam and Elisa bolted past the stricken man down the next flight of steps onto the ground floor, pausing as they reached the door to the corridor.

'The coast looks clear, but there's no way we'll get past the reception area. It looks as though the parking garage is underground. If we can go down there and get a car, we might have a chance of getting out of here.'

Elisa nodded in agreement. They heard shouts from above and the vibration on the metal steps as the clambering of footsteps grew nearer.

'Come on, let's go.'

Before heading down to the next level, Elisa pushed the door to the corridor wide open, knowing the slow close mechanism on the door would mean it would still be closing as the chasing thugs arrived. Moments later, two men dressed in clinical uniforms arrived on the ground floor. Bewildered momentarily by the closing door, they agreed to split up, with one heading onto the ground floor corridor in pursuit whilst the other continued down the stairs to the underground garage.

Elisa and Sam, panting slightly, finally reached the bottom of the stairwell. They felt relieved at the sight of the underground car park beyond the door. Peering through the door window, they saw a large, dimly lit interior. They could make out a Ford sedan parked across from the door, but because of the angle and the light in the garage, they couldn't see much else.

With the reverberations on the metal steps becoming louder, the growing sense of urgency forced them to step into the garage. Once through the door, they flanked either side of it, seconds later a man stormed through, Sam tripped him, sending him flying across the concrete floor onto his face. Before he could stand, Sam placed his knee in the man's back and put him in a choke hold to render him unconscious. The man began to cough and gurgle before a deep voice in a thick Eastern European accent called out from the dimly lit garage.

'Enough!'

Sam looked up to see Darko emerging from the side of a black van, sporting the scar on his face that Sam had given him just a few days earlier in New York. On either side of him, men dressed in clinical uniforms carried pistols that were aimed at him. Sam loosened his grip on the man, who slid out from under him and scurried towards Darko. Two more men dressed in the same clinical uniforms carrying pistols emerged from the stairwell and pushed Elisa towards Sam. They were surrounded.

'Put them in the van.' Darko instructed the two men who had just emerged from the stairwell. Darko, gun raised, ordered Sam and Elisa toward the black van. As they got closer, they could make out two more identical looking vans parked behind. As they neared the sliding door of the nearest van, Darko barked another order.

'Stop.'

Without pausing, he pistol whipped Sam across the face. Sam's forehead oozed blood almost immediately.

'I owed you that.'

Sam reeled from the blow sinking to his knees, blood seeping down his skull, Elisa looking on helpless. As Sam staggered back to his feet Darko nodded to the men, who pushed Sam and Elisa into the rear seats of the van. After Sam and Elisa sat down, the two men sat in the row ahead of them, their pistols drawn. As Darko slid the door shut the tall man, now sat in the front seat, turned around to face them.

'Nice of you to join us. You should still make your appointment on time,' he smiled. 'Your friend will also be joining us. He will follow us in the van behind. He has been much more accommodating to travel.'

'You Son of a…' began Sam before he was pushed back by one of the men holding a gun.

'I suggest you both settle down for the ride. It will be your last.'

The driver started the engine and the vans drove in convoy up the ramp and through the automatic garage door out onto the motel parking lot. Once out in the open, the rain hammered onto the roof of the van and Sam wondered if the tall man was right. Was this the end of the road?

21. The Castle

An unspoken tension hung thick in the air as the van proceeded along the road. The silence was amplified by the hammering of rain on the roof. Sam sat motionless in the rear seat, moving only with the rocking of the van as it negotiated the road. Elisa sat beside him, lost in her own thoughts. Their hands found each other again, as if guided by an invisible force.

Both Sam and Elisa had considered the options for escape and had concluded that any attempt would cause at least one of the guns pointed in their direction to be discharged. In the confined space of the van, the sound would be deafening and there was a high probability that the blast would injure one or both of them, perhaps fatally.

Even if they could overpower the two thugs guarding them, they would still have to address the tall man in the front seat. His position gave him the advantage of being able to shoot them at the first sign of any retaliation. Sam was certain that he would shoot without prejudice in a struggle.

Any successful reprisal in the van would almost certainly be met by an overwhelming response from the vans that followed.

Sam concluded that the only course of action was to do nothing. He was certain, or at least he hoped there would be opportunities for retaliation in the future.

He squeezed Elisa's hand as the van jolted over a bump in the road. They were heading uphill now, and the van was turning and twisting as it ascended the hill. It had blacked out side panels, making it impossible to determine what route they were taking.

After what seemed like an eternity, the van slowed and came to a sudden stop. Men outside shouted commands before the door slid open violently, flooding the van's interior with sunlight. Darko ordered Sam and Elisa out of the van. There were more men all dressed in clinical uniforms, but instead of stethoscopes, they each carried an automatic rifle.

After the darkness of the van, the sunlight was blinding. It took a few moments for Sam's eyes to adjust. When they did, his jaw dropped at what he saw. They stood before a grand red bricked building, at least ten storeys high and the length of a football pitch.

Large turrets formed each end of the building, book ending the behemoth. Ornate wrought-iron balconies, adorned with swirling patterns, graced the windows of each turret and each carefully architected window was arched. The centre of the building protruded outwards and upward as an imposing tower dominated the heart of the structure. A luxurious canopy covered the steps leading up to the building's main entrance at the bottom of the tower. At the front of the building there were acres of well-tended lawn broken only by the twisting drive they had travelled. The back of the building seemed to go on extensively before eventually giving way to the trees on the hillside that enclosed its rear.

Adjacent to the building, Sam saw that the drive led off up into the hillside, where it was just possible to make out the tops of roofs of more structures nestled in the hillside.

Sam was still absorbing the structure's grandeur and surroundings when one of the thugs nudged him and Elisa towards the side of the castle with his rifle. As they walked, it suddenly struck him. There was deadly silence and an eerie stillness. There was nobody else in sight. There wasn't a single sound, no birdsong, no hustle of a working building, especially one of this magnitude. Even the wind seemed hushed. The presence of death hung in the air and, for a moment, Sam felt an intense ball of fear well in his chest. What on earth could this place really be?

The thugs marched them to an ornate veranda that adorned the ground floor. Behind them, Doctor Meadows' body was pushed along on a gurney and they were directed towards a set of large mahogany double doors. The tall man approached an intercom on the building and after pressing several buttons, the heavy doors slid open into the walls, revealing a set of solid metal doors beyond and another security intercom. The tall man presented his eye to a retinal scanner. After a short delay, the doors hissed open.

They were nudged again with the barrel of a rifle into the corridor beyond, as Doctor Meadows and the remaining escorts crossed the threshold both sets of doors automatically slid shut. As they did so, a number of mechanical noises could be heard as the physical security mechanisms were activated.

The interior of the castle was a contrast to the exterior. Instead of brick walls and ornate decoration, the walls were smooth and industrial. Metal, glass and plastic covered every surface and harsh lights illuminated the hallway. It felt much more like a prison than a castle.

Within an instant of the doors closing, the guards moved in to separate Sam and Elisa. Sam was shoved forward further into the corridor and Elisa was manhandled to the side, alongside the guards and Doctor Meadows' gurney. As Elisa was grabbed, she instinctively took a swipe at one of the men, planting her elbow in the centre of his face. A crack of bone was followed by the man's yelp as he put his hands to his face. The other guards quickly gripped her in a tight hold, preventing any further retaliation.

Witnessing the confrontation, Sam moved to intervene but was immediately confronted by the barrel of a rifle and restrained by a guard.

The man Elisa struck cursed at her as he pulled his hands away from his face. Blood streamed down his uniform, staining his once pristine clinical attire. He moved to strike her with his rifle butt before the tall man intervened.

'Stop! There is time for that later. Take her and the body to the infirmary. Darko, Doctor Willoughby asked that you supervise her personally. He said he thought you would want to.'

Darko nodded and in his thick eastern European accent muttered, 'With pleasure, I'll deal with this bitch.'

The guards did as they were instructed, pushing her forward and wheeling the gurney down an adjacent passageway. As the guards manhandled her away, she turned and looked over her shoulder at Sam. 'I'll find you,' he mouthed before she was ushered away in the distance.

'Where are you taking her? What are you going to do with her?' Sam demanded.

'Your concern for her is quite amusing. I wonder if you would feel the same if you knew everything about her.'

'I know everything I need to know. I know she would put you out of your misery.'

'Yes, I'm sure she would. Isn't it fortunate that she wasn't paid to put you out of yours?' he sneered. 'You will see her soon enough, along with your friend, Doctor Meadows. They aren't totally useless yet.'

'What do you mean, see Doctor Meadows again? You bastards murdered him in cold blood. He has nothing to do with this.'

'You really don't have any idea what this is about, do you? What this place is or what is at stake? But I think you will soon enough. I hope for your sake you are a quick learner. Doctor Willoughby does not suffer fools. Now, enough talking, you have an appointment with Doctor Willoughby.'

'An appointment?'

'Yes, that's what you came here for, isn't it? To find out what was going on? Well, Doctor Willoughby is going to give you the opportunity to find out first-hand.'

The tall man nodded subtlety to one of the men stood behind Sam who administered an injection to his arm. He felt the needle too late and was unable to break free from the tight grip he was in. The contents of the syringe began to spread down the side of his body, it felt icy cold and with every millisecond he could feel its effects. He knew instinctively that when it reached his heart, he would pass out. The last thing he remembered was the grip of the guard under his arms holding him up and the face of the tall man leaning towards him and peering into his eyes, examining him as if he were a specimen.

22. The Afterlife

Elisa was marched a short distance at gunpoint before reaching another set of secure doors. Beyond the doors lay an interchange with corridors leading off in various directions, and in the middle of the area, an electric transport vehicle stood waiting. The guards loaded Doctor Meadows' body onto the rear of the vehicle and Darko nudged Elisa into the seats.

The vehicle whirred through the anonymous corridors, and at times, it felt as though they were ascending. Despite the size of the castle, Elisa could not imagine that they were still within the boundaries of the building and thought they must now have journeyed to one of the other building facilities or even underground and into the hillside itself. As the transport continued its voyage, she wondered where Sam was being taken and whether she would ever see him again.

After what seemed an eternity, though in reality no more than a few minutes, the transport came to a halt. The guards ushered Elisa off the vehicle and unloaded Doctor Meadows' body. Through another set of secure double doors they entered a smaller room, it had two rows of control panels littered with various computer control equipment overlooking a dividing glass wall and another room beyond. It appeared to be a medical examination room, but the perimeter was lined with large, upright cabinets resembling coffins, each with a glass front.

A one-way mirror formed the upper left section of the far wall, which she suspected served as an observation deck for whatever went on in this room. A sense of panic suddenly swept over her, and she began looking frantically around for any other means of escape. There was none. Her only option was to fight and find a way to escape Darko's clutches.

As thoughts raced through her mind, the door behind them slid open and the tall, thin man who had been with Sam walked into the room. Darko turned to face him.

'Is it time?' he asked.

'Not yet. He may still want the woman. Either way, you will get your payment.'

One of the men escorting Doctor Meadows' body spoke in a low voice.

'Doctor Sulzberger, the patient is ready for the restore process. It has been over an hour.'

'Then proceed.'

The guards wheeled Meadows' body through the doors at the end of the control room and into the preparation area. Tilting the gurney, the guards wrestled Meadows' lifeless body into one of the coffin-like chambers. Once inside, they began to insert and connect various tubes and equipment to his body.

Elisa looked on in horror as the guards went about their work. Darko stood emotionless behind her, watching with interest at the proceedings.

'What you are about to witness is something of a miracle and something unfamiliar to both of you.' Sulzberger began. The thin, tall man seemed to glow with anticipation. 'You are both experts in death, killing without mercy, killing for pay. Assassins without a purpose. No reason, other than to execute your target at the behest of your paymaster.'

The guards finished their preparation and turned to Sulzberger through the glass.

'The subject is ready.'

'Excellent, start the restore process.'

Feeling restless, Elisa shuffled her feet. She suddenly felt nervous. What on earth could they be doing, and what was this place? It didn't take long to get an answer. The first guard pressed a button on the chamber, causing the machine to hiss, and a large vial of orange liquid above it to empty into the tubes and inject into Doctor Meadows' corpse.

Sulzberger watched on intently, his eyes flittered between Doctor Meadows and a monitor situated on the console in front of them. His body leaned forward and his eyes gleamed with anticipation.

'Wait for it…' he said with the excitement of a small boy about to show off a new trick.

The vial of orange solution drained, and for a moment, nothing happened. Sulzberger continued to stare intently at Doctor Meadows, his gaze unwavering, oblivious to Elisa and Darko's presence. The silence in the room was deafening and the air was filled with anticipation. Then, when it seemed as though nothing was going to happen, a light on Doctor Meadows' chamber illuminated and a corresponding light displayed on the control panel in front of Sulzberger.

He leaned forward with an even greater sense of anticipation whilst, in the chamber room, the two guards took several paces back, in readiness for what they knew was to come.

A second light illuminated on both the chamber and the control panel as a high-pitched beep began to sound in soft rhythmic intervals. Elisa stood bewildered at the events, switching to look between Sulzberger, the two guards and Doctor Meadows. Darko was equally transfixed; his eyes glued to the unfolding scene.

The suspense was broken by a second constant high-pitched tone that was followed immediately by Doctor Meadows' dead body jolting upright in the chamber as if struck by electricity. His head flopped up and down and his whole torso seemed to judder. Elisa let out an unconscious shriek and moved back a pace, bumping into Darko standing behind her. He relented, allowing them both to move further away from the dividing glass wall.

One of the guards pressed another button on the chamber and

injected a second cylindrical vial of orange liquid into Doctor Meadows. Within seconds, his body jolted again and the beeping noise began repeating rapidly. Finally, a guard administered a third vial of orange liquid from the chamber and Doctor Meadows' body jolted again. This time, his head remained upright and his body stiffened as if standing to attention. The rapid beeping stopped and as it did so, Doctor Meadows' eyes burst open and he took a large, gasping breath. There was a look of shock, panic and amazement on his pallid face as if he were staring into the Devil's eyes.

At the sight of Doctor Meadows' reincarnation, Elisa let out another shriek. It was like nothing she had ever seen before. The man had been dead longer than it was possible to revive him. Darko, equally shocked, let out of grunt of shock momentarily losing his Slavic composure. Leaning over the control panel, Sulzberger studied the screen's information intently. Periodically, he glanced up triumphantly to the revitalised body of Doctor Meadows in the chamber beyond.

'You see!' Sulzberger cried to no one in particular. 'Do you see it now?' His voice was triumphant, and he was now so engrossed in his work he seemed oblivious to Elisa's presence. 'Activate the Cryptonasia Cortex,' he ordered.

One of the guards reacted instantly, his fingers flying across a panel of controls; a low hum filled the chamber as a probe extended toward Meadows' neck. Having adjusted the controls, the guard retreated quickly, appearing apprehensive about what was about to happen.

Doctor Meadows remained bolt upright in the chamber. His rotund body had stiffened making him seem at least a foot taller than he really was. His expression had changed from shock to horror. He stared straight ahead, but slowly his gaze softened, and his eyes turned toward Elisa. He stared intently towards her as if trying to communicate a message but unable to.

As the probe entered his neck, a sharp pain pulsed down his spine and up into his brain and a sense of realisation of what was happening appeared in his eyes. His face muscles contorted the pallid skin on his face as his stare towards Elisa grew ever stronger. He grimaced, exposing his yellowing teeth and with an explosive cry screamed in an unholy shrill 'KILL ME!' before his eyes snapped shut and his head locked as rigid as the rest of his body.

In front of Sulzberger, a regular pattern of a healthy heartbeat pulsed on a screen. Doctor Meadows was alive again and in a state of medical stasis. Elisa, still in shock, regained some of her composure. Doctor Meadows' scream echoed in her mind, reverberating around her skull. She glanced at the console and the array of buttons that surrounded the screen that displayed Doctor Meadows' vital signs.

Sulzberger hunched over the glowing screen, and Darko, absorbed in the unfolding events, had released his grip on Elisa. Without a second thought, she scraped her boot down Darko's shin. He cursed at the pain and, whilst he was off balance, Elisa used her body weight to push him backwards. She then launched herself towards the console, shoulder barging Sulzberger to the side. Despite his tall and wiry frame, he was strong, but the surprise helped to knock him off balance and he stumbled and fell over a chair and onto the floor.

Not knowing what to do, Elisa pressed every button on the console.

'No!' yelled Sulzberger from the floor as he tried to pull himself to his feet, but it was too late. Elisa had pressed all the buttons on the console before Darko grabbed her again putting her in a choke hold. Beyond the glass wall, the chamber holding Doctor Meadows hissed a low, guttural sound as all the liquids held in its various chambers were excavated. The power in the chamber shut off and the clamps holding Doctor Meadows upright opened and he fell forward, face first, into the floor.

The guards rushed forward and lifted him onto the gurney in the front of the glass screen. As he lay on the trolley, blood poured from a head wound sustained in the impact of the fall, the orange substance injected into him whilst in the chamber began to ooze from his body with no obvious exit point.

Sulzberger rushed across the control room, through the security door into the chamber room. He and the guards crowded around Doctor Meadows' body. One of the guards, his face etched with concern, asked Sulzberger if they should reconnect him to the chamber. Sulzberger's replied calmly, concealing his rage.

'No. He's dead. He's no use to us now, the information is lost, the extraction at that speed will have fried his brain. Take him to the crematorium.'

Elisa, now out of the choke hold but held in a firm grip by Darko, watched as Sulzberger walked pensively across the chamber room and back into the control room. As he approached Elisa and Darko, he glanced at Darko and muttered.

'Take his body to the crematorium. You can do what you like with her, but make sure she doesn't come back.' He then marched out of the room, leaving behind a lingering silence.

23.Remember Yesterday

Shadows filled every corner of the dimly lit space, but the one cast by the tall cylindrical cabinet at its centre dominated them all. It stretched across the room like a tombstone stretching out its monolithic arm, searching for a place to rest and condemning all that lay before it to darkness.

To the rear of the cabinet, wires ran down from an electrical unit until they disappeared beneath the floor. A yellow light on the unit flashed in a steady rhythm, on and off, illuminating the vacuum of the room that lay behind and creating new shadows that seemed to move and shift across the room with every pulse.

The front of the cabinet would normally be closed to protect the precious content within. But now, the tube was open and the body of the woman, normally held fixed upright in the tube, had been carefully arranged in a comfortable resting position. Life supporting tubes and wires ran from her body and the mask that encompassed her face ran back into the unit and onwards beyond the ceiling cavity where the source of life was both given and taken away.

Behind the mask, the sallow face of the once beautiful woman remained still. Her eyelids hid her once bright blue eyes in the hollow recess of her eye sockets as she slept. Her golden blonde hair now dull despite futile attempts otherwise, rested on her shoulders in an untidy cluster of strands aside her ears and the mask that helped keep her alive.

Doctor Willoughby sat in a chair next to the woman, holding her left hand in his, his head face down, eyes closed resting on his other arm, almost as if he were praying, though this couldn't be further from the truth. He repeated this ritual daily, and it was known that during this time he was not to be disturbed under any circumstances.

Outside the room, a red light shone above the door. It resembled the 'On-Air' warning outside a TV studio during a live broadcast. In reality, the light was unnecessary because everyone knew the consequences of disturbing the ritual, so no one dared.

With his eyes closed, Willoughby couldn't help thinking back to how he and his beautiful wife Francesca had been told about her terminal illness.

On that day a new hurt was born, tears had streamed down their faces when the doctor had confirmed the diagnosis. He had held her, not wanting to let go because he knew that from that moment on, nothing would ever be the same.

In that instant, something died inside him, but the void left behind was not shallow or meek. Something else grew in its place, an energy that burned with such force that in the quiet times it even scared him. It was an energy twisted by sorrow and turned into a relentless evil, determined in its pursuit of redemption and revenge. The once philanthropic cause embedded in his heart and shared by his wife, now replaced by a single-minded quest that would disregard all other morals and consume anything and anyone to achieve its goal.

After everything that had happened to them already, after everything they had done to the benefit of others through their medical research. How could this happen?

When enough time had passed, however long that maybe, only Willoughby really knew, he would slowly raise his head and gaze at the woman's face. He no longer saw the mask and to him the woman's eyes were not sunken and her face wasn't sallow. She was as beautiful to him now as she had ever been.

When the silent thoughts had been thought and the invisible conversation was finished, he would lean into the woman's ear and whisper, '*Remember, I love you.*' before kissing her delicately on the top of her head. He would slowly rise from the chair and wheel it gently across the room to a secure position next to a control panel on the nearest wall. As he walked his shadow would loom large in the room as the blinking light on the tubes electrical unit flashed on and off to its rhythmic heartbeat.

As he tapped various buttons on the control panel, the woman would slide back into the tube, kept in an upright position, nearly as though she was on display. The tube would slide back into place and seal tightly, keeping its precious cargo safe from the outside world. The lights in the room would brighten, although not by much since the lights were kept soft and low on purpose. Willoughby would check the readout on the screen of the control panel and then on a panel on the tube. Once satisfied, he straightened his clothing, checked his hair and face for signs of pressure marks and occasionally traces of tears, for sometimes his thoughts got the better of him, before leaving the room through the automatic doors. The red light above the doors would turn green and it was now safe for others to enter.

24. Gun for Hire?

When Sam regained consciousness, his head was pounding. When he opened his eyes, the light in the room caused him to squint, taking him a moment to adjust. As his eyes became used to the room's lighting, he took in his surroundings. He sat slumped but unrestrained in a plush leather chair, the soft hide moulding to his frame, in a room that could have been mistaken for a luxurious hotel suite.

He adjusted his position to regain his full posture and look around. The room was circular, with modern wooden slatted walls. It was ultra-modern and minimalistic in style but constructed of the highest quality and luxurious of materials. On the walls, there were three large floating shelves, sparsely populated with books that appeared more decorative than functional. Polished wooden floors, gleaming under the light, stretched across the thirty-foot diameter room. The ceiling above was wooden, with an embedded circular light structure that stretched across two-thirds of the room and oozed ambient lighting into the room below.

A circular desk ten feet across sat beneath the central light fixture. The room's flooring transitioned from wood to marble around it. Across the desk, a leather chair sat empty with a panoramic digital window behind it. The screen was displaying a scene of New York at night that Sam could have believed was real. On either side of the panoramic window, a guard of at least six feet stood silently and assuredly securing the room.

The hiss of secure doors sliding open came from behind him. Sam swivelled in the chair to face the sound. A man walked purposefully across the room. Sam noted two more guards at the rear of the room on either side of the doors.

'Good afternoon, Mr Martin, I am Doctor Willoughby,' Willoughby declared as he reached his chair on the opposite side of the desk and sat down, looking directly into Sam's eyes. Sam could feel the weight of his stare. 'I trust you are well and that your journey here was not too unpleasant?'

Sam ignored the question, asking his own instead. 'What have you done with Elisa?'

'Don't worry about her welfare; I'll take good care of her—I hired her, after all.'

'As well looked after as Doctor Meadows?' Sam retorted.

'Ah, yes dear Doctor Meadows, I'm surprised he agreed to accompany you here. He knew far more than he let on.'

Sam shifted in his seat.

'I know you killed him.'

'Death is only temporary and he should have known better.' Willoughby's face was deadpan.

'And what about me?'

'That depends. I'm sure your friend at the FBI told you everything but the truth. But the truth is, he works for me.'

'Morgan?'

'Yes, Morgan, how else do you think I knew you were coming here? Why else do you think I got you involved? I know all about your military background and what you did. That's why I had you brought here. I thought you could be useful. You could be very successful in my organisation.'

'Bastard!' Sam muttered aloud. After all the years he had known Morgan, he had performed the ultimate betrayal. When or if he ever got out of here, he would string him up by his balls. Willoughby had picked up on Sam's disgust.

'Don't think too badly of your friend. He is just a stupid policeman. A corrupt cog in an even more corrupt machine, obsessed with money. He doesn't understand even a miniscule of what really goes on here or the true potential of what I have created. Your friend Meadows did as others like him, and I think you will too. I have an offer for you. Will you accept it?'

Sam was faced with no other choice. 'Tell me more,' he said.

25. Cryptonasia

'Are you a religious man, Mr Martin?' Willoughby asked, staring into Sam's eyes. His own grey eyes were eerily lifeless. They showed no emotion, yet projected a piercing effect that Sam felt boring into him from across the room.

'Not particularly.'

'You know, religious leaders say that God has all our lives mapped out in front of us and is in control of everything that we do. What if that were true? Have you ever thought of that? What if, at birth, everything that would happen to us and everyone else was buried deep inside us, a pre-program, so to speak? The only way for it to work was if everyone was embedded with the same program to know what everyone else was going to do so that you sub consciously reacted to your program and everyone else's. If we could unlock this information, we could see what was going to happen in the future. We could develop new technologies faster, avoid disasters, and cure the incurable diseases. We might even unlock the mystery of how and why we are here and if there is a God. What if we were all pre-programmed and just under the illusion of free will but actually just acting out a pre-programmed set of actions? By understanding and unlocking this power in our brains we could become truly free and reach a higher state of consciousness.'

Sam sat, eyes wide in disbelief. He couldn't believe what he was hearing. He was sitting in an opulent office, conversing with one of the most respected and richest industrialists the world had known. Yet, if they were sitting in his own office back on the Upper East Side of New York, he would be considering recommending that the man should be committed to an institution for some serious therapy for his own safety. He was clearly suffering, despite his enormous industrial success, from delusion of grandeur probably because of some psychotic disorder, most likely some form of schizophrenia. A schizophrenic split personality would, he thought, go some way to explain how Willoughby could operate amongst the world elite without raising alarm by exposing this dangerous alter ego.

Sam responded in a careful tone, he was aware now that Willoughby was a very dangerous individual whose personality could switch instantaneously and who knows what might happen then. Sam was confident he could manage any physical one-on-one confrontation with Willoughby, but his armed security personnel outnumbered him, and they would undoubtedly use deadly force without hesitation.

'I'm sorry, Doctor Willoughby, I don't buy it. If your intentions were purely philanthropic, why would you be deliberately manufacturing defective drugs that have resulted in the deaths of thousands of terminal patients who would otherwise have had their lives extended by their treatment? Why would you flood the street market with drugs that have caused a plague of psychotic behaviours in New York City if you weren't trying to terrorise the US Government to give you what you want? The FBI has you down as their number one on their most wanted list and it won't be long before the US Government manufactures a reason to conduct a military assault on this place to shut you down.'

Willoughby's face contorted, and to Sam's surprise, he began to laugh. It was one of the strangest things he had ever seen. Willoughby's dead eyes remained lifeless whilst the sound of laughter chortled from his mouth, exposing a set of veneers a Hollywood film star would be jealous of. Then, in an instant, he stopped laughing and his face returned to the stern yet placid façade of an emotionless man.

'The US Government doesn't concern me. Let me show you something that might convince you of my sincerity.'

'How do you think I could get all this sanctioned, if not authorised by the US Government? They are complicit in this. They approved the research, even funded it with US tax dollars,' said Willoughby.

'But then they learned of the Cryptonasia process and wanted it for themselves, no longer satisfied with benefits that I gave them through the Liteon drug I developed.'

'You are just a stooge, Mr Martin, a stooge being used by the government to get what they want without creating yet another international crisis. I have no ill will towards you. In fact, the very opposite. I feel I am very near to Cryptonasia being fully realised, but I need a world network of health professionals to support it against the lies spread and funded by the medical association in the pockets of world governments. Imagine the possibilities for humanity if the international community supported Cryptonasia instead of serving the interests of state-supported pharmaceutical companies.'

'With you in control, of course, Willoughby, paying you for the technology and paying you for all the drugs, you would be even richer than you are now, with the power over the future of mankind,' said Sam.

'What would you prefer? Look what your governments have achieved to date with their control. Disease, poverty, hunger, war. I could change all of that, make the world a better place, I could save the world from tyranny…'

'By becoming a tyrant yourself? Can't you see what you are saying? If Cryptonasia is successful, no one person should be in control of it, no one government should be in control of it. If it has the potential to be as powerful as you say, if the wrong person or a government or terrorist agency with less honourable intentions used it, it could do more harm than good. It might not save the world, it could destroy it. Have you ever thought of that? You might not be responsible for saving the world, you could be responsible for the end of it.'

Willoughby sat motionless for a moment. His gaze hung heavily on Sam from across the room. Sam searched his eyes for any hint of inner turmoil or conflict sparked by their conversation, but there was nothing. They remained empty, soulless, devoid of any empathy. Sam remained calm, waiting for Willoughby to say something, to respond to his proclamation.

With a slight head movement and eyes still fixed on Sam, Willoughby gestured toward the guards on either side of him. As he did so, Sam immediately sensed the danger and primed himself in readiness to fend them off, but it was no use. The two guards accosted him with great skill, one twisting his right arm to the point of breaking and the other gripping his neck in a choke hold. A third guard approached with a gun, ready to fire if Sam broke free. There was no escape.

'I am a very busy man Mr Martin, I hoped that given the great effort you went to in coming here to meet me, that you might be more open-minded, that you would be able to see the true value in the work that I am doing here. You are one of only a few who I have ever shared a true insight into the possibilities of my work and hoped that you would see the potential. Instead, I can see you are as blind as the rest of them. A shame.'

Willoughby briefly lowered his gaze while speaking, appearing momentarily disheartened by Sam's rejection. This momentary chink in his armour soon lapsed, his face grimaced as he looked back directly at Sam and continued.

'Perhaps I can make you see it with a first-hand demonstration.' He stood up and turned to the guard nearest to him. 'Take him to the treatment hall and get Doctor Peters. Our guest here is going to be our newest contributor to unlocking the future.'

The guard, twisting Sam's right arm, bent the limb towards Sam's body and expertly applied a set of handcuffs around Sam's wrists in a seamless manoeuvre. With Sam now in handcuffs, the second guard released the chokehold on his neck.

The relief was instantaneous. With the pressure now removed from his neck and his body, Sam was now free to stand upright. He used the freedom to take several deep breaths into his lungs.

Barely a moment passed before the third guard, his weapon held loosely, pointed him towards a plain, dark door on the room's right-hand side. The wooden panelled door slid open with a soft hiss, to reveal a partially lit corridor with walls that, in contrast to Willoughby's plush office, were clinically smooth. The floor, no longer carpeted, was now a cold expanse of grey vinyl, that caused each step to echo. As Sam was ushered into the corridor, the lights ahead flickered to life, casting eerie blue pools of blue light illuminating the path and revealing cold, metallic walls.

The three guards ushered Sam forward into the pools of light, with Willoughby following behind. As they walked forward, the click of the lights ahead as they switched on became rhythmic. After around fifteen yards, the corridor curved to the left and began to slope downwards. As they rounded the corner, the hallway opened up to a widened reception area.

On either side of the hallway, there were bays built into the walls. In each of the bays, there was an electric buggy. Safety notices on the walls warned people that only authorised personnel were permitted, that CCTV was operating, and that they must evacuate immediately in case of fire or Inergen release (A fire suppression chemical).

The guards shoved Sam into the buggy to the left of the corridor. He was then ushered to the side of the bench seat, and as he sat, they immediately secured his handcuffed wrists to the metal frame of the buggy, ensuring he could not cause a disturbance. The guard with the gun sat beside him with the other two sitting upfront, one driving whilst the other sat twisted to face him, now with a pistol in his right hand pointed in Sam's direction. Willoughby sat on the back seat of the buggy on the other side of the corridor. Two more security guards appeared from a set of automatic double doors and sat in Willoughby's buggy.

'Is Doctor Peters on the way?' Willoughby asked the guard who sat in the driver's seat. The guard nodded 'He's on his way, sir. He's going to meet us in the main treatment hall. He was already in the refinery when he received your request, sir.'

Willoughby nodded. 'Drive on.'

Sam's buggy led the way through the corridors, with Willoughby's following close behind. The whirr of the electric motors echoed through the corridors alongside the click of the lights as they activated automatically. They travelled at pace, Sam estimated around ten miles an hour. As they whizzed through the corridors, they passed several uniform double doors that ventured out from the main corridor.

They continued for another two minutes which seemed to Sam like an age. The uniform corridors of white made it difficult to gauge a sense of distance or location. By the time they had stopped, Sam had no sense of where they were. The only sense of direction he could command was that to keep moving ahead would lead to more faceless corridors and onto whatever lay beyond. He had no intention of finding out what lay further down the corridors and kept alert for a means to escape and retrace his way back to Willoughby's office.

Upon stopping, the guards on Sam's buggy dismounted the vehicle in an orchestrated move, ensuring that at least two of them had eyes on him. Once they had all disembarked, the guard who had been driving unlocked Sam's handcuffs from the metal bar and calmly issued him with instructions.

'Get off and stand next to the buggy facing the doors.' The man spoke in a deep voice with a thick French accent. 'Matteo here has an itchy finger and is a very nervous person. You wouldn't want to alarm him.'

Sam slid across the seat and stood up slowly, keeping his eyes on the guard, who held the gun on him. They paused for a moment whilst they waited for Willoughby to join them from his buggy. During the brief pause, Sam examined his surroundings. There was not much to see. The walls maintained the bland, anonymous look of the earlier corridors. The doors in front of the buggy were heavy duty double doors with narrow windows that were blacked out. To the side of the doors attached to the wall was a security pad lit with a red light.

Willoughby strode towards them. The stark illumination and plainness of the hallway emphasised his stature in his expensively cut suit, making him an imposing figure. As he approached, he motioned towards the guard who had been driving the buggy.

'Louis, the doors.' The guard responded promptly. He moved towards the doors and held his wrist up to the security pad on the wall. The light turned from red to green, and the doors opened inwards automatically.

The doors opened to reveal a short corridor leading to another set of doors. Above the doors was a light that glowed red. Like the main corridor, the walls and floor were made of the same simple material. As the doors opened, blue light from ceiling strip lights illuminated the corridor.

The guard, known as Matteo, ushered Sam forward. After several steps he neared the centre of the short corridor where Matteo ordered him to stop. The rest of the party of guards followed him with Willoughby remaining at the rear and the guards providing a barrier between them. The automatic doors they had entered through closed and as they reached their final position, they were secured with an audible click.

Upon the sound of the doors securing, Louis stepped forward and used his wrist pass against a security panel adjacent to the doors now ahead of them. Just as before, the light above changed to green and the double doors opened automatically. This time, the doors opened to a larger corridor. It was the same length as the corridor they were in but twice as wide, enough to house a security post to the side of the room where a large, both tall and round security guard with perfectly greased back hair sat at a desk that housed various equipment.

The doors closed behind them again with the same secure click. Upon closure, Louis greeted the guard with an official-looking salute and presented him with a security pass that the guard subsequently scanned on his computer. Once he'd scanned the card and tapped away at his computer keyboard, he returned the pass back to Louis, standing up as he did so and motioning him towards the next set of double doors. The large rotund security guard then saluted Willoughby as he passed him, which Willoughby ignored.

Sam watched in bewilderment at the proceedings and grew intrigued by what lay beyond the next set of doors. He knew that manufacturing facilities and data centres were subject to strict security protocols, but what he was observing were more like military protocols which made him wonder what was really going on.

The group moved through the second security airlock, following the same procedure as the last, with an additional check with the desk-based security guard. Louis presented his wrist pass to the security door panel. The door light turned amber; then, the large security guard pressed several buttons on his console. After scanning his wrist, the light turned green, and the doors opened.

This time, instead of revealing another security airlock, the door opened to reveal a control room. The room was not large, approximately two hundred and fifty square feet. There were three rows of bench desks in the middle of the room, all with multiple monitors mounted on top. Each terminal was attended to by a man or a woman dressed in a white coat who each intently watched the screens, occasionally tapping away at a virtual keyboard on a screen. Similar screens adorned the room's walls, filling the entire wall space. The wall screens were broken into different sections, each displaying a different type of graph or metric.

Sam stood and paused for a second as he took the room in, trying to decipher what the information on the various screens was displaying. He had seen similar operational monitoring rooms in the military. Those rooms and screens had shown information about enemy targets, position of personnel, along with various other technical data relevant to the military operation that was being undertaken.

These screens were different, they were more uniform, showing the same basic information broken down to hundreds if not thousands of the same set of metrics, repeated again and again. He instinctively took a few steps forward towards the nearest screen to read it. He made out the labels of heart rate and blood pressure before Louis violently pulled him back.

'Those screens are none of your interest,' he said. 'You'll be up there yourself in a minute.'

A tall, thin man with sandy blond hair, narrow glasses and a pointy face approached the group. He held a tablet computer in one hand. He tapped the screen as he walked before looking up and addressing Willoughby.

'Everything is prepared sir.' His voice didn't match his body. He spoke with a deep, gravelly voice. 'Doctor Peters is on the main floor in sector A1 waiting for the patient.'

Before he had finished his sentence, four white-coated men had surrounded Sam. One of the men injected him in the neck, while another simultaneously lifted him into a vertical wheelchair. Within seconds, he began to feel groggy and disconnected from his body, unable to retaliate. One of the white-coated men removed his handcuffs and strapped him into the vertical wheelchair. He was fixed upright, unable to move.

'Move him onto the main floor.' Willoughby ordered. The four white-coated men began walking in unison towards a set of doors next to the desks of monitors and towards a break in the screen wall. Just like the airlock doors, it too had blacked out windows and a security pad that had to be activated by a wrist pass. Once activated by two of the white-coated men, the doors opened.

With a whirring sound from its electric motor, Sam's vertical wheelchair edged towards the door. As he passed the threshold, he saw what lay beyond. At first, his eyes could not take it all in. The doors had opened onto a raised area that gave a full view of the vast expanse that lay ahead. It was unlike anything Sam had ever seen before.

At first glance, the cavernous chamber looked like a data hall from a data centre. It was the size of a football field with rows upon rows of orderly lines of telephone box size cabinets that would, in a data centre house network and computing equipment. As the chair moved forward and into an open lift and down towards the floor, it became apparent that this was not a room filled with computer equipment. Network switches and servers were absent from the cabinets in this room and the overhead gantries were not just lined with just standard network cables. What Sam saw filled him with utter dread and horror.

The overhead gantries had network and communication cables, but alongside these were miles of tubes and pipes that ran down into glass pods. Each pod was a ten feet tall round cylindrical container fronted with glass and a metal backing. The tubes, pipes and cables ran from the gantries above into the metal frame behind.

Inside each pod stood a vertical wheelchair locked into place within the glass compartment. Sam followed the tubes and pipes from above down into one of the glass chambers. He could see liquid moving down one tube and another that appeared to be taking liquid away.

The wheelchair transporting Sam whirred as its electric motor moved him closer to the row of glass pods. As he did so, he began to see shapes through the glass. The shapes became clearer as the chair moved closer until the full horror of what lay before him became clear.

Each chamber held a person locked in a chair identical to the one he was in. The liquid tubes now made sense. They were life support tubes keeping the poor souls enshrined within the pods alive. As his chair moved him along the row of containers, he peered into each one as best his restraints would allow. He saw that numerous wires and pipes held each person in place in their chair and connected them to the pod, both directly into their bodies and indirectly via the chair.

Every person appeared to be asleep, peaceful looking, as they lay propped in position. Their eyes were closed, arms down by their sides, dressed in the same light blue medical gowns. There was something else that they all had in common. They were all old. Not middle-aged old or senior citizen old, they all had the emaciated appearance of a person near death. Sam's mind began racing, trying to consider all the possibilities. Were these pods literally sucking the life out of people? Is this what Willoughby had in store for him?

His chair whirred forward, at the end of the row, the chair turned left and then right. This isle was identical to the row they had just passed, with the same pattern of cylindrical pods with pipes and cables except, a few feet in, stood a man in a white medical jacket.

Doctor Peters was an enormous man standing at over seven feet tall. He was in his mid to late thirties, with blond hair and appeared slim and athletic under his white coat that accentuated his build. Doctor Peters held a tablet cradled in his right arm, which he occasionally prodded with intent, switching his attention from the tablet to the pod as he did so. He leaned into the pod he was working on and after making an adjustment, checked that the readings on the tablet were satisfactory before grunting and nodding to himself.

'Is it ready, Doctor Peters?' Willoughby called out above the sound of the electric chair and the constant drone of fans and electronic equipment that surrounded them. Doctor Peters looked up from the tablet and turned to face the approaching group. A frown was etched on his forehead, he waited for the group to be closer before responding.

'Yes, Willoughby, it is.' His tone was short and gruff. 'It is as ready as I can make it, given the short notice. I have made the adjustments that I think are necessary given the age of the specimen, although I cannot guarantee that he will survive.'

'Thank you, Doctor Peters, Louis, manoeuvre him into position,' Willoughby instructed turning to face the nearest guard. Louis pressed a button on a remote control that stopped Sam's wheelchair opposite the open pod that Doctor Peters had been adjusting. He reached into the chamber and pulled a tube from within, and clicked it into place onto the back of Sam's chair. He then pressed another button on the remote control. The chair made a number of slight movements to adjust its position before automatically moving slowly into the pod. As the chair reached its position within the machine, several clunks and clicks could be heard as it attached to the pod's internal mechanisms.

When the sounds stopped, a light on the chair illuminated amber. Several screens within the pod began to display Sam's health statistics.

'Thank you, Louis,' Willoughby purred as he positioned himself in front of Sam. Doctor Peters stood silently over his shoulder, his impressive height giving him a full view of the activities. His expression remained stern and emotionless. He tapped the tablet again.

'It's ready for organic integration,' Peters informed Willoughby dryly. Sam remained motionless, unable to move in the chair, unable to fight back. Whatever Willoughby had planned, he was powerless to prevent it. His mind raced as he thought about all the other people stuck in the surrounding pods. Was he too going to end up like them, shrivelled and decaying, dependent upon the pod electronics to keep him alive?

'Forget the full organic integration. He won't need it. Just complete a cerebral cortex connection.'

'But…' Peters protested before Willoughby abruptly cut him off.

'Now, please Doctor Peters!' Willoughby demanded.

Peters decided against further protest and tapped at his tablet. As he did so, he activated a mechanism inside the pod. A small arm extended alongside Sam's head. A needle-like probe twisted and turned as the arm positioned itself beside Sam's neck. Its electronic whine fell silent as it paused. Sam felt his entire body tense in anticipation of what would come next.

Without warning, the probe plunged itself into Sam's neck and administered the "Liteon" medication. As the drug took hold, it plunged Sam into a state of sub consciousness.

Sam didn't feel the needle as it pierced his neck. In fact, he felt no pain at all. As the medication began to take hold, a strange, sensation embraced his brain. It seemed to spread from the top of his spinal cord into his cerebellum before bursting simultaneously across his lobes and into his cortex. As it did, a rush of colours flashed before his eyes as his mind raced in a hive of activity. He felt his brain was opening up, slowly at first, but then exponentially. It felt as if his mind was getting stronger. He sensed his thoughts operating faster and new information enter his mind as if his brain was releasing knowledge that had been resting in the far reaches of his mind.

His thoughts were a whirlwind, a cacophony of noise and panic, making him feel like an outside observer in his own head. Then, without warning, the stimulation in his brain increased even further, as if someone had flicked a turbo switch. He felt sharp jolts in his brain as the electrical pulses reverberated around his synapses like an electrical storm.

At first, he felt a wave of euphoria as the increased activity spread around his brain, but this quickly changed. He felt sharp micro pains with each of the thousands of electrical pulses. The pain of each pulse steadily increased until his skull felt like a thousand electrical blizzards combined, threatening to ignite his skull.

His mouth opened involuntarily to scream and his arms and legs shook as his body's survival instinct kicked in, but the straps in the chair kept him securely in place, leaving him to spasm uncontrollably as if he were being physically electrocuted. The pulses in his mind merged into a single electrical fireball of pain searing every sinew of his brain tissue, forcing his body to the limits of its pain threshold. Unable to bear the pain any longer, Sam slipped into unconsciousness.

'Twelve minutes,' reported Doctor Peters as he, Willoughby and the security guards watched Sam's body become motionless in the chair. 'His vital signs are good. His body appears to have accepted the cortex connection well,' he continued as he tapped away at his tablet computer. 'The average time for connection is three minutes on subjects of the usual age profile, with any failed connections and death in the first minute. He should prove to be an interesting specimen.'

'Don't get too carried away, Doctor Peters. I want you and your team to monitor him very closely. We don't want him to become so weak that we cannot successfully separate him from the cortex connection. He is our best chance of our first successful detachment. All the others were too old to survive the process. I don't want him connected for longer than we have to, just long enough that he can tell us of his experience, so that we can use it to advance our research. After that, I do not care what happens to him.'

'From my calculations, two hours should be long enough for him to integrate to the extent that the medication will have had an impact. It should also be a short enough time period to not damage his cerebral cortex or have any longer lasting effects.'

'Very good, two hours it is. After detaching him, send him to recovery and put your best team on him. I want to know immediately when he regains consciousness.' With his curt instructions, Willoughby turned and marched away. The guards promptly followed him.

26. Body Bags

Doctor Meadows' body lay lifeless on the trolley. Elisa had watched as the two men had carefully unplugged the various tubes and connections from the machine. At first she had thought how respectfully they had been undertaking their work, being cautious as they detached each instrument from Doctor Meadows, lifting and adjusting his body with precision. The illusion of care was shattered when they disconnected the final instrument and then slung him back down on the trolley from his upright position, as if working in an abattoir. It wasn't Doctor Meadows they were being respectful of. They were being careful not to damage the machine and its components.

As the two men wheeled the trolley out of the pod room and through the control area, Darko's grip on Elisa tightened as he pushed her forward to follow. Their journey along the anonymous corridors was short. The two guards led the way, pushing the trolley, with Darko and Elisa following behind. Darko's grip was so tight it felt as if he was actually gripping the humerus bone in her upper arms directly.

As they walked, she tried to resist by attempting to lodge her feet on the floor, but Darko's size and strength meant her struggles were futile. His dominance made her feel like a child having a tantrum, being marched away by her parents for misbehaving. As she struggled, she scanned the corridor, hoping to find something she could use as a weapon, but it was bleak and bare.

They arrived at another set of double doors, which were opened by the guards with their security passes. They ventured through the doorway into an open room where Elisa was caught aghast. Tiles covered the entire room, from the floor all the way to the ceiling, which narrowed upwards like a chimney. There were at least a dozen trolleys lined up along the walls on both sides of the room. A corpse lay on each, withered and emaciated, its skin stretched taut over the bones, forever frozen in the grip of death. She scanned the trolleys, feeling the horror inside as her eyes flittered from one to the next.

Three cast-iron muffle ovens were embedded in a brick façade along the far wall. A large barrel hinge attached each door to the façade, and an industrial sized hinged lever latched each door shut. The ovens were spaced six feet apart and in front of each, a metal frame stood with a conveyor belt atop that fed the bowels of the furnace. Next to each of the cast-iron doors, red and green buttons that operated the incinerators nestled in a control panel in the brickwork.

The guards flopped Doctor Meadows' body onto one of the conveyor belts and turned to help Darko with Elisa. A sudden flush of panic overwhelmed her. She searched the room desperately for any sort of weapon, but as she scanned the room, the feeling of panic only intensified. Surrounded by the stench of death and the sight of decaying corpses, with the incinerators looming, and the guards closing in, she screamed in desperation. In a final, desperate act, she kicked out and tried to scratch Darko's eyes in an attempt to loosen his grip, but his strength was superhuman.

As the two guards approached, Darko snapped at them, 'Leave us. I owe this bitch. I'm going to have some fun with her.'

The two guards looked at each other and shrugged.

'Don't forget to turn the oven off after you have finished,' one grumbled as they passed Darko on the way to the exit.

Darko shook Elisa and slapped her across the face, leaving her dazed. He lifted her off her feet and slammed her onto the next conveyor belt along.

'I should have done this in Italy, you bitch!' Darko snarled rubbing the wound on his head from Elisa's attack in the villa. In a fit of rage he ripped at her shirt, partially exposing her breasts. Elisa began to regain her senses as Darko lifted his leg to straddle her. As he did, she lifted her knee with every ounce of strength she had and connected directly with his groin. Darko yelled with pain and fell backwards into the frame where Doctor Meadows lay.

Elisa rolled off the conveyor belt onto the floor and scrambling to her feet ran towards the exit. Behind her, Darko steadied himself before storming towards her, roaring with anger. She fumbled at the door, looking for the release as he closed down on her. As she turned, Darko was nearly upon her, running at full pelt. Instinctively, she used his own force to run onto the palm of her hand and forcing her hand upwards under his chin, sending him off balance again. She shifted to the left and fell into one of the corpses waiting on the side of the room sending the trolley smashing into the wall, and knocking over a tray of post-mortem blades.

Darko got to his feet, lunging forward, narrowly missing her as she flung herself to the side. The man's colossal bulk crashed into the corpse behind Elisa and the sound of bones snapping could be heard as the withering cadaver collapsed under the man's weight. Elisa scrabbled onto all fours, slipping on the surface tiles as she made her way across to the knives that had fallen to the floor. As Darko approached again, she spun a trolley out from its position against the wall to block his path. Enraged, Darko thrust the trolley aside, sending the body on it flying across the floor. The deposed corpse landed in a heap, strewn awkwardly on the tiles, with limbs twisted into unnatural positions.

Darko marched forward, undeterred, his face bulging with rage. As he walked, he appeared to grow taller and wider with every stride. In desperation, Elisa pushed another cadaver laden trolley into Darko's path. The wheels squealed as they spun across the tiled floor towards him. As the trolley neared, he leaned forward, catching the rail and slinging it behind him, sending the trolley crashing into another corpse laden gurney. The corpse flew up into the air with the force of the collision, spinning in the air and floundering before crashing onto the body on the trolley adjacent. Still, Darko marched forward.

Elisa, in a state of panic, desperately scanned the room as she inched backwards away from the oncoming crazed attacker. Only death filled the room, the old in the decaying cadavers, and the new, in the form of this unstoppable man. She took another step back, glancing down as her foot made contact with something on the floor. The surgical knives lay glistening in the light. She grappled them from the floor, losing her balance and falling backwards onto her rear. She scrambled up, grabbed a knife, and threw it desperately towards the oncoming man but her throw had been careless and unconsidered, it bounced off the man's jacket and rattled as it fell onto the tiled floor between them.

She selected another scalpel and threw it with more purpose and precision, as if she were a knife thrower in a circus. The second knife flew through the air, point first. Darko tried to swipe it away with his long arms, but it was travelling too fast. It landed in his neck, its two-inch blade penetrating deep into his flesh and becoming stuck in position.

Darko paused momentarily at the blow of the knife, but seemed impervious to the object now dangling from his neck and the blood that had begun to ooze down onto his collar. Seemingly unharmed and now only further enraged, he rushed toward Elisa. She was trapped, with trolleys to her left, a conveyor belt to her right, and ovens at her back.

Facing certain death and with no other options, she gripped the remaining scalpels in her left hand, blades up, bracing for impact. The next moment seemed to happen at lightning speed and in slow motion all at once. The big man roared towards her, his right arm outstretched to grab her, the scalpel jiggling in his neck but refusing to detach. As he lunged, Elisa took a step to the right and forward and thrust her left hand up and hard, gripping the scalpels together tightly into a jagged weapon. As he reached her, she felt his hand grip her neck. His strength was incredible, powered by his rage. He gripped her larynx and tried to crush her throat.

Clutching the knives with her left hand, she felt them penetrate his shirt and pierce into his flesh, but his fury was so intense that he didn't seem to notice. With his hand squeezing her neck, she found it hard to breathe. In a final act of desperation, she pulled out the cluster of scalpels and thrust them back into his torso, once, twice and a third time with every ounce of energy that she had left. With a desperate scream, she made a final act of defiance and thrust the knives, twisting them with everything she had left.

She gripped the scalpels tightly holding them in position and felt the warm blood from his torso begin to seep over her left fist. They were locked momentarily in a deathly dance step, his grip tightening around her neck, her arm at his waist. Then the dance ended. He stumbled backward, his hold on her neck loosening as his strength failed. As her neck was freed, Elisa gasped for breath and began to regain her composure.

The blood was beginning to leak out of Darko's torso and the pain had finally registered. The rage in his eyes had dwindled, replaced by a look of confusion and even a hint of fear at what was happening. As he stumbled backward, Elisa maintained her hold on the cluster of knives, yanking them from his flesh, causing the gaping wound to bleed out of the man's body. He clasped his stomach with his hands in an attempt to stem the flow, but within seconds, the blood began to seep through his fingers.

Elisa, alert now, watched as he staggered to the side, leaning against one of the conveyor belts to steady himself as the injuries began to take a toll on his senses. She looked for a way past and saw the scalpel still lodged in his neck. In a single movement, she leapt forward, taking the scalpel in her right hand, whipping it from his neck at an angle, cutting a gash into the man's thick neck perforating his jugular vein.

Immediately, the confusion in his eyes turned to panic as the trickling of blood on his neck turned into a gushing river of red. With one hand on his neck and the other to his bleeding torso, he fell back on to the belt. Seizing the opportunity, Elisa pushed the stumbling man further, lifting his legs onto the machine. As the blood drained him of life-force and energy, he was unable to resist. He attempted to get up from the conveyor belt, but Elisa pushed him down with ease, his strength pouring out of him through his neck and body. He tried again to sit up and get off the machine, but was unable to do so. Resigned to his fate, he lay on the conveyor belt, staring up at the bright ceiling lights clasping his neck in a futile attempt to stop the bleeding.

As Darko lay dying, Elisa's focus turned to escape. She moved cautiously towards him, trying to avoid slipping on the blood-soaked tiles as he lay panting on the conveyor belt. His torso and neck were drenched with blood. Blood had pooled on the tiles and was running towards the floor drains which were there for that reason.

Still wary that he might suddenly spring to life and attack her in one last attempt at revenge, Elisa kept her distance from him. She watched as his breathing, fast at first, slowed to a gentle pant.

After a few minutes, the pants slowed, and then stopped altogether. The slow rhythm of his chest ceased, and he appeared to be lifeless. She took a cautious step towards him, watching his face for any sign of movement. His eyes, wide and unblinking, were locked in a death stare at the ceiling. She moved closer still, and seeing no movement in his body was convinced he was now dead and set upon searching his body.

Elisa peeled his blood-soaked hands from his torso and put them to his side. In death, his limbs were heavy and still. She took his gun from its holster and his security pass that she would use to unlock the doors. She tucked the gun into her belt and the security pass in her pocket and felt inside his pockets for extra ammunition or anything else that would be useful.

His clothes were sticky with blood and she started to feel nauseous. She was not used to handling dead bodies. She rarely stuck around after a kill. Fighting the nauseous feeling in her throat, she leaned over his body to investigate his outmost pocket, desperately trying to avoid staining her own clothes with his blood.

She found a spare magazine of bullets in the pocket and withdrew it from its position tight against his leg. Leaning forward to get a better grip, his body suddenly jerked, his arms lifted and closed over her and he tried to lift his head to look at her. A surge of adrenaline raced through her veins. She jumped backwards out of his clutches and instinctively reached for the gun she had tucked in her belt.

She assumed a firing stance and was about to shoot, but his final attack fizzled out as he slumped back down. Darko now lay dead, arms dropped on either side of the belt. Blood continued to drip slowly from his fingers, splattering onto the floor.

Taking no chances, she ran to the big cast-iron muffle oven door at the end of the conveyor belt, prising the catch open and hit the green button on the belt machine. The mechanism jolted into life and Darko's body began to trundle down towards the oven. Once inside, she slammed the big iron door shut with a clang and pressed the ignition. The big oven roared to life as it committed Darko's body to ashes.

Elisa turned away, the nauseous feeling in her stomach almost overcoming her, but she resisted once more and ran towards the double doors in the hope of escape. She breathed a sigh of relief as Darko's security pass activated the door lock mechanism. She bounded into the sterile corridor beyond and filled her lungs with the fresh air they provided.

As she stood taking deep breaths, the inner turmoil raged inside. Her body was flooded with relief and her instinct told her to run for her life, but she felt the need to look for Sam. In the short time she had known him, she had formed a bond with him stronger than she had with anyone else for a long time. She had a choice to make, try to escape alone, or find Sam.

27. Revelations

There was an electronic hum in the room that infiltrated the atmosphere filling the room. It was low in volume, almost calming, like white noise. After a short while, it seemed to fade into the background as if it wasn't there, but it was. It hummed away in the subconscious.

Sam woke with a start. Although it seemed as if he hadn't ever been asleep, his consciousness had just shifted to a different place. He felt confused, yet at the same time, everything was clear. He was sitting upright in a chair. There were two men in the room with him he didn't know, but when he looked at them, he instantly knew them both and all about them. He watched as they went about their business. One was fussing with controls on a panel, whilst the other prepared a hypodermic needle.

The one with the needle looked over his shoulder at Sam and turned to his colleague.

'He's coming around.'

Sam remained still, as if stuck in a strange stasis. He could feel his body from top to bottom, though he was unable to move any of his limbs or even turn his head. In contrast to his body, his mind was more alert than he had ever known. He felt great waves of energy in his brain and an almost insurmountable amount of recall. Yet, somehow, his mind and his brain seemed disconnected from his body.

'It's time, inject him with the revival solution,' the man at the control panel said to the other. 'I'll alert Doctor Willoughby.'

The man with the needle approached Sam with some trepidation. As he moved closer, Sam tried again to lift one of his arms, but it was unresponsive, almost disconnected. Sam watched as the man moved closer to administer the injection. Suddenly bursts of memory flooded Sam's brain, hordes of information engulfing his mind uncontrollably.

Names, faces, places, people, no one or nowhere he knew, but he knew everything about them, just like he did about the man directly in front of him. His name was Francis Brown. He was thirty-two, divorced with a daughter, the names, the places all related to him. He saw his birth, his wedding day, happy times with his child and unhappy times with his wife. Sam saw evil and violence, pictures of aggression. All the knowledge in his mind was as clear as if he had been there. He knew every little detail.

The man was a wife beater, not that you would know from looking at him. His lab coat hung loosely on a wiry frame, thin framed glasses adorned a pointy nose and he had a meek demeanour. But inside he harboured a rage that he kept contained for those who could not retaliate. He would unleash sadistic attacks on his wife until she could take no more. She had left him two years ago, taking their daughter with her and leaving him alone. With nothing else in his life, he worked in this place, disrespected by his peers upon whom he could not retaliate, soaking the sadness in alcohol. Sam saw the man's final hours spread-eagled in a darkened apartment asphyxiated after choking on his own vomit in his sleep. No one would find him for weeks.

Minutes after the man had administered the injection, he began to regain feeling in his limbs and his mind felt more connected to his body. At first he was able to move his toes and then his fingers, slowly at first as if they were stuck, and then gradually the movement came more easily before finally they could move freely. A strange sensation began spreading over his body. It felt like pins and needles. Except the sensation was almost pleasurable and rejuvenating, as if his body were being healed.

He tried to look down at his body but couldn't. His head was firmly locked in place. As the injection continued to take effect the numbness disappeared, he could feel the retaining straps holding him in position. Still unable to move, he saved his energy for what was to come. He closed his eyes and slipped inside his mind. As he slid into the recesses of his memory and into his thoughts, he felt an intense sensation rush through his brain and within the depths of his being. Every turn of the virtual corridors of his mind unlocked new information. At first he saw places he had never seen that he didn't understand, but within nanoseconds he knew what they were and all there was to know about them. He knew everything. He saw the past, the future, every new thought unlocked new information, and he became hungry for more.

He thought of people he knew, his parents, friends and he knew everything, absolutely everything about them, everywhere they had been, everywhere they were ever going to go, how they lived and how they died. His thoughts spiralled uncontrollably. He had unlocked something powerful, and he had lost control of it. He panicked, as if lost in a nightmare. Desperate to wake up, he tried to open his eyes. He couldn't and he didn't understand why, but the information kept coming. He was losing control and then, without warning, it stopped.

His eyes burst open, and he was back in the recovery room. He was temporarily blinded by the light before until his eyes began to adjust. He realised he was panting, and he felt sweat beading on his forehead. He blinked away the light and a hazy image formed in front of him. As his eyes returned to normal and the image resolved, Doctor Willoughby came into focus. He stood staring intently at him from only a couple of feet away and, for a moment, he thought he saw a look of concern on his face.

'Welcome back Mr Martin.'

Sam's mind ignited at the sound of his voice, although this time it was short-lived. The power seemed to dim rapidly, but it was enough time for him to get a burst of information, this time about the man stood directly in front of him but unlike Francis

Brown the information was incomplete. He saw only patches of Willoughby's life, but what he saw filled him with horror. Through the horror, an image of beauty came through, though suppressed as if it was being held back. It was of a beautiful woman, but in pain. He saw flashes of Willoughby and the woman together, happy. The image shifted and faded away, but a name burst through. Francesca.

'I'm sure you must feel disorientated after your experience, but it will pass. What you have just done, very few people have been through and lived to tell the tale. But perhaps now you understand the potential of our work here. You must have questions and given how unique your experience has been and its importance to our work, I have some for you.'

'His levels are returning to normal,' Francis Brown called from across the room.

'That means the Liteon effect will have worn off and you will no longer have the power you gained in your mind. You received a small dose to demonstrate its potential. If you had received a full course, you would have needed to remain plugged in and on life support. I'm afraid that's a downside of the drug; there's no turning back once fully administered, yet the full potential can't be achieved without it. Now, tell me what you saw.'

'I saw everything, everybody, everywhere. I saw too much. It was overwhelming,' Sam began.

'Go on,' Willoughby encouraged leaning in to listen. 'And did you feel the power of your mind?'

'Yes, I felt it, but it was uncontrollable. I saw flashes of everything. It was too much to take in.'

'You see, you felt it and now do you believe in the potential? What you had was just a small dose. Imagine, hundreds and thousands of people fully connected with their minds expanded with Liteon. Imagine what we could capture, what we could learn.'

'But how do you capture it? It is so volatile.'

'We mine minds and use a process that we invented to capture thoughts and index them electronically. It is a form of electroencephalography, we call cortex extraction.'

'But if you can already enhance the power of the brain and extract the thoughts and knowledge that you claim are stored in every one of us, why do you still keep all the people you have and keep recruiting more?'

'You are very intelligent, Mr Martin. I can see you learn quickly.' Willoughby wagged his finger as he talked and now seemed to beam. 'What you have identified is one of the limitations with Liteon and the confines of the brain enhancing process. We have developed Liteon and refined and improved it consistently with much trial and error. As you experienced, the power can be almost limitless, but the human mind can only handle so much, earlier versions were successful but had some flaws.' Willoughby paused as he considered his next sentence.

'Go on,' Sam encouraged.

'Earlier versions were developed out of common psychoactive substances, LSD, methylphenidate and the like. I'm sure you are familiar with them. Whilst these were somewhat successful in unlocking the power of the brain, they had some unfortunate side effects that I believe you may have come across.'

The psychosis, Sam thought, the early batches had been distributed and used as recreational or medical drugs and caused the epidemic across New York and the rest of the country. It suddenly became clear to Sam. Willoughby had disposed of the defective drugs through the MRG network and flooded the underground market deliberately. That's why so many cases had been reported.

He had set up the network of palliative care and dignified end-of-life centres under the guise of benevolence, but the setup was a recruitment network for people to feed his human mind mines and support his need for all knowledge. People were actually volunteering and paying to be used as organic machines, believing they would receive end-of-life care and die with dignity.

When the mind enhancement and extraction process used up the last of their mortality, he simply disposed of them and added more volunteers. The supply was endless. With only limited extraction from each person, Willoughby could need thousands, if not millions, of people to extract the knowledge he craved.

If he was successful, he could be more powerful than God himself. Sam felt revulsion well inside him. Willoughby had to be stopped, but he had no way of escape. He had to free himself from the chair and find a way to destroy his operation.

'As you can imagine, the government would like to obtain the power of Liteon, but I must finish my research. They would only use it to their own advantage,' Willoughby went on. He was in a dreamlike state now, talking almost to himself.

'What about Francesca?' Sam asked during one of his wistful pauses.

At the sound of the name, Willoughby snapped back to attention. His eyes bored into Sam's. He grabbed Sam's arms as if to shake him, with a grip that was surprisingly strong. Within an instant, he realised what he was doing and retained his composure.

'You see, the power Liteon brings, Mr Martin, you were able to see into the deepest recesses of my mind. Secrets locked away for only a few to see, but it doesn't matter. Francesca is my wife, and her predicament only proves that my intentions are sincere. She is desperately ill. She is in this place. Even with my knowledge and great wealth, I have been unable to cure her. I built all this for her, to save her life and bring her back to me. If the government takes this from me, then I may never find a cure and her fate will be sealed, and surely then I will follow as I will have nothing else to live for.'

'He's fully normalised now.' said Francis from the corner of the room.

'Now you must make a choice. I could use your professional

reputation to enhance the MRG network. Recruit others to do the same and help ensure the research continues. You could become a very wealthy man. You don't owe the government a thing.'

Sam shifted in his seat, but it was no use. He was bound too tightly.

'How can I trust you?' Sam asked, stalling for time.

'Perhaps you can ask someone who you know who can vouch for my authenticity,' he replied, smiling.

The beep of the secure door being released echoed in the room and through the door walked Doctor Peters. The man seemed even taller than Sam had remembered. Alongside him, wearing the same suit as when they last met in New York, was James Morgan. He greeted Sam with a smug grin.

'I told you I could get you in here, but I did warn you would have to be careful. Looks like you are in a whole heap of trouble now.'

28. Escape

Having left the horror of the crematorium behind, Elisa glanced down both sides of the hallway, trying to remain concealed within the recess of the doorway. Both ways looked clear but the silence of the hallways was eerie, making her feel nervous. Before moving, she took a glance through the window of the door behind her to check that Darko had not somehow escaped. Though the room remained in disarray, a strange stillness hung in the air.

Remembering which way they had come, she carefully negotiated the hallway. At first she sided with the smooth walls in an attempt to remain as concealed as possible should any on comers approach. She decided that this was futile as the hallways were wide and empty and creeping along the walls would only raise suspicion. Instead, she walked carefully, but with confidence so that anyone who didn't know her would assume she belonged. To reinforce the appearance of belonging, she wore Darko's security pass on its lanyard around her neck. If confronted, she planned to shoot her way out of trouble.

Navigating the twisting corridors and multiple doorways, she proceeded carefully. Thankfully, Darko's pass had security clearance to open all the doors she approached. She reached an alcove corridor with sets of doors on either side and paused to gather her thoughts. She was confident that through trial and error, she could navigate the maze of anonymous corridors back to where she and Sam had been separated and to the building's entrance. However, once outside, if she could get out, she may be faced with overwhelming opposition. She could, however, escape successfully and seek help. But from where? The townspeople all seemed to be working with the asylum and they would surely return her, or worse. It was clear there was no need for her now.

She also felt a sense of loyalty and connection to Sam. Her life until now had been cold and lonely, running from one place to another. Killing and trying not to be killed. Sam had shown her compassion and affection that no one else had, and whilst she was under no illusion that it could be just a romance of circumstance, she felt a sense of loyalty towards him. From the little she knew about him, she was sure that he would feel the same about her and would seek her out if he wasn't already, so that they could escape together. She was certain that the odds of survival were better with two than with one and that she had nothing to lose. Gripping the gun tightly, she ventured out of the alcove and back into the main corridor.

After reaching the point where she had been separated from Sam hours earlier, she followed the corridor in which she saw he had been taken. She arrived at a crossroads and heard voices, one of which sounded familiar.

She ducked into a doorway, hoping they would head in the opposite direction or she knew she'd be caught. The voices became louder as they approached. She could make out at least two men. Pressed hard in the alcove, the voices drifted away. As they grew quieter, she risked a look around the corner. She glimpsed the back of the two men, one in a lab coat who was enormous. Possibly the tallest man she had ever seen. The other in a suit and was unmistakable even from behind. Morgan. That bastard, she thought. He had double crossed them and alerted Willoughby. But what did he have to gain? Was he in league with Willoughby or undercover from the FBI? She didn't know, but she had to find out. With no other option, she set about following the two men, hoping they might lead her to Sam.

She followed at a distance through the anonymous, seemingly endless corridors. They didn't pass any other guards or staff. She occasionally overheard snippets of conversation. They were discussing some sort of deal and Morgan seemed to be concerned about Willoughby's knowledge of the matter. The other man reassured Morgan about his concerns, but Morgan still seemed agitated.

Their conversation stopped as they approached a set of doors. Elisa held back to watch as they activated the security pad and went into the room. She paused briefly to allow for their return, but in order to prevent losing her one and only lead, she rushed to the set of doors. Crouching low with gun in hand, she peered into the room through the door window. She saw the two men approach a man strapped to a chair. She watched as they moved towards the man, blocking her view. As they walked, the tall man veered off to talk to two men in lab coats, revealing the man in the chair. Sam, she had found him. Now she had to find a way to get him out.

29. Escape Trial

Elisa watched through the door window as the group of men engaged in conversation. The discussion appeared animated, with Morgan waving his arms as he spoke.

Willoughby stood watching sternly, arms folded, standing next to Morgan and Sam with the trio in lab coats hanging towards the back of the room, watching events unfold. Two of the men watched with trepidation, whilst the giant man watched with amusement across his face.

She could only hear the occasional word when people raised their voices. Sam's binding to the chair limited him to facial expressions. Rage filled his face, directed at both Willoughby and Morgan. She swore that if it were possible, he would be spitting fire in their direction.

The conversation continued until Willoughby interjected, stopping Morgan from speaking, his patience worn thin. Turning, he barked an order at the three men in lab coats. He then marched towards the door.

As he passed Morgan, he leaned into him, their heads almost touching, and breathed something in Morgan's ear that appeared to surprise him. Without waiting for a response he continued his march towards the doors behind which Elisa was hiding.

With nowhere to hide, she gambled by sprinting down the opposite corridor and around the corner from which Morgan and the giant man had come. Elisa's gamble paid off. The doors opened and Willoughby strode into the corridor away from her. With Willoughby out of sight, Elisa sneaked back up to the door window and chanced a look into the room.

With Willoughby out of the room, the conversation continued. Sam and Morgan were exchanging words intensely. Still bound in the chair, Sam's demeanour remained hostile. Morgan's body language had become defensive, his arms were crossed, and he seemed to fiddle with his cuffs when he spoke.

Towards the rear of the room, the tall man watched on. The meek-looking man checked paper work, whilst the third man in the lab coat approached Sam with what appeared to be a set of syringes. The liquid in the syringes resembled what they had applied to Doctor Meadows when he had been connected to the machine. Elisa felt a sense of horror well inside her as she recalled Doctor Meadows' experience. She could not let the same happen to Sam. There was nothing else she could do, no time to plan, no one to call for help. If she was to save Sam from the same fate as

Doctor Meadows, she would have to act now.

Outnumbered four to one, she knew the odds were against her. She had only two things in her favour, the element of surprise and the gun she had taken from Darko. Releasing Sam would help address the imbalance, but even then, the odds were stacked against them.

She quickly assessed the threat of each of the men in the room. She knew Morgan was likely carrying a weapon, so Elisa would need to centre any attack on him as a primary target as he posed the highest threat. She guessed that each of the men in lab coats were unarmed, but could raise the alarm if not prevented from doing so. The giant man of the three was an unknown entity, his body language did not give off a sense of threat but she could see from the way his clothes hung on his body that he was physically in good shape and could pose a significant threat.

The position of the men was helpful. Sam was nearest to the door and the three men lingered towards the rear. This might give an opportunity for her to release Sam whilst covering the other four men. The man with the syringes started his approach across the room towards Sam. As he neared Sam, he attempted to break free from his constraints in a futile gesture of resistance. It was now or never.

She knocked on the window loudly and scanned her access card against the door security panel. As she did so, the familiar beep of the door release sounded. She repeated the card scan, causing the beep to sound repeatedly.

At the knocking sound, the men in the room turned to face the door in surprise. As the beeping noise repeated, the tall man in the lab coat ordered the meek man in the lab coat to investigate. He approached the door without care. As he opened the door, Elisa stepped out from the side and struck him in the head with the butt of the gun, sending sprawling backwards onto the floor unconscious. One down. It was now three against two.

Slipping into the room she took up a firing position before anyone had a chance to react. As she raised her gun, Morgan unfolded his arms. His eyes narrowed, as if to draw his own weapon.

'Don't even think about it,' she said calmly. 'Arms back just as they were, unless you want me to decorate the wall with your brains.' Morgan did as he was told.

'The same goes for you in the back,' she ordered, referring to the tall man at the back. 'Any movement or attempt to raise the alarm and there's a bullet with your name on.'

'Wait…' began Morgan before Elisa shut him down.

'No talking either. You!' she said to the man holding the syringes. 'Drop them on the floor and kick them to the other side of the room and undo his restraint so he can get out of that thing.'

The man did as he was told. Carefully, he disconnected the implant in Sam's neck before undoing the straps that held him tight in position. Once he had finished, Elisa ordered the man to stand

and face the adjacent wall. He obeyed the order without a word, his shoulders slumped in quiet resignation.

Sam took his time standing up, but found his balance quickly. With Sam released, the odds in the room improved significantly. Sam took a step towards Morgan, his face like thunder. Morgan took a step back, his hands now down at his sides as he began to protest.

'Look…' he began before Sam unleashed a right hook into the man's jaw, sending him sprawling backwards onto the floor against the wall. Still conscious, he reached inside his jacket, but Sam was alert and stopped his hand from going any further. Sam reached inside Morgan's coat and retrieved his gun. A Glock 17M standard issue FBI firearm. Sam was familiar with the weapon. It had a magazine of seventeen rounds and a reputation for accuracy.

Sam turned to Doctor Peters. 'Over here, please Doctor Peters, and don't try anything funny.' He covered the enormous man with the Glock as he crossed the room.

'What's the best way back to the main hall without being seen?' he asked. Before Peters could answer, Elisa interjected.

'You want to go back? Why would you want to go back? We have to get out of this place!'

'No, we have to go back to the main hall. We have to put an end to this. I've seen where this could lead. We have to stop it.'

From his position on the cold, hard floor, Morgan mumbled his agreement. 'He's right. That's what I'm here for, to help.'

'What are you talking about?' said Sam 'It's you that got us into this mess. You double crossed us. We were trying to help you.'

Morgan slid his back up the wall and up to his feet.

'I had to. It was the only way I could get Willoughby to fully trust me. There's more to this than you know.'

'You're lying. You set us up!' Elisa yelled, 'I should shoot you right now.'

'If you do, then you'll never get out of here. You think you will get out just the two of you?'

'Go on.' Sam pushed the Glock towards Morgan 'You've got thirty seconds.'

'Think about it. There was no way you could have got in here incognito. Yes, he knew you were coming, but that was the best way to get you in and get his trust. It was all part of the plan I would get you in, but I would get you out too.'

'Prove it.'

'I have a SWAT team on the perimeter ready to move in on my command. You can speak to them on the communicator. I admit I used you, but it was the only way to gain trust and access. I came here to help you and stop Willoughby. If he succeeds, there is no telling what he will do. All that knowledge and power is not safe in the hands of just one man.'

'But it would be in government hands?' Elisa retorted.

'Your choice. Like it or not, I'm your ticket out of here and your best bet at stopping Willoughby.'

'OK, what's your plan?' asked Sam.

'You can't be seriously thinking about trusting this scumbag again, can you? I should shoot him right here and now after he what he did. You could be dead now, hooked up to that machine!' Elisa yelled.

'I know, but he's right. He is the best chance we have, and we have to stop Willoughby. And if he is lying to us, I promise I'll break his neck with my own bare hands.' Sam turned back to Morgan, lowering his gun. 'Go on, what's your plan?'

'Doctor Peters here is helping me. He knows the way around the facility, how the drugs are manufactured and the process of using it successfully and the best way to isolate Willoughby. The plan is to capture him quietly. We want to avoid an all-out gun fight. We don't want to damage the facility.'

'Go on,' said Sam. 'I'm listening.'

Morgan paused and wiped his brow with his sleeve, exchanging a glance with Doctor Peters across the room. Sam watched as Morgan straightened his jacket, recomposed himself and gathered his thoughts, ready to explain his plan. Sam knew that whatever he was about to say was only going to be half the truth, but also that Morgan had now exposed himself and his FBI connections to Doctor Peters and the other members of Willoughby's team. Did they know who he was and what he was really planning? Morgan was now playing a survival game and was relying on everyone playing along to stay alive. There was no guarantee that men loyal to Willoughby wouldn't turn on him and if that happened, his SWAT team would be too late to save him.

Morgan's plan was simple. Willoughby was unaware of Morgan's intentions and trusted him as a comrade. He was expecting Sam to be returned following his exposure to the Liteon process to discuss joining Willoughby's organisation. If Sam did not agree, then he would send him away to be permanently indisposed. They would use the meeting as a distraction. Morgan would send his SWAT team in ready so that they could ambush Willoughby and capture him alive. Doctor Peters and team could continue their work under the authority of the Government and, with Willoughby removed, distribution of the psychosis inducing medications would be stopped.

Sam agreed to the plan, with one exception. Since Willoughby expected Elisa to be already dead, she would hang back and cover Morgan and Doctor Peters. Any deviation from the plan and she would shoot anything that moved.

With the plan set, Doctor Peters contacted Willoughby. Sam and Elisa watched closely as he pressed the button on the intercom. Elisa held the gun aloft, her eyes boring up into Doctor Peters as a warning. The intercom buzzed, and Willoughby answered.

'Yes, Doctor Peters.'

'He has been successfully restored from the process with no ill effect.'

'Good, I will see him in the main medical hall. Have the medics prepare a permanent pod for him in case he has not seen the light.' Willoughby terminated the connection without waiting for acknowledgement.

Morgan made arrangements with his team and with Sam in front leading Morgan and Doctor Peters, they ventured out into the hall towards the main medical hall. Elisa followed closely behind.

As they walked, Sam wondered if this was the biggest mistake of his life.

30. Execution

A series of anonymous corridors led to the main medical hall, where thousands of pods stood, holding their immobile victims whose last remaining life-force was being mined from them. Their progress was slow, as Sam was still recovering from the ill effects of the Liteon process. He refused to take a buggy as he wanted to have the time to recover further and was convinced that walking was his best chance of doing so.

Morgan and Doctor Peters walked silently behind him, speaking only to give directions. The only other sounds came from Morgan's radio that relayed the progress of his SWAT team. When they had reached their agreed positions, he turned the sound off.

Elisa followed closely behind, wearing Darko's lanyard. She walked slowly, but with confidence. She had taken a lab coat from the recovery room to help her blend in should they come across any of Willoughby's men. Although, if they did, Doctor Peters was under strict orders to confirm their authorisation of passage. It was unlikely anyone other than Willoughby himself would challenge him.

As they walked, in the distance down the long corridor, two

men in lab coats approached pushing stretchers. Sam slowed down to be within earshot of Doctor Peters at a whisper.

'Who are these?' he asked under his breath.

'They are nothing to worry about, just junior porters transporting more patients across the facility. They won't be a problem.'

As the two men approached, the squeak of the stretcher's wheels came into range. Each revolution of the wheels produced a repetitive whine, like a clock ticking down the seconds until their paths crossed. The two men were deep in conversation as they pushed their respective loads, at one point laughing at a joke. As they came closer and recognised Doctor Peters, their conversation fell silent and they resorted to staring ahead, concentrating on pushing the stretchers along the corridor.

When the two groups passed each other, Sam caught a glimpse of the patients on the stretchers. Both were covered with a light sheet that did nothing to hide the emancipated profile of what lay beneath.

Once the two men had travelled far enough down the corridor, they restarted their conversation and the squeak of the wheels faded into the distance.

Sam stopped dead in his tracks and turned to Doctor Peters.

'What sort of patients were those?'

'They were patients who are…' he paused to consider his words. '…no longer treatable.'

'Dead you mean, the last ounces of their life sucked out of their minds to feed Willoughby's machine.' Sam turned back in disgust and carried on walking.

It seemed to take an eternity to travel along the corridors. The bleak white walls and the ever present low, white-blue light illuminating the way ahead gave nothing to show progress. Only the occasional set of security doors gave any indication of advancement. Sam, having been unconscious when he had been transported to this part of the building, had no idea that they had travelled so far. Elisa, having had to negotiate the corridors to find Sam, had begun to pick up on the slight variations of the corridors and sensed that they were near to the main medical hall. Checking that there was no one in sight, she hurried forward and called out to Doctor Peters.

'Hey, this looks familiar. How much further?'

The group stopped mid corridor, Sam turned back to face the other three.

'Well? Is she right?' He tapped the gun under his jacket as a reminder of the situation.

'Yes, she is. It's just around this next corner, through another set of security doors. We may see more medical staff once we approach as they will be going about their duties to maintain the patients.' Doctor Peters looked at his watch. 'The next "maintenance" rotation is in thirty minutes. They are unlikely to say anything as the hall is vast and there are a lot of patients to tend to, they usually start at the opposite end of the hall, checking that all the connections are still in place and that there are no blockages.'

'OK Morgan, it's over to you. Signal your men that we are going in and to be ready to assist, we want Willoughby's men so overawed that they see no point in fighting. And remember, any funny business and I have half a dozen bullets in here with your name on them.'

Morgan nodded and reached for his radio but before he could issue his orders, there was a hiss as the security doors into the main hall opened and a thin, balding man wearing thin rimmed spectacles and carrying a clipboard came scurrying through the doors, a look of worry plastered all over his face.

On seeing Doctor Peters, his face seemed to relax and, ignoring the others, scampered up to the tall man.

'Ah, Doctor Peters, I must speak with you urgently.' His voice was nasally and riddled with urgency. 'Alone, if possible, it's really rather urgent.' Doctor Peters looked at Morgan and then at Sam, who nodded and mouthed silently to get rid of him.

'Doctor Gardner, I'm on important business with these special guests of Doctor Willoughby. Perhaps we can talk later.'

'It's Willoughby I wanted to talk to you about. He instructed the West Coast plant to start with the second generation of the process immediately and expects all other plants to follow as soon as enough of the second generation of Liteon can be manufactured.

He wants to bring forward results at all costs. He seems to have disregarded the instability issues we have been experiencing with the new formula. I wondered if you could talk to him. He won't listen to anyone else.'

As Doctor Peters listened to the man, his eyes widened, lips parted, and the usual reserved look on his face turned to horror. He quickly reasserted himself and patted the man on the back reassuringly.

'Of course, Doctor Gardner, I understand. Why don't you get yourself off home for the day and leave this to me?'

The little man nodded thankfully and scampered away down the corridor, muttering to himself. As the man disappeared round the corner, Sam glanced up at Doctor Peters.

'What was all that about?'

He looked across at Morgan and then back at Sam. 'I think you may be right. He may have to be stopped.'

'But…' Morgan started before Sam shut him down.

Sam turned back to Doctor Peters 'Go on.'

'We've been working on a second generation of the Liteon process. It is designed to be a more powerful version, able to accelerate the mental extraction process. Willoughby has always been keen to push for faster results, but this version of the formula has proven to be incredibly unstable. The successful conversion rate drops by up to eighty per cent and when conversion is successful, the patients survive for only a tenth of the time.'

'You mean it kills more people when they are put into those pods and if they make it into them alive, they don't last as long?'

Doctor Peters' head dropped.

'Yes. I'm afraid so. It means he will need thousands more people to keep up, and so he will flood more psychosis inducing drugs across cities to aid recruitment.'

'And more old and ill people will be put to their deaths under his so-called care centres inducted through the MRG,' add Sam.

Doctor Peters looked crest fallen. He had come to the realisation that his work with Willoughby was no longer for the greater good, it was evil and that he was part of that evil and it must be stopped. There was no longer any justification, if there ever was any, to experiment with the final chapter of people's lives. Willoughby would keep pushing for more and more until he got what he wanted, and even then he would keep pushing further. There was no end unless they put a stop to it.

Sam looked at the big man and watched as the emotions ran over his face, before they disappeared completely, replaced by steely determination in his eyes. Doctor Peters raised his head, pulling back his shoulders and standing up to his full height. He seemed to grow another foot, and his presence became even more imposing.

'We must go, Willoughby will be expecting us by now and we don't have any time to lose.'

Elisa checked her gun and nodded to Sam that she was ready.

He returned her look and, as their eyes met, they exchanged what they wanted to say without speaking. This was no time for emotion or words, even though deep inside, all he wanted to do was to take her in his arms.

Sam checked his own weapon was ready and tucked it into his jacket pocket for easy access. He felt almost fully recovered from the Liteon process, although there was no more time to recover anyway. It was time to act. He told Morgan to issue the final instructions to his men over the radio and had Doctor Peters activate the security pad to open the door. With a final deep breath, Sam led the way, hands in pockets, one on a gun and Morgan and Peters on either arm "escorting" him.

As soon as they passed through the doors and into the foyer of the main medical hall, Elisa quickly stepped to the side into the shadows to stay as much out of sight as possible. The hall was even bigger than Sam remembered. They stood on the same raised platform that Sam had been wheeled onto in a vertical chair. Now standing on his own two feet and able to take in the expanse of the room freely, the terror welled inside him again as he gazed at the rows and rows of pods containing people trapped in Willoughby's human mine.

They made their way down to the main hall to meet Willoughby. Standing in an area at the end of the rows of pods, they turned to see him appear from a set of security doors that led from the main hall.

As he emerged, he took several short steps before pausing.

'So, Mr Martin, you have now had an insight into the power of the Liteon process and you seem to have recovered well.' He looked quizzically at Morgan and then to Doctor Peters, who stood on either side of Sam, holding him in custody. 'Perhaps now you understand the potential or our work here?' A cruel smile spread across his face as his eyes looked past Morgan. From the shadows of the pods Louis and Matteo, two of Willoughby's thugs appeared behind the three men stood before Willoughby. Both men held pistols aimed at Sam.

Seeing the two men, Morgan took a step away to distance himself from Sam.

'You have a simple choice, Mr Martin. I have plenty of room in my facility.' Willoughby sneered. The sneer vanished from his face as two gunshots echoed through the vast hall. The two thugs behind Sam collapsed to the floor, blood pouring from their heads. Elisa, gun held aloft, alert to more danger, eased her way down the steps of the raised platform flanked by two members of the SWAT team.

'It's over Willoughby,' Elisa declared, her gun held steadfast in his direction as she walked.

Willoughby looked confused at the turn of events, looking from Morgan to Peters and back to Morgan again.

Staring intently at Willoughby, Sam was resolute.

'I've seen the potential. It's too much for one man, or anyone to have. We have to destroy this place, starting right now.'

31. Release

Elisa turned to Sam. 'If we destroy this place, then all the people who are connected will die.'

'I know, and it is the last thing I want, but they are dead already. They are being kept alive artificially by their connection so that their minds can be mined. They will be in desperate pain with their minds being torn apart and with no way out until their body gives up. Leaving them connected only keeps Willoughby's work alive to be used by someone else. It has to end.'

Sam turned to Doctor Peters 'What's the quickest way to disconnect people?'

Doctor Peters pondered. As he did so, a pensive look spread across his face as he gathered his thoughts. Together with his height, he looked statuesque for a moment.

He glanced across at Willoughby. Their eyes met, and for a second they seemed to communicate across the air. Willoughby's eyes shimmered and his stare appeared to transmit a plea to his colleague in a final desperate attempt to prevent the inevitable.

Doctor Peters broke the connection, focussing his attention back at Sam. 'We've only ever disconnected a patient one at a time. We have never attempted a mass disconnect before.'

'But there must be a way. What about shutting off the power?' Sam asked.

'Shutting off the power would force the backup power to be activated. This facility was built to military standards of resilience to mitigate such circumstances.'

'There must be some sort of manual override,' Sam probed, getting impatient.

'Indeed, but even the manual overrides have controls built in to prevent a complete shutdown. Despite what you may think, we did not build this facility to terminate patients. We actually want to keep them alive as long as possible.'

'Of course you do. You sick bastards wouldn't want your precious subjects to die before you got your use out of them, would you?' Elisa spat towards Doctor Peters.

'Maybe he has a point Sam, let my men take care of the facility. We can call in experts to decommission it safely.' Morgan interjected. 'Let's just take care of Willoughby and get out of here. We've done everything we needed to do here. It's over for him. This whole thing is finished.'

'No!' Sam snapped 'We have to get rid of it. It's not safe in anyone's hands.'

'Now wait just a minute…' Morgan began before Doctor Peters spoke.

'There is another way. The life support systems and mind

mining is controlled by computer. It maybe possible to issue a command to shut down the system, disconnecting all patients and stopping the mind mining simultaneously. Once the patients are disconnected, it is just a case of physically decommissioning the pods and the rest of the facility. But I warn you, we have never tested this.'

'No!' yelled Willoughby 'You mustn't!'

'I'm sorry,' Peters replied 'Given the circumstances there is no other choice. You've gone too far.'

'Make it happen.' Sam ordered.

Peters was torn. He knew that underneath everything Willoughby wasn't truly evil, but then he had his doubts. He felt like he didn't know him anymore. The experiments were no longer for good, they had become twisted, and he couldn't stand by and let them continue, he had to help stop them, for Willoughby's sake and his own.

'It will take me a minute to initiate the commands, then, once the sequence starts, it cannot be stopped. Because of the number of patients connected, it will take some time before the system is fully shut down.'

Peters walked towards a side room that contained a computer console.

Sam motioned to Elisa. 'Go with him. Give him five minutes to get it done. If he doesn't, we'll burn this place to hell.'

'Look Sam, we've got the situation under control,' Morgan

said, pointing to the SWAT team members now standing on either side of Willoughby.

Sam turned to Morgan. Visibly angry, he prodded Morgan in the chest.

'This ends today. I don't care what the FBI can do. In fact, I worry about what they might do. All this has to go.'

As Morgan and Sam argued, their attention switched from Willoughby towards each other before they were interrupted by the crack of a gunshot. The shot rang out from behind Willoughby and as the sound reverberated, one of the SWAT team members flanking Willoughby collapsed to the floor, having been struck by the bullet.

Sam instinctively dived for cover. In the immediate shock of the gunshot, Willoughby used the surprise to disarm the remaining SWAT team member and rendered him unconscious with a swift blow to the head.

From the shadows, a man in a lab coat emerged holding a pistol aloft in a shooting position. Sam cursed under his breath as he recognised him from the recovery room.

It was clear the man in the lab coat was not used to handling weapons or participating in confrontation. His hands visibly shook and his face was adorned in fear. He slowly padded forward towards Morgan, who was now stranded alone in the centre of the opening, weaponless and totally exposed. Yet, despite his predicament, he remained calm and appeared relaxed.

Sam peered around the pod to survey the scene and noticed immediately that the pistol the lab man was holding was a Glock 17M, the same FBI standard issue weapon he had retrieved from Morgan.

'It's no good Willoughby. Morgan has this place surrounded. You'll only escape here to be recaptured, and killing any of us will only make it worse for you. Put the gun down and we can all get out of here alive.' Sam yelled from behind the pod, the Glock in his hand primed for use.

To his surprise, Willoughby broke out into a laugh, the same maniacal laugh he had witnessed earlier. Its freakish nature sent a shiver down Sam's spine.

'There is no escape. I thought you would have realised that by now, especially after your experience. Leaving this world only moves us onto another.'

As Willoughby spoke, the man in the lab coat neared Morgan, gun still aloft, and Sam waited for the gunshot to sound and for his old friend to meet his end. As the man with the gun neared arm's length, Morgan calmly took the gun from the man's hand, holstering the weapon in his jacket holster. Morgan turned his back on Willoughby to face where Sam was taking cover and shrugging his shoulders said, 'sorry Sam, I can't let this happen.'

A silence hung over the group in the impasse. It was broken by the main lights dimming and the emergency lights being activated. The sporadic lighting made the room darker, with occasional pools of light cast set at precise intervals across the vast expanse of the hall. Upon the top of each of the thousands of pods, a small light flashed like a warning light on the underside of an aeroplane.

'Noooo!' cried Willoughby. But he was powerless to act. Peters had started a total shutdown procedure. A pop and hiss sound began to emanate from the deep recesses of the hall. One after another, a pop of a seal being broken, followed by the hiss of air being released, repeated like firecrackers in the distance. Without warning, the bank of pods nearest the group simultaneously popped as the plastic casing of the pods separated from their fixed positions. Then, as the pods opened, a rush of air escaped, hissing into the atmosphere.

'It's done,' Peters called from his position in the aisle furthest away from the group. 'There is no going back now. The entire system has been shut down.'

Willoughby was physically shaking. His eyes burned with rage and his hand was turning white from the crushing grip he held on the gun.

His eyes turned to Sam, their eyes met briefly in which Sam felt a sense of pain from the man's eyes mixed with confusion and misapprehension.

In the depth of the main hall, the pops and hisses stopped, replaced by a strange pattern of orchestral groans. Shouting followed from the SWAT team stationed further down in the hall. The shouts were panicked, but they were too far away and the room's lighting was too dim for anyone to see what was happening.

Then, without warning, the SWAT team fired gunshots, followed by more shouts as they fired more rounds. Strange wailing screams echoed down the aisles of the pods. Screams of anguish and pain reverberated in the vast hall, some high pitched, some deep and penetrating, but each one filled with horror and despair.

The gunshots stopped, and in the distance, several SWAT team members, armed with rifles, ran toward them in the dim light of the vast room. Occasionally, they would turn and fire a burst of gunfire in the distance behind them. As they ran, they looked left and right at the pods. As they approached the end of the aisle and got closer to the group, Sam saw the sheer fear and horror in their faces.

The SWAT team leader ran up to them.

'They are everywhere! At first we tried to help them, but they started attacking us. It's like they aren't human.'

32. Army of Lost Souls

The popping and hissing sounds grew louder as they moved down the hall. The SWAT team stood poised with their weapons stationed either side of the aisles ready to fire at whatever was approaching in the shadows. As the sounds echoed around the hall, the SWAT team leader turned to Morgan to seek instructions. Peters emerged from the side where he had been working on a computer console, shutting down the system. He looked poised standing calmly amongst the melee, looking across to Willoughby with a contented look on his face.

Morgan, still holding the gun pointed at Sam, called to Willoughby. 'What's going on? What are those noises and who are the people attacking my men? I thought you said the people in these pods were as good as dead.'

Willoughby was now looking more visibly distressed. His face looked panicked and his eyes flittered as the internal conflict in his mind decided on his next course of action. As the psychological struggle raged inside Willoughby's mind, Doctor Peters interjected.

'What you are hearing is the sound of the pods being released.

At first, they unlock and then they automatically open, and as the seal is broken the air escapes. Some have been in place for many months. They open in sequence based on the computer program and the time at which the pods were populated. Those furthest away in the hall were the pods that were populated first and, therefore, opened initially. The other halls will be operating in much the same way. It won't be long before the pods nearest to us open themselves.'

Several shots rang out in the distance, followed by a scream that was abruptly cut short, leaving Peters to continue.

'The patients in the majority were near death, others less so, sent here from various institutions across the country. Hospitals, care homes, psychiatric institutions, prisons or simply just missing persons. People that wouldn't be missed but might free up spaces for other people wherever they might be housed. Most are old, but there are quite a few who are quite young. The Liteon procedure requires the subject to be in a certain level of health in order for the body to remain alive and for the mind to be mined. In order to maximise patient participation, the procedure also includes certain medications to prolong life and enhance bodily functions.'

'You mean that you've pumped them full of steroids and God knows what and they have now been let loose?' Morgan exclaimed.

'Yes, although we know that because of the intensity of the treatment, survival rates for patients disconnected from the process are short, it is something that we have not yet perfected.'

'Oh, my God. It's pure evil,' said Elisa.

From up in his position Willoughby cried, 'It's not evil, you are evil you have ruined it all! I set this up to save lives, but you and the rest of them can't see the real potential. It is only your minds thinking a certain way that makes it evil.' He was visibly shaking.

'Look!' cried the SWAT leader. 'They are coming nearer.'

A sickening sight emerged from the aisles in the gloom of the emergency lights. Dozens of shadows stumbling waywardly. Some limped, some walked, whilst others wandered from side to side. When the light fell upon the walking shadows, their features became visible. Once people, cherished, loved and alive, the skin on their faces was now loose and sallow but on others it was taught and stretched. Their eyes were dark and lifeless, but filled with purpose. As they ventured forward, the frailest looking, some no more than walking bags of bones, faltered and collapsed to the floor. When their bodies fell to the floor, they made a slopping sound as what was left of the structure of their body buckled and crumpled.

As the army of souls marched forward, the SWAT team fired in panic. The gunfire ripped the frail-looking shadows apart, and as their flesh tore, the bodies succumbed to failure and fell to the ground. Yet, when the bullets penetrated the strongest of the shadows, they seemed to have no effect. The bodies flinched upon impact, but the flesh absorbed the bullets and they kept marching forward, eyes still filled with purpose.

As the panic grew, one of the SWAT team sprinted towards a large moving shadow, spraying rounds of bullets into its body. The bullets thudded into its torso, yet it kept moving forward. Even at point blank range, the bullets seemed to have no effect. When the magazine was empty and the rifle clicked harmlessly the large shadow snatched the rifle, pulling the SWAT team member close to it and in the same move grabbed the man by the neck and smashed his body against the side of a pod as if the man were a toy. The impact broke the man's neck and his body slumped lifelessly to the floor. The shadows kept marching, undeterred.

The SWAT team leader stood aghast as the shadows continued their march forward. In the background, more shapes appeared out of the darkness. He ordered his team to fire more rounds into the approaching horde. Several bursts of fire later, the SWAT team paused to survey their work. A few ragged bodies had crumpled to the side, strewn awkwardly on the floor, liquid oozing out of their flesh ripped apart by the onslaught of gunfire, but hundreds of looming shadows kept coming, unaffected by the armed offensive.

'It's no use. We need more powerful weapons. We need to secure the area and prevent them from escaping until we can bring reinforcements. I've never seen anything like it before,' cried the SWAT team leader turning to Morgan with a look of horror on his face. Morgan looked at Willoughby uncertain what to do.

'What can we do to stop them? Put them back in their pods?'

Willoughby stood still, gun aloft, his eyes shimmered with rage and sadness. He spoke with stifled emotion.

'It's over. There is no going back, but restoration must be served.' He looked across at Sam, the gun now held steady in his hand, pointing at Sam's head. He squeezed the trigger, and as he did so, swung the weapon towards Morgan and fired a round into the man's chest, followed in quick succession by a second and a third.

Whilst the group stood astounded, Willoughby turned on his heel and sprinted through the doors behind him. As the doors shut behind him, the SWAT team leader, first to react, sent a flurry of bullets that crashed against the closing doors and adjacent walls.

Free from the stare of Willoughby's gun, Sam turned to Doctor Peters.

'Can we stop them?'

'Maybe, but they are dead already. You will have to blow them up if you want to be sure. The stronger ones are unlikely to feel any pain. But they are unstable, they will not last long before their bodies fail outside of the life support.'

Sam turned to the SWAT leader. 'I suggest you get your men and everyone out of here and secure every possible route to prevent their escape. If Doctor Peters is right, then they will soon self-expire.'

The SWAT team leader nodded in agreement and began calling out orders to his men and relaying the message on his radio to his team in other parts of the building and on the exterior perimeter.

Sam turned away and began towards Doctor Peters.

'You need to come with me.'

'Where are you going?' cried Elisa.

'We have to find Willoughby. We can't let him get away.'

33. The Last Stand

Willoughby heard the bullets rattle against the wall and smashing the window in the doors, but there was no time to stop, no time to falter. It was over. Everything he had built over years had come crumbling down in moments. People he had trusted had let him down again. But this time, he had done something he had never done before. Revenge. He could scarcely believe what he had done. Shooting a man to death. He had deserved it for sure, the ultimate betrayal. He had promised so much, but had let him down just like all the rest.

It was the first time he had ever killed anybody in cold blood. He had dedicated his life's work to saving lives, not taking them. He thought he might have felt differently, guilty perhaps, but the rage that had grown inside him overtook his heart and his mind and now he didn't feel anything.

Now that it was finished, only one thing remained, and he knew it must be done before the place was taken over or destroyed. He ran through corridors and waited impatiently at security controlled doors as he waited for his access card to let him through. He could hear the sound of gunshots ringing in the distance, followed by shouts and cries. It was of no concern to him now. Everything was lost. There was only one hope.

Running through another control room, he paused momentarily. Emergency lighting illuminated the room, providing just enough light to navigate the area. The computer screens littered on the consoles and the large video screen wall that showed the status of the pods that normally shone a green glow of normality, were now flashing red in a state of emergency.

One of his men, wearing a white coat, usually in charge of monitoring the pods, stood leaning over another man lying on the control console. The man lying down was covered in cuts and bruises, his white coat now stained red. He was bleeding heavily from a gash on his abdomen. The other man was trying to stem the flow. He glanced up as Willoughby came in. At first there was fear in his eyes, but upon recognising Willoughby, his eyes flashed a glimmer of hope.

'Doctor Willoughby,' he stumbled 'they attacked him. We went to fix the pods, and they attacked him. He's dying. What can we do?'

Willoughby paused momentarily, his feelings numb. He looked over the man's shoulder at his blood stained colleague dying on the desk before looking up to meet the man's hopeful gaze.

'Get out.' His voice sounded robotic, inhuman. He didn't even recognise it. Without waiting for a response, he ran on. As he ran, his senses began to return, a sense of fear spread throughout his chest. What if they had got to her? What if he was too late? He rounded the corner to the next set of security doors and eagerly presented his security card, cursing under his breath as he waited for them to open.

Finally, the doors opened, and he burst into the room. It was dimly lit with emergency lighting, much like the rest of the building. He paused as the doors closed behind him, staring into the room ahead. In front of him, the pod remained just as he had left it, the door still closed and the precious cargo inside still safe and unharmed. He felt a sense of relief spread throughout his body. The light on the chamber pulsed, illuminating portions of the room. He took a cautious step forward. He felt less urgent now as a sense of occasion began to overcome him, for he knew that this was the end.

More gunshots echoed in the distance as he slowly took more furtive steps forward. The gunshots faded into the distance as his mind locked in on what lay directly ahead of him. As he neared the pod, he glimpsed her hair through the glass panel of the door, and his heart skipped a beat. Even now, after everything they had been through, everything she had endured and her present degenerative physical condition, he was excited to see her and he felt an overwhelming sense of emotion when he caught sight of her.

He was in touching distance. Instinctively, he reached a hand forward to touch her. As he held his arm aloft, something attacked him from the shadows. Two patients, in the shape of walking sacks of flesh, lunged at him. He pushed them away with his arm, expecting them to resist, but they fell away easily, stumbling backwards in a forlorn and desperate way.

They staggered as they approached him again. He watched, in horror as their skin, hanging from the bone, sagged and peeled, their eyes hollow and lifeless. Each of them had a tube dangling from their necks from where they had detached themselves from the pods. As they approached again, their mouths hung open, exposing the darkness of their throat down to their souls. It was then he realised what was happening. They weren't trying to attack him, they were pleading for help, for redemption, for someone to save them. Despite all that they had endured, their human spirit rallied on.

He stood motionless, watching as they approached, knowing that there was no path to restoration. Scanning the room, he searched for a weapon for the only redemption he could offer was death and an escape from their pain. With no weapons, he charged towards them, screaming aloud. Their bodies were thin and effortlessly light and offered no resistance against the weight of his body. The impact of his attack forced them against the wall, smashing their frail skulls upon impact and releasing them from their suffering.

As the lifeless bodies sagged to the floor, Willoughby leaned against the wall, pausing for breath and trying to compose himself amidst the surrounding horror. In that moment he realised it was a horror that he had created.

***

Sam, Elisa and Doctor Peters dashed through the bullet splattered door, but Willoughby was already out of sight. They ran through the adjoining room hoping to glimpse him. The size of the facility was bigger than multiple football fields put together, so without some sort of clue, they would have no hope of tracing him. Whilst Sam and Elisa blindly led the way, moving with urgency, Doctor Peters followed lethargically, although his sheer size meant that he seemed to move a much greater distance with little effort. When they reached a set of corridors, they stopped, uncertain of which direction to take.

'Which way do we go? He could have gone anywhere.' cried Elisa, desperately scanning the corridor for some sign of which path to take.

Sam looked up at Doctor Peters. 'Can we track him using the security system? Every time he uses his access card to open a door, we must be able to see which direction he is heading and then follow him accordingly.'

Doctor Peters nodded. 'We have to find a security console to check. Follow me.'

The security control room was located off a nearby corridor. Doctor Peters' security pass allowed him access. The room was small, only around seven feet by twelve feet. Once inside, the lights came on automatically. The bright fluorescent lights lit every corner of the room and caused them to squint until their eyes could adjust to the new lighting from that of the dingy emergency lit corridor they had come in from.

A secure filing cabinet stood along the length of the wall. Hard hats and high-visibility jackets were stacked neatly and seemingly unused on its top. A desk with a computer terminal stood at the far end of the small, narrow room. Doctor Peters sat in the chair. His size made him look as if he were an adult sitting in a primary school chair. Sam and Elisa stood watching over each of his shoulders.

With a few short clicks, Doctor Peters had logged into the terminal and began tapping away at the keyboard.

'We may actually be able to be more precise with Doctor Willoughby's location,' he began, staring intently at the screen as he typed. 'Each security pass also has an embedded GPS tracking chip built in. As long as he hasn't tampered with it, we should be able to pinpoint his position.'

He tapped a few more keys on the keyboard, which displayed a 3D map of the facility up on the screen. A few more taps later and a red dot appeared on the map and the map automatically zoomed into the marker. It was motionless on the screen.

'Where is he?' Sam asked. 'The room he's in isn't labelled on the map and it looks like he isn't moving.'

'He's not far, just around the corner. The room isn't labelled on the map as it is restricted to only a few selected personnel.'

'Why? What's in there?'

'His wife.'

***

Having regained his composure, Willoughby started towards the pod. He stared desperately through the glass window at his beautiful Francesca. Lying still, her chest showed only the slightest movement, kept alive by the life support machines. As he stood staring, more memories of their happy times came flooding back to him and he longed to be with her.

He had prepared for this moment. The pod was built as a double, allowing a second person to lie side by side. He had worried that when government funding was refused that she might not be saved and that the only way he might be able to be with her again would be by connecting with her mentally through the use of the Liteon process. He never imagined that his facility would come under attack by those he was trying to collaborate with, destroying all that he had built and forcing him to take actions of last resort ahead of time.

He stood staring, imagining what might have been. He pictured the day she would have been cured. Rejuvenated and recovered, he would have been able to have freed her from her confines and together they would have lived the rest of their lives together happily, leaving this place and all the work behind. Now, he knew what really mattered in life and despite his brilliance and wealth, he couldn't have it and his last hope was being taken away from him.

The sound of more bullets being fired in the distance broke his daydream. Fully focused again, he prepared the vacant pod. He took three vials from a secure cupboard. They were all super-sized compared to the vials used on Sam and Doctor Meadows and seemed to glow in colour. Willoughby slotted them into position within the pod mechanism. He then punched several keys on a computer console set against the wall. When finished, a timer appeared on the screen and began counting down.

He rushed across the room, throwing his lab coat to the floor and stripping naked to the waist, tossing his shirt to the side. With a desperate leap, he jumped into the pod and began connecting himself to the tubes and various apparatus. He struggled with the connections, as they were not designed to be self-administered. Driven by the desire to reunite with the only person that truly mattered to him, he choked on the orogastric tube as he inserted it in his throat and winced at the pain of self-administering a catheter into the vein of his arm.

Finally, he pushed a button in the pod to lower his side of the door. Knowing what was to come, he reached his right arm across to hold Francesca's hand in his. He lay back and waited for the process to begin. The pod hummed as the automated process began and the probe for connection into his cortex began its journey towards him. The pain of the needle as it penetrated the skin of his neck did not prepare him for the agony he felt as it drove deeper into his neck. He screamed, but no sound came out and then as the needle drove deeper and delivered its formula, he was no longer in a normal state of consciousness and the pain disappeared.

A kaleidoscope of colours flashed before his eyes, his mind seared open, and he felt it begin to race and pulse. His brain was opening up, he felt could go anywhere, and do anything. The world as he knew it seemed so insignificant and miniscule, in this moment he could see the big picture.

His thoughts raced as new information bombarded his senses. He struggled at first to control the flow, such was the intensity. He learned quickly and made intricate changes to his thought patterns to manage the deluge of knowledge he was now exposed to.

Once the initial onslaught had passed, he concentrated, for concentration was the key to control and he knew he had to control his mind or it would control him. He searched his mind and, once in command, he searched beyond his mind onto the plain that he knew existed between those whose minds had been enhanced by the Liteon process. They existed not as bodies but as cortex entities joined by a greater power and understanding.

As he journeyed through the cortex connections, he recognised people, patients he had worked with in his institutions and those still connected in his treatment locations across the world. Some were echoes of those connected, but who were no more. He felt their anger towards him, a pure hatred. He moved as quickly as he could to get away from them.

Drifting through memories of billions of people, past, present and future, images and thoughts flashed through his mind and buried themselves deep into his memory. His knowledge was growing exponentially, yet he still could not find what he sought.

Concentrating harder, he blocked the incoming messages and focused his own mind pulses out into the cortex. He suddenly received a flood of responses. Not facts and figures and memories, but feelings and emotions. Cries for help, tears of joy, despair, doom and elation until amongst the millions of responses, there she was, a signal amongst millions of others. He focused harder and her signal became stronger and louder. He blocked out all the other pulses, responding to his own until there was only one.

They drew each other closer until they were together. She was whole again, as beautiful as she had once been, and she pulled him to her, their minds together where their bodies could no longer be and then there was nothing.

***

Amidst the sound of gunfire echoing in the distance, the room was eerily calm. An electric hum of the large double pod emanated around the room, and the lights on top of the pods glowed intermittently to an electric rhythm. Sam and Elisa watched as Doctor Peters checked console readings on the computer screen.

Willoughby and his wife lay still, his hand on hers outstretched across her body.

'Well?' Sam looked across at Doctor Peters. The big man shook his head.

'According to the computer, he administered a concentrated mix of the Liteon solution. It was the new formula we had been working on that required dilution before administering. He took it all. There is no way he could have survived. We are too late.'

Sam checked the health monitor on Willoughby's pod. It showed no signs of life.

'Then it's over.' Elisa looked across at Doctor Peters. The enormous man was hunched over, his face strained with emotion.

'Come on,' she said. 'It's time to leave.'

34. An Offer

A week had passed, and the onset of early fall had begun. Central park was awash with tawny coloured leaves littering the pavements. The bite of the change in season was felt by the drop in temperature, although the day was bright with sunshine and the sky was clear blue.

The elevator hummed as it ascended the floors of the FBI building in New York City. Sam and Elisa stood patiently, almost sentry like as they waited to reach the twenty-third floor. Agent Daniels, who had introduced himself at Sam's apartment the previous day, accompanied them. He was of average build, late forties and, despite his greying hair, was relatively young looking.

Although he looked serious, he had been friendly and inviting. However, Sam had no doubt that Agent Daniels possessed a ruthless streak beneath his pleasant facade. The man had a scar on his forehead above his right eye and carried himself with the air of a man who held no fear. In Sam's experience, men like Daniels were more dangerous than the bravado-laden type. They were much more predictable, whereas men with Daniels' understated demeanour often hid the most cold-blooded of operators.

Sam and Elisa had spent the last week since returning from upstate New York, feasting daily on New York City's finest dining experiences, living the ultimate indulgent experiences that the city offered before returning to Sam's Upper East Side residence to share more time together.

They had agreed to stay under semi-house arrest, confined to the city until such time the FBI had cleared Willoughby's facility and decided on the next steps. A pair of NYPD cops were assigned to watch over them. They were a pair of plain clothed cops who were easy to spot and easy to lose, but Sam and Elisa humoured them rather than antagonise them, occasionally providing them coffee in their residential Chevrolet in which they were stationed on Sam's street.

The visit from Agent Daniels was therefore not a surprise. He did not call for long. He simply agreed to pick them up the following day for a debriefing session in the FBI building on Federal Plaza. They weren't expected to bring anything, but were told the session may take a couple of hours. The exchange was pleasant and Agent Daniels left before returning the next day as arranged.

The elevator reached the twenty-third floor, and the doors eased open. Agent Daniels invited them through the doors, and they passed through the security control that Sam had negotiated with Morgan only a few weeks ago. This occasion felt less tense, providing a feeling that they were guests instead of suspects.

Although the atmosphere was relaxed, Sam and Elisa remained guarded, although outwardly they participated in the pleasantries.

As they walked along the corridor, they passed the office Sam had been summoned to before. They continued down the corridor until it opened to reveal several glass-walled meeting rooms arranged in an oval. Agent Daniels knocked on the door of the nearest room. It was the only room where the glass walls were opaque having had the privacy feature activated.

'Come in,' a familiar voice responded.

Agent Daniels opened the door and invited Sam and Elisa into the room.

'I'll leave you at this point. I'm sure I'll see you later,' he said, nodding as he left them to enter the room.

The meeting room contained a large desk encircled by modern, comfortable-looking office chairs. There was an expensive-looking coffee machine in the corner and on the solid side wall there were several picturesque looking landscapes. The room was as close to comfort as FBI rooms got.

As they entered, Sam recognised a familiar face sitting calmly at the end of the table. Special Operations Director Keating.

He looked up from the desk and stood up, welcoming them in. 'Good morning Sam, Ms Guisti.' He grumbled in the most pleasant tone he could muster. They accepted his offer of seats, opting to sit together at the table instead of facing each other.

Keating sat back down. He offered them a drink in a

mechanical it's the polite thing to do type of way and was unmoved when they declined. Sam noted that unlike his visit to Keating's office, there was no security detail present in the room, although he was sure that they were being filmed and there would be men on standby should they make any sort of unwanted motions towards Keating. He took the lack of visible security as a good sign. If they were in immediate trouble, the Director wouldn't have invited them to the building through the front door, and certainly not to an audience without his security staff present.

'You probably want answers, so I'll get straight to the point.' He shuffled some papers and put them to one side in a neat pile on the desk. He didn't wait for a response before he went on. 'We've cleared the castle on the hill and removed Doctor Willoughby and his wife from the facility, along with the other patients. We are making the most appropriate and dignified arrangement for the patients that were residents in the facility and considering the ordeal that they endured. Where appropriate, we are agreeing those details with the families who, I am sure you will recognise, are somewhat distressed to learn that their family member is either deceased or in some cases still alive. Therefore, we will maintain strict privacy regarding most patients' arrangements, and we will not share the facility's details. Given the circumstances and the threat to national security, I'm sure you will understand.'

'Of course.' Sam agreed. Elisa remained silent, listening intently to Keating and anticipating what he was about to say next.

'We will decommission the pharmaceutical manufacturing facility in due course, and we are investigating his remaining facilities, both here and abroad, with the relevant foreign authorities to ensure they do not fall into the wrong hands.'

'That's nice to know,' said Elisa, breaking her silence. 'But what about us?'

'I was just coming to that,' he began.

'And Morgan, what about him?' interrupted Sam.

'Ah yes, James Morgan,' he rumbled. The name seemed to stick in his throat. 'I think you knew him quite well, although at least you thought you did, as did we.'

'The bastard double crossed us,' spat Elisa through gritted teeth. 'I should have killed the slimy bastard.'

'He double crossed us all. It seems he was a multiple agent. He was certainly in it for himself, but trying to keep all his masters happy was his ultimate downfall.'

'I had known him awhile. He never showed any signs that he might be in trouble. What exactly happened with him?' asked Sam.

'Well, you know he worked for us and a damn fine agent he was, too. What we find sometimes is that agents get too close to the people we are investigating. He was leading an investigation into narcotic operations in New York, but he became too close to some of the big time dealers. They gave him money, gifts at first, which he should never have accepted. He should have at least declared them so that he could have been put under watch to protect him from what ultimately happened. His drug lord paymasters began to expect more than him just turning a blind eye to some of their operations. They wanted him to help with securing some of their supplies. Foolishly he agreed.'

'But don't you have protocols to stop this sort of thing from happening?' Elisa asked.

'We do, but Morgan was a smart man, blinded by greed and arrogance he decided against following the internal protocol that would have saved him from getting in too deep with the drug overlords and instead thought he could use his position to his own advantage. He had been leading on the case of the defective batches of drugs hitting the streets and had started work with Willoughby as part of the investigation.'

'But why Willoughby? He was a leading industrialist helping to push new medical boundaries.' Sam chipped in.

'Indeed, he was, and he was in no way suspected of being involved in what we would consider a relatively small but important defective drug situation. Things like this can often occur, usually through gangland turf wars or disagreements between those on the streets and the cartels in Mexico, but on rare occasions, they are the tip of a bigger issue. As was the case here. Morgan originally engaged Willoughby as part of some consultancy work he is contracted to for the US government, to help with analysis, possible manufacturing sources, that kind of thing. We were aware of a dispute he had with the FDA, but again, these things happen all the time and usually resolve themselves one way or the other.'

'So what happened?' Elisa queried.

'It appears that Morgan's routine engagement with Willoughby triggered the man, I think you know about his wife now, he thought the game was up and that we had sussed him out, which was as far from the truth as it could be, we were merely seeking his assistance. Apparently thinking the game was up he had a breakdown and confessed to Morgan that it was him supplying the defective batches onto the streets in revenge for the FDA failing to authorise his new drug and the US government refusing to support further research into therapies he believed would help save his wife. In that moment of weakness, Morgan saw the opportunity to exploit the situation for his own benefit.'

'At which point Morgan became the Kingmaker.' Sam interjected.

'Exactly,' continued Keating. 'He convinced Willoughby that the only way he could get the government to agree to fund his research without giving up the intellectual property to Liteon was to eliminate anybody who knew about the Liteon process giving him the monopoly on the intelligence and forcing them to give into his wishes. If the government were still unconvinced and continued not to support his work, Morgan convinced Willoughby that he could fund the work by supplying the cartels via his vast production facilities and legitimately through the MRG network.'

'And that's where I came into it?' Elisa probed.

'Yes. Morgan convinced Willoughby to hire you to eliminate the men who had worked with Willoughby to develop Liteon.'

'Although there are still elements that are still somewhat…'Keating paused, searching for the right words, 'unclear to us. Morgan used a number of connections on the continent to conceal the connection back to Willoughby and himself but more concerning than that is that it appears there was another party that was aware of the information he ultimately shared with you and made legitimate attempts to stop you from getting the information.'

'The explosion at the hotel?' Elisa stated.

'Yes.'

'And what about the two men? Darko and the other man? Why were they after me?'

'We think they may have been connected to this group on the continent that was monitoring Morgan, but when you secured the information, Darko went to ground and followed orders, working within, so to speak. We don't believe Morgan was aware that who he thought were working for him were themselves in effect double agents. Ultimately, we believe if they had obtained the information about Willoughby's key contacts they would have disposed of you and Morgan and infiltrated Willoughby's operation in order to take control. Thankfully, because of your actions that did not happen and Willoughby's operation is now safely in the hands of the authorities.'

Elisa contemplated for a while, taking it all in before Sam broke the silence.

'And now you want our help to track down this party on the continent?'

'I head up a new secret special operations division of the FBI that investigates international crime and I'm offering you both a position in the team. We think that you both have a set of attributes that would make you excellent for the role. I can guarantee that the terms and conditions will be favourable to anything you might be used to.'

'What makes you think we will accept?'

'And what if we don't?' chimed in Elisa.

'If you don't accept, you are free to go on about your business. Whatever it is, you choose to do.' He paused before continuing. The air hung heavily in the room. 'However, I think that there are advantages to you both if you did accept. For you, Ms Guisti, I think you will find being part of the Bureau will give you the freedom that you seek. It will give you a level of protection against the dissatisfied client base we understand you have accumulated in your current profession and would struggle to find elsewhere.'

Elisa's skin crawled at the thought of her situation being known to the authorities, but in her heart she knew that this was not unexpected and that he had a valid point. Who would dare seek an assassin now working for the FBI? Even the most vengeful of her clients that she failed to deliver for would not want the attention from the authorities that a hit on her life would bring. They would conveniently forget about her and most likely actively avoid her. She looked across at Sam to gauge his reaction. He looked stoic, staring directly into Keating's eyes.

'I think Sam, for you, the offer needs little explanation, your indiscretion in the military forgotten, the opportunity to serve your country again and, if nothing else to get away from the academic role you have chosen for yourself and get your hands dirty again doing what you are best at. Well, what do you both say?'

***

An hour later, they sat in the dusk on a bench in Central Park. The evening was closing in around them, but the autumn air was warm, as if summer was trying to hold on before the inevitable change in season. They had been dropped off by an unmarked dark coloured Cadillac Escalade and as they walked into Central Park discussed in silent tones the offer they had been made. Eventually there was nothing left to say except what sometimes didn't need words at all. They had sat for a few minutes in silence, watching the occasional passer-by across the park and the sun as it set over the New York skyline before Sam broke the silence.

'I knew that would happen,' he said.

He suddenly felt tense.

'Really? What happens next?' she said, smiling.

'Don't you know?' he asked.

For the first time in her life, her mind was still. There was no noise, no inclination or worry about what might happen in the future. She felt a deep welling of excitement inside that was totally new.

Elisa looked into Sam's eyes and felt as if she were looking deep into his soul. She finally felt totally at ease. There was no need to panic. No need to think about what might happen. All she felt was the need to live for the moment.

'No,' she whispered. 'Do you?'

He gazed back at her sparkling eyes and cupped her soft hair and the back of her head in his hand. Should he tell her what he had seen, what he knew? What could he do? After everything, he felt more confused than ever before. He kissed her forehead gently and drew her head to his chest.

For a moment in the warm night, beneath the moonlight, the events of the past couple of weeks disappeared into the ether. They had all the time in the world, he thought.

'Let's find out together,' he said, pulling her closer.

THE END

Acknowledgements

Special thanks to my wife and family for supporting me in the process of writing this book. I couldn't have finished it without their input and support. Their patience, time and encouragement is something I am grateful for.

Thank you to Alys J Clarke for her guidance and input, her books can be found at all the usual online retailers and on her website: www.alysjclarke.co.uk

Thanks to the design team at www.getcovers.com for their excellent work on the book cover.

The poem "Sorrow" was written by Edna St. Vincent Millay and was first published in Renascence, and Other Poems (1917).

Printed in Dunstable, United Kingdom